"I'll get the bloodstones," Viv said. "How many do you think we'll need?"

"Twelve should do it."

"I'll bring sixteen. Always better to have more than not enough, right?"

Nikoli gave her a sultry look. "It's always better to have more."

Viv cleared her throat and rummaged through the bloodstones, but she felt her breathing quicken. There was no ignoring Nikoli's scent—a mixture of leather, musk and fresh, rain-kissed air. No one had ever affected her this way. Viv narrowed her eyes and tried to concentrate on the bloodstones.

"I think we're good," she said, chancing a look at Nikoli's face. Big mistake. When she'd turned to him, they were but a breath apart.

Both of them froze, eyes locked, and in that moment the rest of Viv's world disappeared. All that existed was the scent of him, the brawn of him. The only thing either of them had to do was move a fraction of an inch and...

Award-winning and bestselling author **Deborah LeBlanc** is a business owner, a licensed death-scene investigator and an active member of two national paranormal investigation teams. She's the president of the Horror Writers Association, Mystery Writers of America's Southwest chapter and the Writers' Guild of Acadiana. Deborah is also the creator of the LeBlanc Literacy Challenge, an annual national campaign designed to encourage more people to read, and Literacy, Inc., a nonprofit organization with a mission to fight illiteracy in America's teens. For more information go to deborahleblanc.com and literacyinc.com.

Books by Deborah LeBlanc

Harlequin Nocturne

The Wolven
The Fright Before Christmas
Witch's Hunger

WITCH'S HUNGER

———

DEBORAH LeBLANC

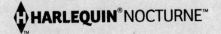

Recycling programs
for this product may
not exist in your area.

ISBN-13: 978-0-373-13993-4

Witch's Hunger

Copyright © 2017 by Deborah LeBlanc

Printed in U.S.A.

Dear Reader,

Out of all the choices at your disposal, thank you for choosing this book to add to your library. I hope you enjoy the story as much as I loved writing it. Quite the task, weaving a new breed of triplet witches along with those I named the Originals—Nosferatu, Loup Garou and Chenilles. Add four hunky males who inherently carry the power of lightning, and you have all the ingredients needed for havoc, mayhem, lust, love and the need for more!

With heartfelt thanks,

Deborah

DeborahLeBlanc.com

For Pookie and Sarah. It's been a long, hard road without you...

Prologue

The triplets had known trouble since birth.

Near the north wall of a vast cavern southeast of Marseilles stood a wide stone table. Behind the table sat the Council of Elders for the Circle of Sisters—Magda, head of the council, Bayonne and Palmae.

Magda, shaking with fury, glared at the three young women standing before them. Esmee, the eldest of the triplets and most outspoken, and her sisters, Lisette and Julianne François. The girls' shadows danced across the stone walls from the multitude of candles that illuminated the dank cave.

They were forced to wear sackcloth and walk the many miles to the meeting area. They stood dirty, sweating and trembling with fear at what they were about to face. They were identical in appearance save for their eyes. Each held a unique color. Esmee's were brilliant blue, Lisette's a shiny copper and Julianne's blacker than any shade of night.

All three pairs of eyes were now downcast, the girls' heads bowed in sorrow and submission. Coal-black hair fell across alabaster skin. The cave smelled of their sweat, burning candles and the earthy scent of the dirt beneath their feet.

Magda, as head of the council, held the staff of judgment so tightly in her right hand her knuckles had turned white. Her fury was undeniable. The staff of judgment was eight inches long, made of thick, pol- ished Elder-wood and topped with a bloodstone the size of a small woman's fist. The staff was the ballast used only in severe cases, of which this was definitely one.

Being responsible for an entire clan of witches spread throughout France, especially in the fifteenth century, was no small feat. She held fast to being firm and fair, and unwavering from protocol. Despite her anger, looking at the triplets made her heart ache and cluttered her thoughts.

This wasn't the first time the sisters had stood be- fore the council. Mostly for misdemeanors on other occasions. Their youth accounted for the majority of the dismissals of those cases.

Magda knew the council granted special favors to the triplets out of pity. Years ago, their parents had left a theater late one evening when a band of thieves shot out from a dark alley and murdered both of them. The triplets had only been two years old at the time, and by vote, the Council of Elders decided that Bayonne would take responsibility for them. They'd had no other choice. It was part of their culture. Neither adoption nor abandonment existed in their code of ethics. The Circle of Sisters took care of their own.

Magda always suspected Bayonne had been too lenient on the girls throughout the years, and today's fiasco seemed to attest to that. At sixteen years old, with a full fourteen years under Bayonne's tutelage, the young women should have known better.

"But, Elders, we beg of you," Esmee said. "Please consider reason. Would you not have done the same? Would you have allowed such boldfaced betrayal to go unpunished? Would you not have sought revenge? How can you judge us when we were the ones wronged?"

"You demonstrated complete misuse of your powers," Magda said gruffly. "Granted, your years may still be tender, and in many ways the three of you still inexperienced with many spells, but you are not naive to our laws. What you did changes the face of the human race. The monstrosities you created will not only kill and destroy other humans, they will breed and mutate, producing subspecies, and their numbers will become endless. Their nightmare will never end. You have executed your revenge, but these creatures will never know peace. They will never have the opportunity to make amends. You chose to be judge, jury and executioner, all of which you had no right. Punishment is due for this atrocity. And the punishment must match the crime."

Magda glanced at Bayonne, whose eyes brimmed with tears, then at Palmae, who sat ramrod straight, eyes wide with shock. "Are we in agreement here, sisters?" she asked them.

Both gave almost imperceptible nods.

"Very well," Magda said. "So shall it be." She held the staff of judgment outright, its tip poised over the stone table.

Suddenly a sensation caught her attention, and Magda cocked her head slightly to one side to listen intently. She heard water dribbling from somewhere within the cave, the ragged, anxious breathing from the triplets and the other two Elders, but little more. Despite that, she felt certain…no…*knew* that someone was listening to their conversation from the mouth of the cave.

Trusting her instincts, Magda felt that someone was Tenebrus Cray, one of the most self-serving, power-hungry sorcerers she had ever known. Magda thought about storming out to confront him, then considered a better idea.

They might have gotten away with it, but there'd been too much blood. The entire city raged over the incident. It hadn't taken long for the Elders to find out. Stupid girls.

Gnawing on that thought, and the piece of clove he had stuck in his mouth earlier, Tenebrus Cray squatted near the entrance of the cave. He leaned in as close as he dared to the opening so as not to miss one word spoken by the women.

The witches had gathered secretly in the stone belly of a hillside, far from prying eyes in Marseilles. He knew their location because he had spotted Magda, Bayonne and Palmae clomping out of town on horse- back, each wrapped in their signature, floor-length capes—black, purple and red, respectively.

The three were master witches and all but recluses. They lived in a hovel away from the bustle of the city. Tenebrus had only seen them come out to work in their herb garden. To watch them head out of town was a novelty. To have them retreat so hastily, and on horse- back, was unheard of.

Tenebrus knew that Magda had the power of tele- portation. Why have an animal bear one's weight when all one had to do was wave a hand, cast a spell and the three would have immediately teleported to their destination?

Wherever they were going, whatever they intended to do, had to be significant. And Tenebrus was not about to miss the event.

Magda pounded the stick of judgment on the stone table once. Then decided to complete the trial in their tribal language, Kaswah, a language rarely spoken and only understood by those within the Circle of Sisters.

They had been speaking in French until now. Any- one eavesdropping would only hear gibberish, includ- ing Tenebrus. Magda considered casting a silencing boundary, then dismissed the thought. The sorcerer would immediately open it.

She glanced briefly at Bayonne, noticed the tears trickling down her cheeks. Palmae's expression was one of sheer dread.

Sitting arrow-back straight and lifting her chin, Magda scowled at the triplets. "Step forward."

The triplets complied, instinctively grabbing a hand of the sister nearest her.

Magda pointed the bloodstone at each young woman, then looked over at the other two Elders and said, "Sisters…"

With that single word, the three Elders recited in unison.

"Jealous lovers,
Vengeance sought.
Defiling nature,
Havoc wrought.
To chastise thee,
We Elders three,
Bind ye now for eternity."

Palmae and Bayonne slumped back in their chairs but Magda remained straight and focused and let out a sigh.

"From this day forward, you will be responsible for the creatures you have created," Magda commanded, pounding the staff of judgment once on the stone table. "No longer will you have the freedom to live life as you please. Your purpose and your powers will be used to contain these monstrosities so they do not multiply and exceed the number of humans on earth. You will establish boundaries, you will set binding spells for control. You will supply them food, but only from natural sources."

Esmee dropped her head wearily. Lisette and Julianne began to weep.

Magda pounded the staff of judgment on the table again to emphasize yet another consequence for their actions. "You and the generations of triplets to follow shall be called Triads from this day forth. The name will serve to identify your wrongdoing. And because you have altered the human race, you and the triplets of future generations are no longer allowed to marry a human nor live intimately with a human."

Esmee, Lisette and Julianne gasped in unison, as did Palmae. Bayonne let out a sob.

"Magda, this punishment is far too harsh," Palmae said. "We must consult as Elders before casting such a spell upon these young women."

"I will hear no more!" Magda shouted. "Did we not agree as a council that the punishment must fit the crime?"

"Yes," Bayonne said. "But you cannot call this punishment on your own, Magda. Where is your mercy?"

"As head of this council, I am allowed to call the punishment, if punishment is agreed upon, as I see fit. And mercy, you ask? The men whose lives these women have altered are changed forever; who gives them mercy?"

Bayonne lowered her head and Magda immediately turned her attention back to the triplets. "The creatures you have created shall be named accordingly. The one condemned to thirst for blood shall be known as Nosferatu. The one doomed to hunger for flesh yet never be sated shall be known as Loup Garou. And the one you have caused to eternally search for the marrow of bone shall be known as Chenilles. You and future

Triads shall protect humans from them, and with the passage of time, as each species interbreeds and mutates, you will assign constables and shepherds to help manage them."

"But—" Esmee said.

"Silence," Magda demanded. "Along with those tasks, you and every Triad generation to follow until the end of time will bear the mark of *absolutus infinitus* on their body as a reminder of this day." She pointed the bloodstone at Esmee, and the cave echoed with the sound of sizzling flesh.

Esmee hissed in pain, lowered the coverlet of the sackcloth to examine her left shoulder and saw the mark of *8*. The *absolutus infinitus*, at first red, faded quickly to black.

Julianne and Lisette huddled closer to Esmee, but it did not stop Magda's mission. She aimed the bloodstone at Lisette, who let out a shriek of pain and clutched her right hip. Julianne came next, only hers Magda placed on her right ankle. Julianne bore the pain through gritted teeth.

"Now," Magda continued, "to minimize the chances of this occurring again, each of you will compile separate tomes. Your tome must include every spell within your knowledge, whether innate or taught. You are to identify each spell, its purpose and the consequences that occur with use of each spell. These tomes will be known as Grimoires. Once they are completed, you will bind each Grimoire in Elder-wood for preservation."

Magda waved the bloodstone over the stone table

that separated the triplets from the Elders. Three palm-sized mirrors appeared on the table, one in front of each triplet. "Behind the front cover of your Grimoire, you will notch out an indention in the wood. One large enough to securely hold one of these mirrors. Understood?"

The triplets only stared at her.

"I said, do you understand?" Magda said loudly.

Esmee nodded slightly, and Lisette and Julianne quickly imitated her acknowledgment.

Seemingly satisfied, Magda continued. "You and every generation of Triads to follow must review your Grimoire daily. The first thing you will see upon opening your tome, however, is the mirror. It will reflect the death and destruction that will befall the world should you or any Triad not live up to her duties."

Signaling the triplets closer, Magda pointed at the mirrors. "Come closer now and look at what your irresponsibility has set into motion, and why the consequences besetting you are so severe."

All three sobbing now, the triplets drew closer until they stood at the edge of the stone table. Bayonne and Palmae leaned over to look within the mirrors themselves.

With another pounding from the staff of judgment, the reflective surfaces began to dance with a myriad of colors, swirls of red, purple, green, black. Within seconds, the colors settled into indescribable scenes so vivid it was as if they were seeing them firsthand.

Reflected in each palm-sized mirror was a sea of blood, dead bodies, some mid-decay, some fully decayed. Men, women and children, all strewn about the land like garbage. Blowflies, maggots and buzzards fed on the little bits of flesh that remained on corpses. From within these images, they heard great wailing and gnashing of teeth.

When Magda waved a hand over the mirrors, erasing the images, the triplets fell to their knees, sobbing. Bayonne and Palmae looked visibly shaken.

The shadows within the cave deepened, casting purple and dark gray lattices over each triplet. They were in shock, lost, a terrified look in their eyes.

Although her position as head of the council made it necessary for Magda to execute such punishment, she couldn't help the pain she felt in her heart for the young women. She had handed down a life sentence that would change not only their lives forever but every generation of Triads to follow.

Still squatting near the mouth of the cave, Tenebrus, frustrated, strained to understand the words being spoken inside. From the occasional sob he heard coming from inside the cavern, Tenebrus assumed the punishment meted out was harsh. That angered him. Whatever limitations had been imposed on the triplets would limit him, as well.

He had known the three sisters since they were babies, and even back then he'd known something was different about the tiny witches. Triplets in any race seemed an anomaly, but in a tribe of witches, they were nearly nonexistent. So it only made sense that the three held special powers.

The day the triplets were born the Elders of the Circle of Sisters seemed perplexed as to what to make of the unusual birth. It was the beginning of a new race within their tribe. From each set of triplets, one triplet would bear triplets of her own, and so it would be until triplets no longer existed, which probably meant until the end of time.

Tenebrus had been right about them having special powers. All three girls had needed little training from a very young age. Most of the spells they conjured as children took many witches years to learn. Each triplet had special gifts in her own right, but he'd often wondered about what might happen if their powers were melded together. Well, he had to wonder no more. He had witnessed it firsthand the other evening.

The night of the incident, the one that resulted in the trip to this cavern, happened at Lord Chermoine's castle. A prenuptial gathering prepared for the intendeds of the triplets—the wedding scheduled for the following day— and Tenebrus had garnered an invitation, which came as no surprise. He'd cast a simple yearning spell to make certain his name appeared on the roster.

An unfortunate delay, or fortunate depending on one's point of view, caused Tenebrus to arrive at the castle late. Just in time to see the triplets standing outside the castle beside their intendeds, screaming about unfaithfulness. Women Tenebrus knew to be of ill repute ran out of the castle and scattered from the estate on foot, obviously not wanting any part of the tumult taking place outside.

Tenebrus hid behind a tree and watched as each

triplet pointed to her intended, railing him unabashedly with obscenities.

Then the girls quickly gathered, joined hands and
uttered words Tenebrus had never heard before. They
swayed and chanted and from where he hid, Tenebrus
felt the air thicken and begin to vibrate. Even with so
much distance between him, he saw fear in the eyes
of the men meant to marry these women.

Suddenly, Esmee pointed to the man she was to
marry the next day and proclaimed, "You blame the
drink for your actions, for your unfaithfulness. So let
it be. From this day forth, you will thirst from your
very core. You shall thirst for that which does not come
easily and you will never know satisfaction."

No sooner were those words uttered than the man's
face began to contort, widen and turn white. The hair
on his head fell away as if someone with shears had
been working behind the scenes, waiting for this very
moment. His scalp was now white and bulbous with
a large vein running up from the center of his forehead then branching out on top of his skull like tree
branches. His mouth opened wide as he cried out
in pain. His two front teeth became thin and sharp,
incisor-like, and grew to unimaginable lengths. His
eyes turned ruby red. The tips of his ears grew long and
pointed. He stood frozen for only a moment, watching,
feeling his own transformation, then ran for the woods
behind the castle.

The two other men looked on in bewilderment and
fear. Lisette pointed to her intended and proclaimed, "If
you want to act like a beast, then you shall be a beast

for all eternity. Your nights will no longer be your own. You will crave flesh like an animal."

Her words caused an immediate transformation in the man. Her intended cried out in pain as fur covered his entire face, and his mouth and nose elongated, creating a snout. His body seemed to explode in width and height. His teeth were no longer those of a man but the fangs of a wolf.

The sisters appeared unaffected by the transformations taking over the men.

The man-wolf howled, confusion obvious in his eyes, and he, too, ran for the woods.

Julianne's intended had evidently seen enough for he, too, began to run. Even if he had gained twice the speed, it would not be fast enough to escape Julianne's spell.

She pointed at him, "You claim your excuse for unfaithfulness to the mindlessness that comes with drink, so you shall remain mindless. Always controlled by another. No longer will you have a mind of your own that allows free will, and you shall hunger for the bone marrow of the man you once were before engaging with that harlot."

Instinctively, Tenebrus knew the sisters had no idea about the seriousness of what they had just done.

When Julianna completed her spell, the sisters joined hands. They raised them to the heavens and proclaimed that by the power of three and every element that made up the universe, no witch or sorcerer could break their spell, no matter how powerful he or she might be.

The mutation of the third man did not appear as hideous as the former two. Oddly, he simply grew taller, thinner, but something in his eyes went empty, like the life within him had drained away. Not even fear registered in them.

Tenebrus wanted that kind of power. Absolute control over the elements of fire, water, earth and air. Over all who existed on this planet.

He had studied the triplets for years and for the past ten years, Tenebrus had become obsessed with finding a way to combine their power with his own. A sorcerer could not drain the power from this special breed of witch. But if he studied them, then took what he learned and joined that with his own superior power, he'd be ruler over every being on earth. His power would be supreme. Ultimate.

Sensing Tenebrus's presence even stronger caused Magda's anger to boil in her veins. If for nothing else but spite, she would stop this event immediately. But she couldn't. As head Elder, she had to set an example for the fifteen-hundred plus witches she, Bayonne and Palmae were responsible for.

Magda cleared her throat. "Should you or your siblings, including the generations to come, shirk their responsibilities, that Triad shall lose her powers. And the creatures they are responsible for will be freed upon the earth to kill and destroy at will."

"But you are condemning us to be alone for the rest of our lives," Lisette cried. "If we cannot marry nor live in intimacy with a human, nothing remains. Our lineage will die. Who will we marry? Who will father our children?"

Bayonne nodded in agreement and looked over at Magda. "Who?"

Magda pointed the staff of judgment at Lisette, giving her a stern look. "You will have at your disposal what remains. Fae. Sorcerers who have transcended, or one of the creatures you have created."

Palmae gasped so loudly it sounded like she'd nearly swallowed her tongue. "Magda, no! This is far too harsh and—"

"Enough!" Magda proclaimed. "It is done." She struck the stone table once more with the staff of judgment. "*Isonno, funjusa, orlato*—so it is said, so shall it be done and so shall it ever be!" Then under her breath, Magda recited another incantation, only this one was for that nosy, good-for-nothing Tenebrus, who dared to eavesdrop on such a sacred meeting. After slamming the shaft of judgment on the table for the last time, the bloodstone atop it shattered. Everyone in the cave gasped in shock, and the collective sound reverberated throughout the hollow space.

The shattered bloodstone came as no surprise to Magda. In fact, she'd half expected it—for she had just done the very thing to Tenebrus that she had placed judgment for on the triplets who stood before her.

Only this time no one but she would ever know.

Chapter 1

Vivienne François stood behind a forty-foot gate that was topped with silver-tipped barbwire, watching blood, fur and some chunks of flesh fly in every direction, and wondered where she'd gone wrong. The air smelled of dirt, blood, urine and musk.

It was mid-October in Algiers, Louisiana, but witnessing this much brutality made her break into a sweat like it was high-noon in August.

Wearing jeans, boots and a light blue pullover work shirt, Viv took a fighting stance. Feet spread apart, fists at her sides. She closed her eyes, gritted her teeth, then said loudly, "I bind thee now, powerless until released by my word. So shall it be. So it is by my command!"

She opened one eye slowly and groaned. The blood and fur still flew.

"I don't understand what the hell is going on," she said to Socrates, who sat beside her right foot. "That's the fifth damn binding spell I've tried and it's like everyone has gone deaf, including the universe. Either that or I have turned into a frigging toasted marshmallow." She kicked angrily at the ground with the toe of her boot.

"Do you always have to be so abrasive and surly when you're upset?" Socrates asked. He was a pompous Bombay with gold eyes and had been Viv's familiar since her birth. He yawned and gave a swish of his tail. "Truly, Viv, can you not see why your spell isn't working?"

"No." She huffed. "The way it works is I do a spell and the recipient responds immediately. This isn't a show-and-tell game or three-card monte. I'll be damned if they're not going to listen."

"Oh, for heaven's sake," Socrates said with an exasperated sigh. "Must I point out every detail to you?"

"With that attitude, buddy, you're lucky if I don't ship you off to Siberia." Not that Viv would really ship Socrates anywhere, but she was so frustrated she didn't know what to do with herself.

She stood out here alone, behind a gate that served as the compound entrance to a fenced-in, five-hundred acre lair. The compound held the North End pack of Loup Garou, whom she watched over herself, since she didn't live far. Just north of the compound was another three hundred acres that served to feed and grow livestock she and her sisters used to feed the breeds they were responsible for.

Viv was one in a set of triplets, the oldest by ten minutes and responsible for the Loup Garou. The middle triplet, Evette, took care of the Nosferatu, and the youngest, Abigail, dealt with the Chenilles. All breeds were netherworld creatures that she'd had to work hard not to resent over the years. For Viv, it was like baby-sitting a gigantic pack of prepubescent teens.

To feed their factions, they raised cows, goats, pigs and mules specifically for that purpose. Fortunately, Viv had three humans whom she trusted to handle the cattle in the farm area. One of them was Charlie Zerangue, a fifty-two-year-old cowboy who'd worked with her for the past ten years buying cattle. He made sure his two hands sent that cattle through the feeding shoot that led them directly to an area south of the Loup Garou compound. This was the feeding territory.

Once the cattle were sent through the shoot to the feeding area, the Nosferatu were ferried from New Orleans near the river bank to Algiers. There they were loosed upon the cattle to gorge on as much blood as they wanted. The idea was to have each so satiated that they would be easier to manage around humans during their daily or nightly chores.

Once the Nosferatu were ferried back across the river, the Loup Garou from the North, West and East packs were allowed into the feeding area to rip through as much meat as their stomachs could handle for the exact same reason.

And lastly, the Chenilles, Abigail's brood, were ferried across the river to the compound and allowed to feast on the marrow of all the bones that remained.

This maniacal ritual occurred every day without fail between 3:00 and 4:00 a.m., when most of New Orleans was either asleep or too drunk to understand or care about what was going on. They used a family-owned ferry for the transports, something not easily obtained in New Orleans. But it was nothing that a little magic and a lot of money greasing the right political palms couldn't manage.

Aside from tending the feeding shoot, Charlie was also responsible for a thirty-one-year-old, hard working farmhand named Bootstrap from Ville Platte, Louisiana, and Kale Martin, a forty-six-year-old wrangler from East Texas.

The men were paid well and had free housing in a two-story ranch house near the front of the property. The one thing Viv appreciated most about Charlie, Bootstrap and Kale was that they never asked questions. They worked hard and kept their mouths shut. Not once had any of the men asked about the cattle sent through the shoot. Their job was to keep the livestock area full, the cattle healthy and fat, then send whatever was ordered through the shoot each morning.

The North End pack of Loup Garou that lived beyond the gate where Viv stood now clocked over three hundred strong, all of them Originals. Not the watered-down version of werewolves that existed in other areas. Viv was responsible for all of them, but she had worked hard at putting together a strong team of leaders to manage different territories.

Viv let out a heavy sigh. Some job she had. People thought that just because you were a witch, a real witch, not a Wiccan wannabe, all you had to do was snap your fingers and everything became beautiful. You got exactly what you wanted when you wanted it and how you wanted it. Nothing was further from the truth.

"Miss Viv," called Whiskers, a small female Loup Garou with blond fur. She peeked out from her den, a bramble of bent tree branches that wasn't far from the fight taking place center court. "Please make it stop. Warden and Milan I mean. They're going to kill each other!"

"Aw, let them have at it," said Moose, another Loup Garou hiding fifty feet away. "It's healthy to see a good fight every now and again. Puts a little spark in you, you know?" Moose was one of the largest Loups in the Northern pack, but not the brightest bulb in the lamp.

Yazdee, a female Loup who denned with Whiskers, gave Moose a little growl. "You're sick, you know that? Leave it to a guy to watch two other males fight to the death over a little tail. I mean, I don't get it. It's not like there aren't plenty of females to go around."

"Yeah," Moose said, "but we're talking about Stratus here. Everybody wants a piece of that alpha female when she's in heat. Hot stuff there, baby doll. Hot stuff."

"Pervert," Whiskers barked.

"Prude," Moose shot back.

Yazdee snorted. "Better a prude than pitiful. If you're so hot for it, why aren't you in the middle of that tangle?"

Moose grunted and ducked back behind a thicket of trees.

Amid the chaos, Stratus lay with her head resting on her paws at the door of her den, which sat on the opposite side of the compound in direct view of Whiskers and Yazdee. She watched the fight, her expression flickering from curiosity to boredom.

A growl rumbled so close to Viv it made her jump. The mauling, biting and clawing were reaching a fevered pitch. She threw a quick glance around the compound. It seemed most, if not all, of the Loups in camp had gathered in a wide circle to watch the fight. Everyone kept a safe distance away.

The two alphas in combat were Warden, the North End alpha, whom Viv had chosen to mate with Stratus; and Milan, who belonged in the East End pack. Evidently, Milan had found a way to sneak in, hoping to get a piece of Stratus's action.

Viv thought about having Socrates go fetch Jaco, who oversaw the East pack, but the last thing she needed right now, leader or not, was another alpha thrown into this mix.

Finally, after attempting another binding then a freezing spell, both of which failed, Viv let out her own little growl. She ran her hands down her arms, mumbling words beneath her breath. Immediately, all that was visible of her was the vague silhouette of the tall, slender, black-haired woman who stood there seconds ago. Invisibility was a hard accomplishment for any witch, yet at thirty years old, she nearly had it down pat. Partial invisibility was better than none at all.

"And just what do you think you're doing?" Socrates asked, suddenly standing at attention. "Do you think you can simply walk in there and physically stop those two alphas from ripping each other apart?"

Viv grabbed a two-by-four that leaned against the gate and said, "Watch and learn how simply, cat."

She reached for the huge latch that bound the gate to a silver pole but before she could pull it up and open, Socrates rammed into her shins and began to hiss. He darted in and around her legs, threatening to trip her if she took a step.

He hissed again, loudly. "Don't be ridiculous, Viv. Some things are stronger than magic. Put your anger aside for a moment and feel what's coming from that lair. You'll see and understand why your spells have been ineffective."

"Get out of my damn way or you'll get a swift kick that'll land you right in the middle of that mess." She put a hand on her hip, knowing full well, as did he, that her threat was empty. For once, she gave in to his suggestion. She reined in her anger and allowed all of her senses to stretch to full alert.

She knew what was going on and for all intents and purposes, there was only one way she could see to stop it. She couldn't call Charlie, Bootstrap or Kale out to help. They had never even seen the Loup Garou. They had never been allowed on this end of the property. Her sisters would be useless, for their spells only worked for their own broods.

Pondering all of it put Viv in an even crappier mood. It was eight o'clock in the morning, when normal people usually sat down for coffee and eggs, and here she was dealing with this. She just wished for a normal life.

Often dreamed about what that might be like, feel like. Just as she often wondered why certain people were born a certain way. Some rich, some poor, some white, some Asian. Others Chenilles, another Nosferatu. Or as Socrates had so aptly put it moments ago—a Triad.

It was hard enough having been born a triplet when life seemed to be about "finding" oneself. How did you find yourself when you were a tether of three? And an odd tether at that; a tomboy prone to wrangling cattle and sharing a beer with one of three cowboys. Her sisters carried themselves with grace and reeked of femininity. She, on the other hand, usually reeked of sweat.

Even as children, Viv and her sisters never dressed alike, each seeking their own identity. Aside from the need for singularity, they had always remained very close. Oftentimes, if one of the sisters wasn't feeling well or even experienced a startle, the other two felt it just as strongly. In fact, she was surprised with all she was going through right now that Abigail and Evette weren't here standing beside her. Surely they had to know something was going on with her.

Maybe the universe had gone deaf. Whatever the case, with her senses heightened, the intense sexual charge in the air didn't help matters one bit. She hadn't had sex in over a year, all because of some stupid curse that had been handed down too many generations ago.

Because of that curse, every mother or Elder responsible for a Triad lived out their days twisting and turning just to keep them chaste. They weren't supposed to be intimate with humans and marrying one was a huge no-no.

Chances were, the other no-goes for a Triad had gotten twisted around so much that their literal meaning had been tweaked in one manner or another as they made their way to the twenty-first century. She knew they couldn't marry a human, but having sex with one was something she considered left to interpretation. Not that she or her sisters had tried it…yet. They were too chicken to tempt fate.

All Viv knew for sure was that every damn morning before she came down to the feeding shoot, she had to look through her Grimoire and face the horrid mirror. That mirror showed the most horrific scenes regarding the devastation of the world if they shirked their duties. The book itself listed spell after spell, consequence after consequence. And if that wasn't enough to shove her tainted ancestry in her face, she and her sisters each bore a birthmark. An *absolutus infinitus*. Viv's was about two inches long and sat on her right hip. An ugly reminder of some big bad no-no done a gazillion years ago by a grandmother thirty times removed.

Taking that into consideration, all that remained for Viv and her sisters when sex came to mind—which was often—were Fae, leprechauns, one of their brood or a sorcerer who had taken the dark side to devilry and had paid for it with his humanity. Fae and leprechauns did nothing for Viv. Both were too short, and short turned her off. As for sorcerers, there were only three that she knew of in the area. Trey Cottle, a weasel and whore-monger, Shandor Black, who always had his nose stuck so far up Cottle's butt, Viv didn't know how he breathed. And there was Gunner Stern, a sorcerer, but a nice old guy. There being the problem. He was old, like seventy-something old. That certainly didn't make Viv's nipples tingle.

When too much time had passed, and it was either have sex or go blind, she'd have a row with one of her Loups. When not matted with fur and fangs, many of the males were quite handsome. Big and muscular, with long, flowing hair, and they knew what to do with genitalia. There was always something missing, though, when having sex with a Loup. The act felt animalistic, which wasn't all bad at times, but she was a woman, damn it, and a bit of romance would be nice occasionally. Romance, however, was not in a Loup's vocabulary. All they knew was get it while it's hot, then sleep it off until it's time to eat.

Sometimes, though, as Socrates said, some things were stronger than magic, and she gave into her urges and had sex with a Loup. She couldn't get attached to any one of them in particular because the other males would see that as a weakness in her leadership abilities. She certainly wasn't going to marry a Loup Garou, much less a sorcerer.

Viv kicked the dirt again, angry she'd allowed herself to jump on that train of thought. Her frustration level now matched Everest's peak.

Here she was watching two alpha males fight over a female Loup Garou just because she twitched her tail. Viv wanted to beat the two males upside the head with the two-by-four to mellow out her own sexual frustrations. Also so she wouldn't have to babysit them.

It was far from easy being on twenty-four-seven watch over a bunch of sniveling, whining, horny wolves. And when Viv François had enough, she had had enough.

She picked up the two-by-four, gave Socrates a little nudge with her boot when he hissed at her, then unlatched the gate. She immediately closed and locked it behind her.

Still partially invisible, she didn't think she had to worry about the warring Loups turning on her. Even if they glanced her way, they'd only see a shimmer in the air, like heat rising from a desert highway. There was the two-by-four that appeared to be floating in midair, however.

Viv walked slowly toward the alphas, realizing she probably could've stepped up to them in full view. They were too wrapped up in which one would go down first so the other could hop Stratus, who seemed unable to care less about who won the fight. Really.

Socrates started caterwauling, weaving through the bars of the gate, going inside of the compound then quickly back out, as if not knowing what to do or how to stop Viv.

Milan was a large black Loup with a mane that reached to the middle of his back. His ears were long and pinpoint straight, and his bared fangs were at least six inches long. He stood upright like a man, though his paws were those of a Loup, and he swiped at Warden with long, sharp, black claws. Warden was a blond Loup and nearly twice Milan's size. Yet he showed the worst of the wear simply because of his color. More blood stained his fur. It was difficult to tell if most of it came from his own wounds or was splatter from his opponent's. Suddenly, Whiskers and Yazdee started whooping and jumping up and down with excitement. Evidently Socrates's noise had caught their attention and they had zeroed in on the floating two-by-four.

Viv dared to move faster, fearing the racket stirred up by her cheerleading squad might capture Warden's or Milan's attention.

It did rouse Stratus. The alpha female lifted her head from her paws, looked past the two-by-four and directly at Viv as if she were in full view. Viv could've sworn she saw Stratus smirk. She hated when that Loup went into heat. It always turned the compound upside down. Throw in a stray male alpha from a different compound, and she had World War Seven.

Viv kept her focus on the alpha males, inching closer, dodging left, back, forward in rhythm with their fight. It felt like an odd war dance as she juggled around the fight, trying to avoid getting clawed, yet get close enough to make impact.

She took aim. Whichever Loup cleared first was the one she planned to whack.

They tumbled, clawed, she dodged left. Blood from one of the Loups sprayed across her shirt and jeans, then again before she felt it splatter across her face and slide down her neck. These guys were really getting out of control, and if she didn't do something soon, one of them was going to die. And that was not an option.

The closer she moved in, the harder they fought. She ducked left, more blood sprayed across her face. She felt it splat onto her head and through her hair, which she kept in a braid that reached the small of her back.

Finally, seeming to gather what strength he had left, Warden leaped out and took a huge swatch of flesh from Milan's chest, turning him in place. Blood sprayed everywhere, especially over Viv, who now looked like she'd bathed in it. Milan's eyes appeared dazed as he whirled about from the blow.

Before he could refocus for the fight, Viv grabbed the two-by-four in both hands and swung at him, whacking him across the head as hard as her tall, slender body would allow. That pitched him off balance and dropped him to the ground.

As Milan scrambled to get upright, Warden had enough time to race over to Stratus and attempt to mount her even before she stood.

Milan mewled when he saw Stratus begin to take all Warden had to offer.

Viv allowed herself to return to full view, tossed the two-by-four aside and snarled at Milan's mewling. "Oh, grow the hell up," she said, then whirled about and headed back for the gate.

En route, Viv pointed at Stratus, making sure she had her attention. "You want to play games with these guys, sistah? Then get ready to play hard because I quit."

Viv stormed off for the gate, her head buzzing with an ache so painful she could barely see.

No sooner did she unlock the gate, let herself through and relock it than Socrates started yelling at her. She ignored him, catching only a word or two from his rampage because of the buzzing in her head.

"You can't just leave, Viv," Socrates yelled after her.

She stormed past him, turning her back on the fortress bound with silver-tipped barbed wire. In the distance, she caught the sound of Whiskers fretting.

"Wait, wait! What do we do? Stop! Yazdee, what do we do now? What? Our leader has absconded!"

Socrates scrambled to the other side of the gate and watched Viv storm off. He knew he couldn't stop her, not when she was this mad, this disgusted. It worried him that her spells hadn't worked. Even under the circumstances, with all that just happened, leaving hadn't been the answer.

If Viv thought things were bad now, she was about to discover a new definition for worse.

Chapter 2

Nikoli Hyland and his cousins, Lucien, Gavril and Ronan, sat in brown leather captain's chairs across from one another in pairs. A small dining table separated them.

They were flying from New Zealand to New Orleans on the family's Gulfstream G200 jet as instructed. They'd received the alert yesterday evening with orders to leave immediately. The orders came from their fathers, who were brothers and retired Benders.

Although involved in the family business for the past ten years, the onset of a mission always settled hard in Nikoli's gut.

He was thirty-five years old, and his cousins only a year or two younger than he. It was still hard for him to intellectualize that they were the new generation of Benders. The tenth generation, to be exact. And, as usual with the onset of a mission, Nikoli pondered what that *something* was. Sometimes it felt like pride— heavy responsibility—purpose.

Tuning out his cousins' banter about the witches they were about to meet, he glanced out of the plane window, soaking in the sight of dawn beginning to light a blue-black sky. A finger snap brought his attention back to his cousins.

"Where'd you go, bro?" Lucien asked, grinning. "Neverland?"

"No, I heard everything you guys said. But it doesn't matter what these women look like," Nikoli said, knowing full well the appearance of each woman. His father had given him pictures to verify their identification. Each one was drop-dead gorgeous. He'd kept that information to himself, knowing how crude a couple of his cousins could be. "We're going over there for one reason and one reason only. Remember our mission creed. Keep your dick in your pants and your eyes and ears sure and mindful."

"Right," Ronan said.

Now it was Gavril's turn to roll his eyes.

"This is our biggest job ever," Nikoli continued. "And from all indications, it'll get even bigger before we land. We've been nickel and diming Cartesians for the past three years. One here, three there."

"Hey, don't forget about the fifteen we knocked off in Brazil last year," Lucien said. "That was no small bite of potato."

"It is when compared to what we're about to face," Nikoli said.

"How many we talking, cuz?" Gavril asked.

"From what I hear, we might be talking a hundred or more."

Ronan turned his attention back to his cousins and let out a low whistle.

Lucian grimaced. "How in the hell are just the four of us going to handle a hundred or more of those monstrosities? Especially if they pile up into one big-ass troop."

"Like we always do," Nikoli said. "We get 'em one at a time, bro. One at a time."

Cartesians were a nonentity to almost every human and many breeds from the netherworld on the planet. Reason being, Cartesians were rarely, if ever, seen. Nikoli didn't understand the entire story about how his family had initially gotten involved with fighting them, but he did know the enemy. He'd seen them.

Massive creatures. Some Cartesians stood eight to ten feet tall. Their bodies were covered with long thick scales like an armadillo's, only a hundred times thicker, and those scales hid beneath a heavy mat of black and brown fur. Six-inch, razor-sharp claws served for fingers and every tooth in a Cartesian's mouth was a lethally sharp, four-inch incisor.

One didn't simply stab a Cartesian in the heart or brain to kill it. In fact, Nikoli didn't think any Bender knew for sure if they could be killed. To destroy a Cartesian, Benders had been taught to shock it back into another dimension. The farther the dimension, the better.

Somehow Cartesians were able to cross over the wrinkles of time and space from one dimension to another through the smallest dimensional tear. And they traveled swiftly, always on the lookout for other netherworld creatures. Their purpose appeared to be total netherworld domination, no matter the kill. Vampire, werewolf, fae, leprechaun, djinn, anything and everything that did not make up the human race. A Cartesian killed any and all it found to absorb its victim's power.

The creatures had a leader, of that Nikoli was sure, but no one knew his name, not that it really mattered. It wasn't like someone could Google him.

What they needed to do was destroy him, by pushing him into the dimension of no return. The eleventh. Vanquish the head, the rest of the body dies. From all accounts, this so-called leader stood nearly twenty feet tall, but Nikoli would have to see that with his own eyes to believe it. All he had to worry about was destroying whatever Cartesians he found in his missions, hoping that luck or fate might hand him that leader one day.

It wasn't that Benders had any particular liking for vampires, werewolves and the like. But the secret society of Benders knew that if the Cartesians dominated the whole of the netherworld and became one sole power, that power would then take on the human race in order to achieve world domination. And with all that power wrapped up in an army of monstrous, furry armadillos with fangs and claws, world domination would be a cinch. Every Bender had sworn a solemn oath to do all in his power not to let that happen.

Not letting on his thoughts to his cousins, Nikoli secretly worried about the mission that lay before them. It was hard enough to destroy a Cartesian, but even with their massive size, they were difficult to spot due to the speed with which they traveled between dimensional folds.

Benders were trained to recognize a Cartesian's proximity by scent. The creatures emitted a horrendous odor, a mixture of sulfur and cloves. And for some odd reason, on occasion, Nikoli had picked up a vibration that ran up his spine right before he caught a whiff of the odor. He thought it might come from the disturbance of a dimensional fold, right before a Cartesian made its way into their world.

A Bender's job was to push Cartesians back through the dimensional rift with a scabior, an odd-looking tool that for all intents and purposes looked like a child's toy. It was an eight-inch-long metal rod with a marble-size bloodstone topping one end of its one-inch circumference.

Harmless-looking, but if held in the right hand and used in the right manner by a Bender, the scabior let out such a strong current of electrical power that it refolded the dimension from which the Cartesian had entered, pushing him back inside. With each dimensional backward thrust, the scabior emitted a loud, sizzling pop, heard only by the Bender. The number of pops told the Bender the number of dimensions he had been able to push the Cartesian through. To date,

Nikoli had only managed six, still the highest number among his cousins.

Each cousin sat quietly, staring off into the distance, probably thinking about what lay ahead.

A full five minutes went by before Lucien broke the silence. "Any of you have an idea about how those ugly mother-effers were created?"

Gavril cleared his throat. "All I know is that eons ago somebody pissed somebody else off, and that somebody else turned somebody number one into a Cartesian. How they multiplied from there, I don't have a clue."

Ronan leaned over and crossed his arms on the small table. "The first one was created as punishment, for what I'm not sure. I don't think any Bender still alive really knows for sure. But Cartesians multiply by kills."

Frowning, Lucien cocked his head to one side. "Huh?"

"Kills," Ronan repeated. "When the first Cartesian made his first kill in the netherworld, it gave him enough power to create another one just like him. That new Cartesian makes a kill, it now has the power to reproduce itself, but only if the original Cartesian allows it. And you can bet he does. Who wouldn't want the biggest army in the universe?"

"You mean they don't breed like everybody else?" Lucien asked.

"No," Ronan replied. "As far as I know, and this comes from two of the oldest Benders I know in Switzerland, Cartesians don't even have sex organs. Not only do they not procreate, they don't even have genders."

"That's fucked up," Gavril said. "No wonder those things are always out hunting, killing, destroying shit. I'd probably be that way, too, if I never had sex."

"But if they're genderless, why are they usually referred to as male?" Lucien asked.

"Probably because they're big sonsabitches," Nikoli chimed in.

Gavril shook his head. "Well, all I've gotta say is whoever or whatever did the punishing sure screwed up. Bet they didn't count on the bastard wanting and working toward ruling the entire universe."

"Did everyone get the info on why so many suddenly hit New Orleans?" Ronan asked.

"One of the Triads," Nikoli said.

"You mean those witches we're supposed to meet out there?" Lucien asked.

"Yes," Nikoli said, then signaled for the steward standing at the back of the plane to bring drinks to the table.

"Why are they called Triads?" Lucien asked.

Nikoli waited for the steward to place four glasses of cold, sparkling water on the table then head back to his station before he responded. "Because they're triplets."

"Oh, man, sweet!" Gavril said, twitching in his seat.

"Down, boy," Nikoli warned. "Remember the code. No funny business while on a mission."

Gavril groaned and tossed his head back against his seat. "Spoil sport."

"Do these triplets run their own coven?" Ronan asked.

Nikoli shook his head, then took a long, much-needed drink of water. "Triads belong to a sect of witches called the Circle of Sisters. They don't have covens like other witches. The Circle of Sisters is small, comparatively. Maybe fifteen hundred worldwide."

"All of them sets of triplets?" Lucien asked.

"No. There's only one full set of Triads per generation, and each triplet has a specific duty."

"I'd like to give one a specific duty," Gavril said, then turned his head quickly when Nikoli scowled at him.

"One of them is responsible for the Loup Garou, another for the Nosferatu and the third the Chenilles."

"Wow," Gavril said. "You're talking original breeds there, cuz. Before vampires, werewolves and zombies and shit."

"I know," Nikoli said. "That's why this mission was put together so quickly. Those breeds have never been hit by Cartesians. The Triads always kept a tight rein on them."

"So what happened," Lucien asked. "Who screwed up and how?"

Nikoli shrugged. "No idea. Guess we'll find out when we get there."

Lucien whistled through his teeth. "Must have been a pretty huge screw-up to cause a rift big enough to let that many Cartesians through."

"Not necessarily," Nikoli countered. "All it takes is a miniscule tear. Once one gets through, any number that want to follow can."

"How many of the Originals have been destroyed so far?" Ronan asked.

"By the time we land and get to the Triads, over a hundred Loup Garous."

"Since they're witches," Lucien said, "can't they just cast some hoodoo spell and close the rift themselves?"

"Nobody can mess with a Cartesian except a Bender," Gavril said proudly.

"True, but they don't even know what's about to hit them," Nikoli said. "The tear hasn't been completed yet."

Ronan leaned back in his seat. "Are they ever in for a surprise."

"Sadly, yes," Nikoli agreed. He felt bad for the Triad he'd yet to meet. Chances were she'd created the rift by accident. Probably didn't even know that rifts existed—or Cartesians for that matter.

As they closed in on New Orleans, Nikoli sensed a circling of sorts. Like the four of them were pioneers, traveling out west by wagon and surrounded by a massive tribe of banshees they could not yet see.

Nikoli sensed something big was about to break loose. He feared this fight might be bigger than any Bender generation had encountered before, and there had been many.

He looked over at his cousins, who were talking softly among themselves. Except for Ronan, of course. Mr. Sole Man was staring out the window, probably thinking about the quest ahead.

The four cousins couldn't have been closer if they'd been brothers. And in his heart of hearts, Nikoli trusted each one with his life. They were equally strong, talented and vicious warriors against the Cartesians.

Regardless, a small nagging voice inside his gut warned that four of them were heading to New Orleans ready to fight, but only three would be returning home.

Chapter 3

By the time Viv had ferried to the opposite side of the river, it was almost ten o'clock in the morning. She smelled coffee and beignets from nearby cafes, and it made her stomach rumble. What she wouldn't give for one of Evette's special hickory-blend coffees and chocolate-drizzled beignets right about now. But food had to wait, she realized as she hurried to her home in the Garden District.

She shared the Victorian with her sisters. It sat on the corner of St. Charles and Washington Avenue. The house had belonged to their mother, who'd died in an airplane accident when they were nineteen.

They never knew their father, as was often the case with Triads. For some odd reason, the fathers of each generation of Triads took to the hills as soon as they discovered their wife was pregnant. Wrong men? Wrong timing? Who knew. Not that it made any difference to Viv.

Although she was definitely heterosexual and struggled with raging hormones from times to time, she didn't need a man to make her life complete. She had enough on her plate. Maybe her ancestors had felt the same way for none of them had remarried, which was why the François name still held strong today. Although exhausted, Viv picked up her pace, anxious to get home. Each sister had a floor with a bedroom and bath to call her own. Evette, whom they called Evee, had the first floor; Viv, the second; and Abigail, whom they called Gilly, had the third.

Evee owned a café off Royal Street called Bon Appétit. She opened at eight o'clock in the morning and closed at two o'clock, right after the lunch crowd dispersed so there was a good chance she wouldn't be home.

Gilly, on the other hand, would be home. She owned a bar-and-grill off Iberville Street called Snaps. It opened at two o'clock in the afternoon and closed at two o'clock the following morning. Those long hours gave Viv some confidence that Gilly would still be sleeping right now, which meant she had a good shot at getting into the house and into her bedroom undetected.

Thinking about her sisters and the broods they were responsible for made the twinge of guilt Viv carried for her Loup Garous grow stronger.

She'd left without tending to those who worked during the day at construction jobs or city maintenance. Certainly by now, especially at this hour, many would be wondering when they would be released from the compound to go about their chores. The only good thing was that Loups were infamously resilient. If no one released them for duty, they'd make use of the day by napping, prowling or watching Stratus get her fill of Warden.

It seemed to take forever for Viv to finally make it home. Just as she pushed open the back door, Socrates ran past her into the house. She hadn't noticed him on the ferry nor on her walk to the house, yet here he was, skittering around the kitchen toward the hallway, where he started caterwauling at the top of his lungs.

Viv released her partial invisibility spell, which was useless around her sisters anyway.

"Stop that!" she demanded in a loud whisper. "What kind of familiar are you, trying to get your own mistress busted?"

Gilly slept on the north end of the third floor, so although Socrates was loud, Viv doubted Gilly heard him. What she didn't count on was Elvis, an albino ferret with ruby eyes and a pink nose and ears. Gilly's familiar.

Viv barely made it to the stairway when Elvis came streaking down the stairs like a bolt of lightning. The moment he spotted Viv, he came to an abrupt stop, flipped over one step, then jumped up and started racing back up the stairs, letting out a shrill chirping sound as he went. She knew he meant to fetch Gilly, and Viv tried to outrun the inevitable by taking the stairs to the second floor two at a time.

She raced into her bedroom but before she had a chance to close the door, Gilly shoved against it and pushed her way inside.

Dressed only in a pink silk sleep shirt, with her black pixie cut spiked from sleep, Gilly's mouth dropped open when she saw Viv.

Before her sister uttered a word, Viv had a peculiar thought about Hollywood and witches. Had anyone been watching a movie, they would have expected Gilly to immediately cast a spell that would wash the blood from Viv and have any wounds appear in purple neon so they'd be easily detected.

But there was no spell-casting, and this wasn't Hollywood. Witches were human, just a different race, and just as each race had their distinct features and culture, witches were no different.

A witch's potential for power often depended on the clan from which she was born. Viv and her sisters came from the Circle of Sisters, a relatively small, close and extremely secretive group with maybe fifteen hundred witches worldwide at best. Viv, Evee and Gilly were even a subgroup within the Circle, since they were triplets.

"Wh-what the hell?" Gilly said, snapping Viv out of her daydream. All three of the sisters had olive complexions, but right now Gilly's face blanched as she took in all the blood covering Viv.

"What happened?" Gilly demanded. "Who attacked

you? Where are you hurt? Heavens, look at all that blood!"

Elvis scurried around his mistress's feet as if trying frantically to weave a web around them. Then in the blink of an eye, he scampered up Gilly's right leg, across her back and came to rest on her right shoulder.

"I'm going to call an ambulance," Gilly said, and Viv grabbed her by the arm before she had a chance to whirl about.

"Stop, it's not mine," Viv said. It took a few seconds for frenzy to leave Gilly's eyes and settle on Viv's face.

"What do you mean, it's not yours?"

Socrates rubbed up against Viv's left ankle then made his way between the sisters and politely sat as if to create a boundary. Elvis leaned over Gilly's shoulder, watching Socrates's every move. Socrates hissed at him, gold eyes blazing. "Just that," Viv said, obviously a little too nonchalant for Gilly's taste. In that moment, she saw her sister's black eyes turn auburn, which meant only one thing. Gilly's specialty was astral projection, and whenever she zoned off somewhere, the telltale sign was the change of her eye color. Right now, Viv would bet dollars to horseshoes that some ghost of Gilly present was at Bon Appétit summoning Evee home.

"Then you'd better start explaining really quickly," Gilly demanded. "Whose blood is it? Where did it come from?"

For the next ten or fifteen minutes, Viv tried to explain what happened at the compound. She kept stumbling over her own words, uncertain how to tell her sister why her own spells hadn't worked against the Loup Garou. Truth be told, she didn't know why they hadn't worked. Back at the compound, she thought her crappy attitude might have played a part in making the spells ineffectual. But after giving it much thought on her way home, the only thing she knew for sure was that the spells *should* have worked despite her mood. And how was she going to tell her sister why she'd whacked Milan upside the head with a two-by-four, then walked away?

Viv had circled the conversation back to Milan in the compound and how he and Warden had gone to war when Gilly blew out an exasperated breath.

"You covered that already," Gilly said. "Just spit it out. All of it."

Suddenly Viv heard a loud squawking followed by the entrance of Hoot, a copper-and-white horned owl. Evee's familiar. He swooped down, barely missing Socrates's head, then rocketed back up, nearly knocking Elvis off Gilly's shoulder.

"Damn it!" Gilly yelled and swung out an arm to keep Hoot from flying at her.

That sent Hoot into a high-pitched screech, which pushed Elvis's squeal button to top volume. Socrates stood with his back arched, teeth bared, and hissed like a bucket of snakes.

"Y'all shut the hell up," Viv shouted to no avail. The room continued to vibrate from all the hissing, shrieking, squawking and yelling.

The sisters looked at each other, perplexed. Time seemed to stand still in a deafening vacuum that neither of them could quiet. It wasn't unusual for their familiars to snap at one another from time to time, but normally they got along like brothers and sisters. But this was as though each familiar was out to protect their own territory.

Finally Viv held her arms out at her side, hands out, palms up, and said, "Silence is all I care to hear, I command this noise away from here."

Immediately, all three familiars went silent. Gilly blinked rapidly, then said, "Why didn't I think of doing that?"

Socrates meowed, then said to Viv, "If I'm not mistaken, this is our domain. Would you please get that intolerable ingrate of a bird and elongated rat out of this room?"

Viv nudged him with a foot, signaling for him to hush. Fortunately, to Gilly, Socrates had only caterwauled since only the mistress of a familiar understood its voice.

She didn't know how much time had passed after the racket died down, but it felt like only seconds before Evee burst into the room, out of breath, dressed in a smartly fitted, powder-blue pantsuit and black pumps.

"I—I left Margaret in ch-charge of the café and hurried over as fast as I could," Evee said, panting. "What… Look at you! All the blood! What happened? Where did this happen? Did somebody attack you? We need to call an ambulance. We need to call nine-one-one! No, I'll get the car. It'll be faster."

"We don't need an ambulance," Viv assured Evee.

"She said it's not her blood," Gilly added.

Evee's copper-colored eyes grew wide. "Did you kill somebody?"

"Of course not," Viv said, feeling guilt twist a bit harder in her gut. That answer might have been different had she hit Milan any harder with the two-by-four.

Now that all three sisters were in the room, Elvis, Hoot and Socrates settled down next to their mistresses.

Viv's reassurance may have calmed Evee's voice but seemed to do very little for her nerves. Evee reached out to touch Viv with a shaking hand, then quickly drew it back.

"Really," Viv said. "I'm okay."

Gilly grabbed one of Evee's hands and pulled her sister to the edge of Viv's bed, where they sat.

"Okay, enough bullshit," Gilly said. "Tell us what happened."

Viv sighed, glanced around for a place to sit. Then decided to remain standing so as not to get blood on anything and told them what had happened that morning.

"Why didn't you just open the damn ground up where they were fighting and drop the dumbasses into a hole," Gilly huffed after she'd finished. "If they wanted to kill each other, they could have done it in there. Saved you a lot of grief. And a pair of jeans and shirt."

"Oh, please," Evee said with a shake of her head.

Now that Gilly had mentioned it, Viv didn't know why she hadn't thought about opening the ground while at the compound. The shock of that might have stopped the fight. Once again, she blamed the brain pause.

"I didn't want them dead," she said to Gilly. "They were only fighting for some alpha tail."

Gilly narrowed her eyes. "Wait—you mean those two alphas were fighting so close to the gate where you were watching that you got doused in blood?"

Evee nudged Gilly with a shoulder. "Stop interrogating her like you're some kind of detective," she said. "Give her a break. I mean, look at her. Don't you think she's been through enough?"

Gilly nodded slowly and clicked her tongue between her teeth. "Let me guess. You did that partial invisibility thing and went inside the compound to stop them didn't you?"

Viv looked down at the highly polished oak floor beneath her boots.

Evee and Gilly stood up simultaneously.

"My word, please don't tell me that's what you did!" Evee said.

Viv glanced up at them. "I couldn't think of anything else to do."

Gilly stomped a foot. "I told you what you should have done. You had no business being in the middle of that compound. You could've gotten yourself killed. Two big alpha males like that. What were you gonna do, slap some sense into them?"

"What did you do?" Evee asked shakily, as if not really wanting to know the answer.

Viv glanced away, vividly recalling the scene as she described it to them.

When she was finished, Evee suddenly snapped her fingers. "This whole thing about your powers not working at the compound… Did you remember to read your Grimoire this morning before the feeding?"

"Now who's playing detective?" Gilly said with a snort.

Viv glanced down again. "Yeah, well, it's what we do every morning, right?"

"She asked if *you* read yours," Gilly said, her eyes narrowing again.

"Okay, so maybe I didn't this morning," Viv admitted. "But that doesn't mean I wasn't going to when I got back. I mean, we have this routine where we read it before feeding every morning, but that's not like a hard and fast rule."

"Oh, Viv," Evee said. "You know the rules. That particular one may not be hard and fast, but it's one we've stuck to for years. We have to stay sharp with study. Always armed and ready for anything."

Out of nowhere, Viv felt a nudge in her gut, an urgency that they had to look at their Grimoires right now.

As if picking up on the unspoken message, Gilly and Evee suddenly raced out of the room, and Viv knew they were going to get their books. Hesitantly, she went to the top bureau drawer and pulled out her copy. It was nearly eight inches thick, the heavy parchment pages worn, its cover weathered Elder-wood. She placed it on her bed and within moments Gilly and Evee were standing on either side of her, books in hand. They each placed their Grimoire on either side of hers.

Without a word, the sisters reached for the front cover of their book and opened them simultaneously. The three gasped in unison. Recessed in the front cover of each book was a four-inch oblong mirror. Instead of the apocalyptic scene they were used to viewing each day, the only thing reflecting from the mirrors now were swirls of gray, like billowing smoke.

"What does this mean?" Evee whispered.

"I have no idea," Gilly said. "It's the first time I've ever seen it do this." She leaned over and sniffed at her Grimoire, then Evee's and Viv's. "You smell that?"

"What?" Evee copied her sister's motion and sniffed her book. "It's…" She frowned.

"It's what?" Viv asked, following suit. Her Grimoire did smell a little funny. It not only carried its usual aged, worn-wood scent, there was something different, albeit faint, mixed in. "Is that nutmeg I'm smelling?"

"Cloves," Evee said. She put her nose to Gilly's Grimoire, then Viv's. "Definitely cloves."

"When the hell were these books ever around cloves?" Gilly asked. "Did you bring some back from the café?"

"Why would I do that? To stick cloves between the pages of our books?" Evette said smartly. She tsked. "That's absurd. Absolutely not."

Gilly shrugged and sniffed again.

Viv glanced at her sisters. "Do you think the gray in the mirrors has something to do with why my spells didn't work at the compound?"

Gilly gave her a serious look. "It could be because

of what happened at the compound. You're the clairvoyant. What do you intuit from this?"

Viv studied the mirrors, the swirls of gray roiling ever faster. "That the future is uncertain because of something that must unfold. That's why we can't see anything. Something must've happened to change the order of what was to be."

Gilly clamped a fist on her hip and turned to Viv. "Tell us exactly what happened when you were at the compound."

"What are you talking about? I already did."

"Do it again," Gilly demanded. "Don't leave anything out. It could have been something you did or something you said without realizing it that made this change."

With a heavy sigh and slow shake of her head, Viv retold the story. Only this time, she included the very end. "So after I whacked Milan over the head, I turned around to leave, pointed at Stratus and told her if she wanted to play games she was on her own because I quit."

Evee gasped.

"Wait. Wait one damn minute," Gilly said, holding up a hand. "You said *what*?"

"How could you say you just quit?" Evee asked. "That's why these mirrors are gray. I mean, did you really mean that, Viv? You're not going to watch over the Loup Garous? You're just going to leave them at the compound?"

"No," Viv said. "I was just pissed off. Was in a real

crappy mood. It's not like I really meant I was quitting this whole gig for good. I just had enough for the day."

Gilly closed her Grimoire and held it close to her chest. "Do you think the universe knows the difference between a bad mood and truth when it comes out of your mouth? You might have set something in motion, and we have no idea what that is."

"I said I'd fix it," Viv said, growing frustrated.

"It has to be done immediately," Evee said, closing and picking up her own Grimoire. "Viv, you forget how powerful your words really are. When you said 'I quit,' you rubbed up against the aura that covers the Circle of Sisters. The universe itself. So if you're really going to fix this, you have to go back there now."

"I intend to," Viv said through clenched teeth.

Neither sister responded.

Viv looked from Evee to Gilly. "Look, tell me the truth. Don't either of you get tired of all this sometimes? What we do is not normal, even for witches. We can't even use the spells we know to enrich our own lives. Everything gets sucked up taking care of the broods we're responsible for. We have to babysit them because of something our great-great-times-thirty grandmother did. Why do we have to be punished for it? Don't you get tired of it?"

"Of course I do," Gilly said. "But quit acting like a martyr. We all get sick of it, just like any human gets sick of their job from time to time. But it is what it is. We have big responsibilities, and you can't just throw words around like 'I quit,' then pretend you can just walk into your boss's office the next day and say, 'Oh, I really didn't mean it. I take it back.'"

"Fine. Got it. Enough already!" Viv said, and whirled about, ready to leave the room. She had more than her fill of her sisters ragging on her.

Chapter 4

Any silence was short lived because Hoot, Elvis and Socrates started a cacophony of squawks, hisses, chirps and shrieks.

Amid the noise, the sisters heard someone pounding on the front door downstairs. Pounding hard, as though they meant to break the door down if it wasn't answered right away. The sisters glanced at each other, then ran downstairs as quickly as possible.

Viv made it to the door first. Already angry and half expecting to see a wayward missionary standing on the front porch ready to show them the error of their ways, she yanked it open. "What in the hell do you—"

The words died in her throat when she saw four men standing side by side on the porch. For more than a few seconds, she stood mesmerized. As a clairvoyant, she didn't sense danger. As a woman, she saw trouble times four.

All four men appeared to be in their early thirties, stood over six feet tall and were dressed in black. Black jeans, black T-shirts pulled taut over huge, muscular chests and biceps that rippled when they moved. Their shirts were neatly tucked into their pants and held in place by wide black belts with ornate silver buckles.

Although there were four, Viv seemed incapable of taking her eyes off one in particular. He had gray eyes the color of storm clouds and smoke. Walnut-colored hair fell to his shoulders. A cleft accented his chin, and his beard and mustache were trimmed into a perfect Van Dyke. Had he been ice cream on the lawn, Viv would've gladly licked him away from every blade of grass.

"May we help you?" Gilly asked, stepping up alongside Viv.

Viv blinked quickly, surprised and a bit unnerved by her sudden and blatant hunger for the man. Remembering she was still covered in blood, she darted away from the door and ran for the stairs, leaving her sisters to deal with the strangers.

"Is she all right?" Viv heard one of the men ask as she took the stairs two at a time. She wanted to hide in a closet for the rest of the day from embarrassment.

After showering and washing her hair in record time, she dried off. Although her long black hair was still damp, she whipped it into a braid, then headed to the closet, where she pulled out a pair of white linen pants and a light blue pullover to wear. She slid her feet into sneakers then bounded out of the room and down the stairs.

Viv found her sisters and the four strangers in the sitting room. It was a spacious area that Evee had tastefully decorated in mahogany and leather antiques. Two Chippendale couches covered in delicate beige fabric needled with gold-and-maroon filigree faced each other in front of a stone fireplace.

Three of the men sat on the couch to her left. The fourth, the one with the storm-gray eyes, sat in a maroon wingback chair beside it. Her sisters sat on either end of the couch on the right.

Six pairs of eyes locked onto her the moment she entered. Everyone looked cordial but grim.

"If you don't mind," Evee said as Viv walked toward her sisters, "would you please start again so our sister can be brought up to speed? This is Vivienne, by the way. You can call me Evee, her Viv, and Abigail goes by Gilly."

On her way to the couch to join her sisters, Socrates suddenly darted into the room and ran between Viv's legs, causing her to stumble. He jumped onto the couch between Gilly and Evee, while Viv flailed to find purchase.

A strong arm caught her mid-stumble, and she held back a hiss. In that second she felt ready to combust. The heat that abruptly shot through her body from his touch made her feel like she'd spontaneously combust. Viv didn't have to see his face to know the arm belonged to Storm Eyes. She glanced up to confirm. Oh, it was him all right.

Regaining her composure quickly, Viv gave him a brisk nod, then hurried over to her sisters. Socrates scurried off the couch to make room for her, then darted out of the room as quickly as he'd entered.

When she sat, her heart thudding in her chest, Viv tried to appear nonchalant.

"Are you all right?" Storm Eyes asked Viv.

"Quite all right," she said. "I apologize for disappearing so suddenly when you arrived. An incident at work… Well, I'm sure you noticed my appearance. I wasn't injured. And as for the stumble just now…" Viv shrugged. "Cats will be cats. They have minds of their own."

"They certainly do," Evee said, tossing Viv an odd, questioning look. She turned back to the men. "Gentlemen, if you would continue…"

Storm Eyes smiled and nodded. "Once again, I do apologize for intruding without prior notice. We came as quickly as possible, directly from the airport. My name is Nikoli Hyland, and these are my cousins." He motioned to the men sitting on the couch and named them from left to right. "Lucien, Gavril and Ronan Hyland."

Each man looked like he deserved a front cover on *GQ Magazine*.

Lucien's hair was the color of gingerbread, shoulder-length, and his emerald green eyes seemed to hold a perpetual sparkle. He had full lips and sported a well-trimmed beard and mustache.

Gavril had collar-length, tousled, soot-black hair.

His eyes were violet and set deep into a well chiseled, lightly bearded face.

Ronan sat and moved with the precision of a drill sergeant. His serious black eyes were hooded by long-thick lashes, and his collar-length black hair was neatly groomed. His square-jawed face held the hint of a five o'clock shadow.

"Why are you here?" Viv asked Nikoli bluntly.

"According to them, they're here to help us," Gilly said, not giving him a chance to answer.

Viv felt her blood run cold. "What do you mean?"

"Allow me to explain," Nikoli said. "As we were telling your sisters—"

"It's complicated," Evee said to Viv. "I'm still not sure I understand everything."

Lucien nodded. "It certainly is complex, but we're more than happy to go over everything again with you."

"We're Benders," Gavril said to Viv. "And we've been commissioned to you."

Viv frowned. "What's a Bender, and who do we know that would commission you to us? How do you know us?"

"We're the tenth generation of Benders assigned to keep watch over Triads," Ronan said.

"Ten generations?" Gilly said. "Why haven't we heard of you before? Our Elders would've told us about someone like you."

"Not necessarily," Nikoli said, then looked at Viv. "There are many generations of Triads who never knew we existed."

"That doesn't make sense," Evee said. "If you're

supposed to help us, how does anyone get that help if they don't know you exist?"

"They didn't know because they didn't need us," Nikoli said. "Unless there's an emergency, we tend to be more of a blend-into-the-background sort of group." He smiled, and his dazzling white teeth and full lips made Viv shift uncomfortably in her seat.

Gilly shook her head. "You're going to have to start from the beginning because I'm totally lost."

"If we were here to con you," Ronan said, "wouldn't we be asking for something?"

"Yeah, so?" Viv said, in Gilly's defense. "We haven't gotten the whole picture yet, so the bullshit might easily be hiding in the back story, and you just haven't gotten to it yet."

"Good point, Viv," Nikoli said, his smile broadening. "But I know you're a clairvoyant, so you already know we mean you no harm. Isn't that true?"

Viv looked at Gilly then Evee. "Did either of you tell him that?"

Both shook their head.

"We know of the Triads," Nikoli continued. "The Circle of Sisters is a very cloistered group, and they keep knowledge of you close to their chest." His eyes moved ever so quickly down to Viv's covered breasts before he turned away and shifted in his chair. "Just the fact that we know all about you—where to find you, what you can do, what you're responsible for—should tell you something."

"If what you say is true," Viv said, "then what are Benders supposed to help us with?

Nikoli's eyes darkened and his face hardened. "Serious trouble is headed your way. An attack on one of your factions. More attacks will follow."

All three sisters sat staring at him, open-mouthed.

"A-attacks?" Viv said.

Nikoli nodded slowly. "What's expected is total annihilation of each of your sectors."

The sisters moved to the edge of the couch like they were about to spring off it.

"Whoa!" Gilly said, holding up both hands. "What the hell?"

"All of them?" Evee asked, her hands beginning to tremble.

"H-how do you know this?" Viv asked, trying to keep her voice level.

"Because our job is to find, keep tabs on and kill Cartesians, many of whom are planning attacks on your territory," Nikoli said.

Viv got to her feet and gestured for a time-out. "Hidden Benders, too much knowledge of what you should know nothing about, now you throw in these…these Corinthians?"

"Cartesians," Gavril corrected.

"Whatever," Viv said, starting to pace. "What are they?"

"Cartesians are monstrous creatures," Nikoli said. "Many stand ten feet or taller. They have incredibly thick scales that cover their body, and the scales are hidden beneath a dense mat of fur. The scales and fur protect them from any form of human weapon. Even a grenade wouldn't faze them. Their teeth are all massive incisors, made to rip and shred, and their claws are four to six inches long and butcher-knife sharp. They travel through dimensions and get into our world through rifts. Their sole purpose is to destroy the whole of the netherworld so they will have absolute power. Every time they kill a creature, be it a vampire, werewolf, djinn, or anything from the netherworld, they absorb that creature's power into themselves. That power allows them to multiply in numbers."

"That can't be possible," Viv said, her head buzzing with all the information. "If creatures that size were roaming around this planet, surely we'd know of their existence."

"I remember the Elders talking about them," Evee said, biting her lower lip. "When we were little. Much, much younger. Remember? Taka told us. She didn't call them Cartesians, not that I recall anyway, but it sounded like bogeyman-talk to me. You know, something to scare us into being good."

"I don't remember any of the Elders or even Mom talking about that kind of creature," Gilly said. She turned to Viv. "You?"

"No."

"Wait," Gilly said, standing up and whirling on the balls of her feet to face Nikoli. "What's this about traveling through dimensions?"

"The reason Cartesians are not as widely known as others from the netherworld is because they hide between dimensions." Nikoli placed one hand atop the other, indicating layers. "They're able to travel through the folds of time and space, move from dimension to

dimension. They attack, then simply vanish into another realm. Like they never existed at all."

"How many dimensions are there?" Viv asked.
"How much hiding space do the bastards have?"

"Ten dimensions," Lucien said. "But we've only
been able to push them back to six."

"Actually, there are eleven dimensions," Ronan said.
"The eleventh is still controversial in today's scientific
think tanks, but it exists."

"What causes a rift in a dimension?" Viv asked.

Nikoli slid to the edge of his seat, giving her his full
attention. "Anything that produces a large amount of
atmospheric, electrical static. Like a tsunami, Category
Five hurricane… Words from a powerful Triad. Once
the tear is created, one or many Cartesians will plow
through it, capture whatever netherworldly creature it
can, kill it, then return the creature's power to the Cartesian's leader to do with as he sees fit."

"The creeps have a leader?" Gilly asked.

"Yes," Nikoli said. "He's the one all Benders truly
seek. He wants to possess the power of every netherworldly creature in existence. Once he's accomplished
that, we fear his ultimate goal is to control mankind.
To be the supreme power of the universe. He'd be able
to control the very structure of planetary alignment
with that much power."

Gilly and Evee looked over at Viv, who lowered her
head. She knew they were thinking about her saying
she'd quit this morning. She wondered how Nikoli knew.

"Ten—eleven—dimensions, does it really matter?"

Viv said, to get her sisters' eyes off her. "How do you kill what you can't see?"

"Oh, we can see them," Lucien said, "but only after we track them by scent."

"What kind of scent?" Evette asked.

Gavril wrinkled his nose. "Like rotten eggs and cloves mixed together."

Evee's head whipped in Viv's direction. "Cloves?"

Viv swallowed hard, eyeing Evee and Gilly. She turned to Gavril then to Nikoli. "We've smelled it. The cloves, I mean."

The cousins looked at each other, appearing puzzled.

"*You* smelled it?" Nikoli asked. "Where?"

"Here, in the house," Evee said. "In our Gr... Our books. We opened three books and caught a whiff of it."

"Why did the four of you look so...I don't know... out of sorts when we mentioned the scent?" Viv asked.

"Because, normally, humans can only pick up a whiff of that scent at the time of a Cartesian's entry or right after an attack. It concerns me that you smelled it in your home. What kind of books were you referring to?" Nikoli asked Evette.

The triplets eyed each other. No one knew of their Grimoires except the Elders or those within the Circle of Sisters. They were taught from a very young age that the books and their contents were not to be shared with anyone except another Sister.

"Personal books," Viv finally replied. "Doesn't matter what kind of book. The point you're trying to make is that we smelled it in here, right?"

Nikoli stared at her, and Viv saw something in his eyes that made her insides feel hot and quivery. "Right."

Suddenly a loud, frantic pounding came from the front door. Without a word, Viv, Gilly and Evee ran toward it.

Through the side windows that bordered the heavy front door, Viv saw Jaco, her East pack leader, standing at the front door, his face serious and drawn. In human form, he stood over six-four with a massive chest and a long mane of black hair that reached below his shoulders. He wore jeans and a white T-shirt. His eyes, usually a brilliant green, looked faded, dull. The sight of him made Viv's heart stutter to a stop. Even though he had access in and out of the locked compound as one of her generals, Jaco *never* came here. For him to come directly to her home meant something had to be seriously wrong.

Jaco pounded on the door again and was about to give it another hit when Viv opened it.

Jaco took one look at her and took a step back. "I must speak with you immediately," he said.

She motioned him inside.

He shook his head. "I think it is best if we speak privately."

Viv motioned him inside again. "Whatever needs to be said can certainly be said in front of my sisters."

Jaco nodded. "As you wish." He stepped inside, and Viv closed the door behind him.

"Is there a problem at the East lair?" Viv asked.

"No," Jaco said. He looked uneasily at Gilly and Evee. "May I speak freely?" he asked Viv.

She glanced toward the sitting room, saw the four cousins had remained inside. "Absolutely."

He nodded, then lowered his eyes slightly. "The problem is not at the East lair. The problem is at the North compound, where you were this morning." He hesitated and Viv signaled for him to continue.

This time he looked her square in the eye. "There has been a breach in the North compound. We have at least a hundred and fifty Loup Garou dead. The front and back entries were wide open and there are many gaps throughout the fenced territory."

Gilly moaned and Evee gasped. Viv simply stared at him.

"If a hundred and fifty are dead," Evee said, her eyes wide with panic, "then that means at least two hundred might be loose in the city."

"Or dead farther back on the feeding grounds," Jaco said. "I didn't have a chance to check every inch of the territory." He looked at Viv. "I had gone there to get Milan as I had been notified he was missing and suspected he would be near Stratus. I spotted the massacre as soon as I arrived. Did a quick check along the entire fence lines, then came here to let you know."

Viv nodded, feeling like someone had thrown a fifty-pound boulder into her stomach. "Go back to the North compound. I'll meet you there and get this figured out."

Jaco nodded, turned on his heels, opened the front door and disappeared in a flash.

As soon as the front door closed, Gilly whirled about and faced her. A cocoon of hot air wrapped tight around Viv. Always an indicator of Gilly's fury.

"Viv François," Gilly said in a low, trembling voice. She took a step closer to her sister. "What the fuck have you done?"

Chapter 5

The first emotion to hit Viv full in the heart when she made it back to the ranch and the compound with Nikoli was shock. A huge sob suddenly locked up in her chest, and she feared if she released it, she'd be changed forever. She didn't know what to think—how to think.

She didn't even remember leaving the house. Somehow in the midst of the scramble to get to the compound, Nikoli appeared to take charge, ordering Lucien and Ronan to go with Evee to check on her Nosferatu, and Gavril to go with Gilly to check on her Chenilles. Gilly had started to protest, but instinct told Viv Nikoli was right and she told her sisters as much.

Viv stood, holding a hand over her mouth. Still a sob escaped. "Who could have... How did... Oh, this can't be. It can't."

Socrates sat between Viv and Nikoli, his head lowered. Then he let out a loud mewl and said to Viv, "I told you not to leave! Oh dear, oh dear. This is so terrible, so horrific." He sounded like an old, fretting, English butler. "What shall we do, Vivienne? What shall we do?"

Reflexively, Viv turned her head away from the scene before her and buried her face in Nikoli's shoulder, never giving a thought to the fact that they'd only met hours earlier. He cupped her head with a hand. "How?" she whispered. "Who?"

"The Cartesians," Nikoli said, his voice hard.

Viv forced herself to turn back. The very gate that she'd opened earlier, and knew she had locked before she'd left, had been torn away from the fencing that held it up. Rips and gouges ran throughout the fencing as far as the eye could see. Far worse were the bodies of her Loups strewn everywhere. Many lay in the area where Milan and Warden had been fighting earlier that morning.

With Nikoli beside her, Viv took a tentative step inside the compound, beyond where the gate should have been. Her tears refused to be held back any longer and started to flow profusely down her cheeks.

When a Loup died, it immediately transformed to its human body. It made her think of all the wars that had been fought by countries around the world and how their battlegrounds must have looked a lot like this. Body after bloody body. The air reeked of blood, urine and feces. A putrid, solid scent that forced her to hold a hand over her mouth and nose.

She whimpered when she spotted Whiskers. Her timid, sweet Whiskers. Death stealing her beautiful blond coat and leaving behind a young woman who appeared no older than twenty with long, blond, blood-matted hair. Her body was so mutilated she was barely recognizable.

"No," she mumbled between her fingers. "Heavens, no…"

To her left, Viv saw Warden, or what was left of him. Stratus lay beneath him, both positioned as if they still copulated. But that was far from the case. They lay in what looked like a swimming pool of blood. Stratus was on her stomach, but her head had been twisted about so it faced the middle of her back.

"Moose," Viv groaned between sobs when she spotted her big, lovable oaf crumpled and flattened beneath a tree. It looked like he'd been run over by a semi.

So many bodies everywhere. Certainly they couldn't all be dead. Not all…

Dropping her hand from her mouth and nose, Viv let out a shrill call to her Loup Garous. The sound wasn't audible to the human ear, but any Loup Garou within a reasonable distance would hear it and recognize the sound as her beckoning call.

When nothing stirred, Viv called again, cupping her hands around her mouth so the sound would travel as far as possible through the five hundred acres. She called and called until her throat hurt.

Still not getting any response, Viv closed her eyes and sent out her own vibration, sent it through the earth, causing the ground to rumble with it. *"Your mis-*

tress desires your presence. Your mistress demands your presence."

Nobody came.

"I really didn't mean it," Viv said, turning to give Nikoli a sorrowful look. "I was just upset, you know? Tired of fighting with them." Fresh tears poured down her face.

Nikoli put an arm around her shoulders and pulled her in close. "I know. We can't bring these Loups back, but we can damn sure make certain it doesn't happen again. Trust me."

Viv lowered her head, sobbing, and gave a slight nod. She had no other choice but to trust because she and her sisters had no idea about the enemy targeting them.

"Right now, we've got to give these guys a proper burial. If we don't, the stench will only grow stronger, cause people downwind to start investigating." Nikoli lifted Viv's chin. "You up for that?"

The question added starch to her back, making Viv stand taller and lift her head higher. "Yes. They're my Loups, and I won't leave them rotting here like garbage at a slaughterhouse."

Nikoli nodded, and he and Viv walked back to the outside of the compound.

When they stood just past the entrance, Viv closed her eyes and released the same vibrations that she'd sent out to summon her Loups, only stronger. She held her arms out in front of her, hands out, palms up, and pulled from deep within herself, seemingly from her soul, a call to Mother Earth to bring her dead brood front and center.

In that moment, the ground began to rumble and roll like soft waves on an ocean. Within the five hundred acres, the ground rolled gently from North to South, then East to West, then vice versa. Viv opened her eyes and watched as body upon body rolled into a heap near the tree where she'd found Moose. She lost count after ninety.

When no more bodies found their way center, Viv lowered her arms and scrubbed her hands over her face to keep the sobs at bay. Then she held out a hand, gave a quick twist of her wrist and pointed her index finger toward the heap of bodies.

Instantly a spark of fire roared to life in the middle of the pile and within seconds it consumed the entire death toll with a flash of white-hot flames.

The air quickly clogged with the scent of cooking meat.

Viv lowered her hand, and the fire blinked out as quickly as it had started. All that remained was a pile of ashes.

"Do you smell that?" Nikoli asked.

"How can you not? The stench is horrid."

"No, not just that. Something else mixed with it."

As much as she hated to, Viv drew in a deep breath. What filled her lungs nearly gagged her, but she caught on to what Nikoli meant. "It's the same thing we smelled on our Gr—our books" she said.

Nikoli nodded. "Cloves."

"Only it smells stronger here than it did in our books. Where is that scent coming from?"

"I'm not certain yet. Let's finish this so I can find out." Nikoli gave Viv a light rub on her back, which sent electricity and guilt racing through her body.

Viv stepped away from him and held out her arms once more, only this time she held her hands together as if to pray. "Open now by my command," she said aloud. "Let all that's gathered enter this land. *Surah— mobdin—garnesh*." Then Viv opened her hands like a book, and the earth emitted a rumble, then a loud cracking sound. The ground within the compound split open, creating a narrow ravine that swallowed up the entire pile of ashes along with the trees that stood near it.

When Viv closed her hands back into a prayer position, the ravine zipped closed like it had never been there, sealing the ashes and blood far below. With that done, Viv then held out her left hand, palm up, and drew a swirling motion with her right index finger. Layers of dirt within the compound began to churn and flip like a grater had been set in motion. Every drop of blood that hadn't been touched by the fire was soon covered over with fresh soil.

"I was wondering how we were going to clean everything up. Was afraid the smell would get people's attention."

Viv whirled about, startled by the sound of Jaco's voice behind her. "Shit! You know better than to creep up on me like that."

"Forgive me," he said. "I really didn't creep though.

The man standing over there saw me walking up. You were just…busy at the time." Jaco's eyes grew hard. "Who's the man?" He motioned to Nikoli standing a few feet away.

"A—a friend," Viv said, for lack of anything better to say. "He's here to help."

Jaco let out a soft snort and turned his attention back to her.

As Viv's heart rate lowered from its shot of adrenaline, she said, "You have no idea who did this, Jaco? You didn't see anything? Anyone?"

"Nothing and no one. I came here looking for Milan. His lair companion came to me and claimed he'd gone missing. I figured with Stratus in heat, he might have slipped out and found his way here. That's when I saw…well, all that was here. But let me show you something else I found."

He motioned for Viv to follow him as he walked about a hundred yards east of where they stood, outside the compound area. Viv signaled Nikoli to follow. When Jaco stopped, he pointed to the ground.

"See?" he said. "Tracks."

Tracks were there, just as he indicated, but from what, Viv couldn't decipher. They looked more like dog prints than footprints, only the pad markings were five times the size of a man's hand. Above each pad track were claw marks that dug into the ground at least four inches deep.

"Shit," Viv whispered loudly. "I've never seen prints that big before. What is it? Bear?"

"Oh, no," Jaco said. "Even if we had grizzlies down here, their prints wouldn't be that big."

Viv felt fury roiling in her chest. "I'm going to go talk to Charlie and the boys over in the cattle area to see if they noticed anything out of the ordinary."

"You shouldn't be alone out here," Jaco said. "Whatever did this to the Loups is no joke. The Loups are powerful in their own right and for something to take down that many… I can't even imagine a creature capable of that."

"I won't be alone," Viv said. "Nikoli will be with me. I want you to check on your brood. Make sure everything is as it should be. Get a head count. Make sure we're good there. Also let Aaron running the West pack know what's going on if he doesn't already. Have him do a count, as well. Then meet me back here." Viv pointed to the North compound's entrance. "But make it quick. I've got other things for you to do once I get the all clear on West and East."

Jaco nodded. "I'll take care of it quickly."

Nikoli offered to drive Viv's old blue Chevy pickup, which she kept in Algiers to haul around supplies and to trek from the compound to the ranch. When they were about two hundred yards from the ranch house, Viv signaled for Nikoli to stop.

"It's best you stay here," Viv said to him. "The hands out here aren't used to seeing other people with me. Don't want to get their hackles up."

Nikoli put the truck in Park, shut off the engine and turned to her. "Hackles?"

"Just stay put, okay?"

Viv was making her way to the ranch house when she heard a loud whistle in the distance. She looked toward the sound and saw Charlie Zerangue waving at her from the back of his battered pickup. From the looks of it, he and his two helpers, Kale and Bootstrap, had been tossing salt blocks out of the truck into a cow pasture south of the ranch house.

She sent a wave back and started to walk in their direction but the men scrambled into their truck and headed her way.

"How you doin', Miss Viv?" Charlie said through the open truck window when he drove up. It wasn't until all three men were out of the truck that Charlie did a double take.

"You got somebody with you, Miss Viv?" Charlie asked, surprise in his voice as he squinted at her truck parked in the distance.

Viv threw a quick glance at her truck. "Oh, just a friend from out of town."

"You okay?" Kale, an ex-wrangler from Texas, asked. "Looks like you been crying."

"Did somebody hurt you, Miss Viv?" asked Bootstrap, the youngest of Charlie's helpers. "If'n so, we can take care of 'em quicker than spit."

Viv held up a hand and shook her head. "Nobody hurt me," she said and looked away. "Allergies."

Charlie shook his head. "Must be one hell of an allergy for your eyes to be all swollen up like that."

"Mmm," Viv said and left it at that.

"Odd world we live in today," Charlie said, for the

simple sake of saying it. "Lots of crazy people. Odd everywhere you turn."

"Talking about odd," Viv said, "have any of you noticed anything out of sorts out here? Anything or anyone heading to the back compound? Weird noises, people?"

"No, ma'am," Charlie said. "We don't let anybody out this way much less out to the compound. Not even us. We know you don't want us out that way."

"Now that I'm thinkin' on it," Bootstrap said, "I did hear some weird noises coming from back that way."

"When?" Viv asked.

"Early this morning," Kale said. "I heard it, too. A weird high-pitched sound."

"Yeah," Bootstrap pitched in. "Sounded like a bunch of ghosts yelling at the same time."

Charlie gave Bootstrap a shove on the shoulder. "Shut up now, boy. Don't be making up stories like that in front of Miss Viv."

"I ain't makin' it up," Bootstrap said, then held up four fingers. "Scout's honor."

"Sorry, Miss Viv," Charlie said. "Don't know what these boys are talking about. I sure didn't hear anything like that."

"You didn't hear it 'cause you was out picking up those ten head of Brahmas," Bootstrap countered. "I'm tellin' you we heard it, didn't we, Kale?"

Kale gave a quick nod, then tapped his cowboy hat low over his eyes. "Heard something. Could have been a bunch of coyotes, though. Not unusual out in these parts."

"So neither one of you went back there to see what was making the noise?" Viv asked.

"No, ma'am," Bootstrap said. "Seein' how you told us never to go back that side, we did just like you ordered. Nothing."

"Saw your man Jaco head back that way a bit later," Kale said. "Figured if something had gone sideways back there, he'd let us know. Guess he went and told you first though, seeing you're here now."

"You got troubles back there, Miss Viv?" Charlie asked. "Need us to go tend to anything for you?"

"No, just do your job right here, guys. If I need you, I'll give you a call. I just wanted to check in with you. Make sure nothing or no one had been out that way."

"No, ma'am," Bootstrap said. "Hand to God. Been just us three. Well, 'cept when Charlie went out for the Brahmas this morning. We been pitchin' hay and salt most of the day."

"Sorry we couldn't be more help, Miss Viv," Charlie said.

"No problem," Viv said. "But I'd appreciate if you'd keep an eye peeled."

"For sure," Charlie said. "I see anything, I'll make sure you're the first to know."

"Thanks, Charlie."

As Nikoli drove her truck to the landing where the ferry was moored, Viv rode along in silence.

She didn't know what to do, but she vowed to find out and to take back what was hers, even if it meant losing her own life in the process. Whatever was out there causing that much damage was no small ordeal.

She might have thrown in the towel during Warden and Milan's fight, but she'd be damned if she'd let her entire city-wide brood of Loups be slaughtered. They were her responsibility, just like they'd been her mother's and her mother's mother's. She wasn't about to let this go without a fight.

She closed her eyes for a moment and saw Whiskers's innocent face. It took all she had to keep her tears from running anew.

As they bounced along the highway in the battered pickup, she felt a searing heartache for all she left burned and buried behind her. Now she was heading back to a city that most people thought existed for one big, continuous party.

Nothing could have been further from the truth.

Chapter 6

"We're going to have to change the time we have lunch. This simply will not work. They give me indigestion," Vanessa Crane said. She crinkled her nose at the three gentlemen who sat four tables away from them in the Bon Appétit Café.

She sat with the other two Elders of the Circle of Sisters, Arabella Matthews and Taka Burnside. They lunched at their usual table at the front window, where they could watch the pedestrians go by.

Arabella, who was spearing a grilled shrimp from her Caesar salad and drinking tea sweetened with marmalade and sugar, turned her head slightly to have a look at what had Vanessa so flustered. She frowned. "They're just eating like we are. Why do you let them bother you so much?"

Taka, who was munching her way through a cheeseburger with curly fries and enjoying a Diet Coke said,
"We can't change the time we eat. You know that we
have to be here at 11:45 a.m. If we come later or earlier, I'll get indigestion. I have to eat at this time, and
we have to come here. They can go and eat somewhere
else if something has to change. I'll go tell them myself if I have to."

Arabella, head Elder of the Circle of Sisters, said,
"Don't be ridiculous, Taka. Let's enjoy our lunch, and
they'll be gone soon enough."

The café was packed with people, everyone chat-
ting in cheerful, low tones with forks clanking against
china plates, glasses tinkling against one another and
waitresses buzzing about tending to customers. The
small establishment was decorated in blues and silver with white linen tablecloths. Whether you chose
a cheeseburger or a filet mignon from the menu, the
food was always served on china and crystal. Evette
exuded class when it came to serving her customers,
which was why the café was always so full.

Despite the cheerfulness of the place and the beautiful day radiating through the window, Vanessa kept the
sneer on her face as she took a bite of her crab cake and
roasted green beans. Every few seconds, she'd throw a
look over at the three men and wrinkle her nose.

Arabella shook her head. They had so much more
to worry about than the three sorcerers sitting nearby.
But once Vanessa got something stuck in her head,
there was no reasoning with her.

At sixty-five, she was the same age as Arabella.

Today, she wore a black polyester pantsuit printed with red and yellow flowers and pink slippers. It was the only type of shoe she ever wore. She was a constant worrier and often forgetful. She wore her auburn-dyed hair in a chin-length sweep-over, had an aquiline nose, brown eyes and always wore wine-red lipstick. Vanessa loved costume jewelry and a lot of it. Her ears weren't pierced, so she had black-and-white baubles, the same size and color of her necklace, clamped to her earlobes.

Taka, on the other hand, wore an electric blue over-shirt on top of a black blouse along with a string of pearls and a turquoise necklace. Her earrings were turquoise, as well, but the size of broaches. She was a week shy of sixty-nine, had snow-white hair that she wore in a tousled pixie cut, blue eyes and a snub nose.

Arabella had chosen to dress a little more conservatively for lunch. She wore a light pink silk blouse and white linen pants, which, when eating at Bon Appétit, wasn't always a great idea, especially when sitting beside Vanessa and Taka. Something was bound to be spilled. She had to work at enjoying her salad and ignoring Vanessa's constant smirks at the sorcerers.

Vanessa called them "the three amigos." Regardless, they were the only real sorcerers in New Orleans.

The trio included Trey Cottle, who looked to be in his late sixties or early seventies, and was someone Arabella absolutely abhorred. He had a bulbous beak, wore thick, black glasses, had a bald head save for a three-inch wrap of hair around the back of it, and sniffled every few seconds. It wasn't his looks that bothered Arabella as it was what he stood for. Arrogance.

He used his sorcery for personal gain. He owned the law firm of Cottle and Black, was part owner of a casino, and he drank like a fish. No matter the time of day, you could always count on Trey having a bourbon close at hand.

Across from Trey sat his law partner, Shandor Black. Shandor looked to be in his midsixties, had a hawk nose, wore wire-rimmed glasses and had a badly wrinkled face with thin lips that held a perpetual scowl. He was well-groomed in a new brown suit, but no matter what Shandor wore, it didn't change his face.

Arabella didn't care for Shandor either, but for different reasons. Just two weeks ago at the café, Arabella had noticed him eyeing Evette like she'd been a juicy, four-inch ribeye. What a letch. And even worse, he was Trey's yes-man. Had his nose so far up his partner's butt, Arabella didn't know how he breathed.

Beside Shandor sat Gunner Stern, a handsome gentleman who looked to be near seventy years old. He had a Greek nose, a wide forehead due to a severely receding hairline, a well-trimmed mustache and was always well dressed and well spoken. His bright blue eyes always seemed to sparkle, and the crow's-feet around his eyes gave testament to a man who smiled often.

He glanced over suddenly and caught Arabella staring at him. She blushed and he smiled. She returned the smile and quickly looked away. She didn't have any idea why Gunner hung around Trey and Shandor. He owned his own art gallery, which did quite a brisk business. Maybe it was simply because the three men were sorcerers and like attracted like. For lunch and breakfast anyway.

"We have business to discuss," Arabella said and took a sip of her marmalade tea. She leaned toward Taka and Vanessa. "The Triads are in trouble," she said, keeping her voice low.

"Again?" Vanessa said. "Who'd they piss off now?"

"Not that kind of trouble," Arabella said. "We're talking serious. Very serious."

Taka's mouth dropped open, revealing chewed-up curly fries.

"For heaven's sake, close your mouth," Arabella told her.

"What happened?" Vanessa asked, then looked about conspiratorially. "Should we be talking about this here? Someone might overhear, like those nosey sorcerers. They'd love to know some of our sisters are in trouble. They'd revel in it."

"I don't have specifics. Picked it up this morning during meditation and wanted to give both of you a heads-up."

"Why didn't you tell us then?" Vanessa asked.

"You've known me long enough to know the answer to that," Arabella said.

"'Cause she wanted to make sure, that's why," Taka said, a bit too loudly. "But if they're in trouble, why aren't we doing something about it?"

Arabella shushed her, then leaned in closer. "Because they have to come to us, you know that. You both know how this works. We can't interfere in their business and control every move they make. They have to stand on their own feet. We can't intercede until they come to us."

"I need to go to the bathroom," Taka said suddenly and got up from the table, clutching her purse to her chest. Arabella watched as she wove her way through the tables to get to the back of the café.

"Surely there has to be some kind of dispensation if the matter is serious like you said," Vanessa whispered.

"There isn't."

Vanessa shoveled more crab cake into her mouth, her brow furrowing deeper. "Did they kill or kidnap somebody?"

"Oh, please. Now you're starting to sound like Taka," Arabella snipped. "I didn't sense anything like that. All that feels certain is that we need to be prepared to help as best we can."

What Arabella didn't tell Vanessa was that she felt the Triads would indeed be coming soon, and she dreaded the hour. Something big was about to go down. She couldn't quite put her finger on it, but she knew the situation was dire. As high-strung as Vanessa and Taka were, she wasn't about to share that bit of information with them until the triplets arrived.

"My word, look," Vanessa said. "Here come the three amigos." Abruptly, she sat up straight. She took the linen napkin from her lap and dabbed the corners of her mouth with it.

Arabella threw a side glance to her right and spotted Trey, Shandor and Gunner getting up from their table and heading over to the cashier's podium. Mid-route, however, Trey turned on his heel with Shandor following closely in step and walked right up to the Elders' table.

"How lovely to see you again, Arabella," Trey said. "Vanessa."

"Hello, Mr. Cottle," Arabella said briskly. "Mr. Black, Mr. Stern." She smiled when Gunner nodded at her with a grin.

"So wonderful to see you, Arabella," Gunner said. "I must say, you look quite lovely today."

Arabella felt her cheeks flush. "Thank you."

"We don't want to interrupt your meal," Trey said. "But we saw you sitting here and didn't want to be rude and not at least say hello." He turned to his brown-noser. "Shandor, why don't you go ahead and take care of the bill?"

Shandor, with his perpetual scowl, simply nodded and left to do as he was told.

"You know," Trey said to Arabella, "since my office is so close to the café, we eat here often. And more times than not, we see the three of you here. The six of us should schedule a lunch date. Catch up on old times and all the new things happening in the city since Katrina. You know, we do have some things in common. We may be on opposite sides of an odd fence, but we both water the same type of lawns."

Vanessa grabbed Arabella's hand under the table, her signal for, *Don't you dare say yes!*

Arabella worked up a smile, knowing Trey to be a snake in the grass. She needed a second to come up with a polite excuse. Chances were if she had caught wind of the fact that the Triads were in trouble and something was about to go down, so had Trey. The reason for his invitation was obvious. He wanted to milk them for more information.

"We'll see what we can manage," Arabella finally said. "Thank you for stopping by. Enjoy the rest of your day.

Trey grinned, and it came across as a sneer. "We hope you can manage something soon," he said. "Have a nice day, ladies." Then he turned and walked away in his black slacks, white dress shirt and pink tie.

Gunner didn't follow Trey right away. He stayed behind and held out a hand to Arabella. She took it without thinking and enjoyed the warmth and strength that exuded from his palm.

He shook Arabella's hand gently, holding her gaze. "Hopefully we'll be seeing you again soon." He released her hand and nodded at Vanessa. "Good day, Miss Vanessa." He smiled, then walked away.

The front door had just started to close behind the men when Arabella spotted Taka waddling back to their table. The timing couldn't have been better. Taka often had trouble holding her tongue, and there was no way of knowing what she might have said with the sorcerers around, especially considering the issue with the Triads.

"He's sweet on you," Vanessa said with a smirk.

Arabella frowned. "Who?"

"Gunner, of course. I saw the way he looked at you and shook your hand."

"Don't be silly, and hush, Taka's coming."

"The hand towels," Taka said, when she reached the

table, still clutching her purse to her chest. "There's a shortage of hand towels in the ladies' restroom. That would upset Evette greatly if she knew. We should alert someone."

"Let's finish our meal," Arabella said. "Then we'll let Margaret know about the towels and ask her if she's seen Evette." She said that more to console Taka than anything. She knew Evette wasn't here. She was somewhere with her sisters at this very moment. Arabella could almost feel them roiling in whatever chaos they'd clashed with.

Arabella went back to her meal, eating slowly. She wasn't looking forward to the Triads' visit.

Not at all.

Chapter 7

After parking the pickup under a lean-to near the ferry dock, Nikoli killed the engine and turned to Viv. She sat at the far end of the bench seat with her head back and eyes closed. Dusk had pushed against the sun, causing shadows to play over her face. He wanted to touch her cheek, soothe the weariness on her face, the worry lines from her brow.

The first time Nikoli had seen Viv back at the Triads' home, when she'd yanked her front door open obviously madder than a hornet, he'd gone numb. When she'd shot out of sight, Lucien had asked her sisters if Viv was all right, given the blood splattered in her hair and on her clothes. For some reason, Nikoli had instinctively known it wasn't her blood.

In fact, all he'd really seen were her large, cobalt

blue eyes, heart-shaped face with high cheekbones, and full lips and small nose, all of it orchestrated over a flawless, olive complexion. When they were offered entrance into the house, Nikoli had caught sight of Viv bolting up the stairs, long, slender legs clad in blood-stained jeans. A Bombay cat with gold eyes had followed at her heels.

Viv looked a lot like her sisters, but they were not identical triplets. All three had black hair and the same basic facial features, but the color of their eyes varied greatly. While Viv's were heart-stopping cobalt, Gilly's were as black as a moonless night sky and Evee's the color of well-polished copper.

When he first caught sight of Viv, Nikoli had felt the air charge with an electrifying energy. His heart began to beat so hard he feared his cousins might hear it slamming against the inside of his chest. Vivienne François was one of the most beautiful women he'd ever seen.

During the time they'd spoken in the sitting room, despite the severity of the conversation, Nikoli had caught Viv's scent. Lilac with an earthy undertone and latent sexuality that seemed ready to explode at any moment.

Not only was she beautiful, but he admired her mind, her wit, her confidence and determination. It took extreme willpower to keep his mind on business whenever she was near.

When they'd met up with Jaco again at the North compound, Nikoli had stayed near, on alert for more Cartesians, while Viv tended to business.

Jaco had told Viv that he'd spoken to Aaron, her

West pack leader, and filled him in on what had occurred at the North compound. He also gave her a head count of the remaining Loup Garou as she'd requested.

She told him to put his second in command in charge of his pack and then have Aaron do the same. She wanted Jaco and Aaron to return to the North compound and, using protective gloves that she'd pulled out of her pickup, they were to repair the fence and gate surrounding the compound.

Nikoli knew Loups to be fast and strong, so it made sense for her to issue the command. The gloves made sense as well, for a Loup couldn't tolerate silver. It shocked their hearts into arrhythmia or, depending on the degree of contact, stopped their hearts altogether.

Nikoli shifted ever so slightly, and Viv opened her eyes and sat upright in the truck.

"Sorry, I didn't mean to wake you," Nikoli said.

"Wasn't sleeping," she said, staring out of the windshield. "Worried about leaving the Loups."

"Having Aaron bring his troop to the North compound was a smart idea," Nikoli said.

"Tell Jaco that," she said with a shake of her head. "He wasn't exactly thrilled about it."

When Viv had told Jaco to have Aaron bring his pack to the North compound so all her Loups in the city would be in one place, Jaco had argued vehemently against it. So much so that for a moment, Nikoli thought he'd physically attack Viv. But she'd held her own. Even when Jaco told her, "Why do you want us to bring all the Loups here when you couldn't even protect the ones who *were* here?"

"I thought you were going to punch him," Nikoli said.

"Wanted to," Viv said, then turned to him. "Why the hell are you here, Nikoli? You and your cousins claim you came here to help, yet a large group of my Loups were slaughtered. What kind of help is that?"

Before he could respond, Viv opened her door and jumped out of the truck. He had to hurry to reach her before she took off on the small ferry without him.

As the engine hummed and water lapped against the sides of the ferry, Nikoli stepped closer to her. Viv turned away from him, which sent an odd, sharp pain through Nikoli's heart. "I was in your home when the attack happened. As well trained as we are, there was no way for me or my cousins to pick up their scent and prevent the attack."

She whirled about to face him, and they were nearly nose to nose. Nikoli gritted his teeth to keep himself in check. Despite the circumstances and the fury on her face, he had an overwhelming urge to kiss her.

"According to your story, the four of you were summoned here. Scent or no scent, shouldn't that have given you a clue that an attack was imminent?"

Reluctantly, Nikoli took a step back to make room for her anger. "What would you have had me do? Go right to the compound without talking to you and your sisters first?"

"To save my Loups, yes!" This time she stepped toward him, and he saw tears trickling down her cheeks. "Look, buddy, if this is the best you and your cousins have to offer, you can get yourself right back to the airport. We don't need you."

"You will."

"Yeah, right," Viv said and moored the ferry on the city-side dock.

Nikoli stepped off the ferry, took the key fob to the black Camaro he'd rented at the airport out of his pocket and pressed the unlock button. The car beeped a welcome just as Viv stepped off the ferry. She marched past him and the car, never looking back once.

"Viv, where are you going?" Nikoli asked. "The car's here."

"I don't need your damn car. I'm walking home," she said. "Have a safe flight."

Nikoli forced himself to remain in place. He wanted to run after her and shake the hardheadedness out of her. Viv only thought she had a bad incident at the compound. She had no idea as to what lay ahead.

As he watched her pace quicken to a stoic march, Nikoli realized just how much trouble he'd walked into. If he didn't get his head out of his ass where Vivienne François was concerned, they very well might all end up dead.

By the time Viv reached home, it was late. Gilly had left a note for her, stating all was well with her Chenilles and she was headed to Snaps to make certain her managers were in place. Evidently, Evee had other matters to tend to as well because when Viv walked through the house, she found it empty.

With exhaustion seeping through every bone in her body, she couldn't help but feel grateful for the solitude.

Viv climbed the stairs slowly, aching with every step

and feeling sorry for herself. She really had no business being responsible for anything, much less having the powers of a Triad. The last thing she should be doing was managing others. Hell, she couldn't even manage her own mouth. What was she doing with the responsibility of an entire breed that depended on her for food, direction and safety?

When she reached the bathroom within her master suite, she washed up quickly, trying not to think about all the blood and bodies she'd had to incinerate earlier.

It was impossible. When she looked in the mirror, all Viv saw was the person who let down her Loups.

Her poor Whiskers. She'd seen the fear that death had locked in her Loup's eyes. How her beautiful Loup must have pleaded for help. The scene played over and over in Viv's head—Whiskers—Moose, so much innocence in a massive body. Her heart broke. She'd miss them all—so very much.

Trying to stanch her tears, Viv pushed away from the sink. Tears wouldn't help her Loups now.

She made her way into her bedroom and stretched out on the chaise near her bed. A fierce headache throbbed behind her eyes from all her crying. It felt like the frontal lobe of her brain had split wide open. Viv closed her eyes.

No matter how hard she tried, she couldn't get the images of the dead Loups out of her head. Nor the fact that the binding and calming spells she'd attempted on Warden and Milan had bombed. Something she still couldn't understand. She had cast those spells a thousand times before, and neither had ever failed.

Of course, this was the first time she'd been confronted with two alphas from different packs fighting over a strong alpha female in heat. Still, the spells should have worked, and her clairvoyant abilities should've warned her about the attack.

The explanation Evee had offered regarding her spells and the sexual energy being strong enough to override a Triad's spell didn't sit right with her. She needed to see the Elders. They might have some answers to help make sense of it all.

Suddenly, Viv felt something jump onto the chaise beside her right hip. Startled, her eyes flew open, and she saw Socrates snuggling up next to her. He pressed his body close to hers without a word, as if to assure her that she wasn't truly alone. She laid a hand on his head and softly thumbed his fur.

Rolling hillsides, meadows free,
I summon your energy to comfort me.
Lazy river, soothing sea,
I summon your energy to quiet me.
Licking flames and warmth of fire—

Before Viv had a chance to finish her spell, her eyes, heavy and burning from exhaustion, closed against the deep ache in her head. Sleep soon caught her unawares, and she allowed herself to fall into the sweet blissful darkness of it. A clean, blank slate.

It was an illusion of course, just like the ones Evee knew how to conjure with a small wave of her hand and a short list of words. The only time a person truly held a blank slate was at birth. And even then, Viv had been screwed out of that deal. Being born a Triad, she carried a curse that had followed each triplet born into the Circle of Sisters for the past thirty generations.

She moved her hip closer to Socrates and thought of Nikoli. The worry in his eyes, the firmness of his jaw, the size and feel of his hands when he'd caught her after she'd stumbled when they first met.

Unable to shake the thought, Viv drifted off to sleep, bringing Nikoli with her.

Chapter 8

He loved it when a plan came together, especially one that hadn't necessarily started out as a plan. Once it got started, all it took was a little push here, a nudge there, and the dam holding back her frustration had cracked. That had been enough to allow the slightest rift in the fourth dimension, where his army had been collecting.

Granted, it had taken some doing. The rift had been small, eye-of-a-needle size. Regardless, it had been enough. He'd picked, tweaked, pulled, nudged until that tiny snag had grown large enough to release a Cartesian. And once one made it through, the rest had been a cake walk.

He wanted to celebrate but felt it a bit premature. Just getting that snag in place so he'd have this opportunity had taken centuries. He could be patient and wait a bit longer to reward himself for a job well done. Better to save the real party for when the entire quest was completed.

Later meant a larger army, which meant more awareness of his greatness and supremacy. Then he'd be able to command the very stars in the sky to dance, to bow at his feet and call him Master... God.

He hadn't decided yet which term he preferred. There'd be time for that later.

Now that the proverbial ball had started rolling, he'd make certain it picked up speed. This moment's priority was to make sure his army, each squadron and its leader knew their position. To make certain they were committed to the fight and, more important, to him. To be at his right hand, ready to inform and infiltrate, to ingest the true purpose of his being in this operation. And that they would do so without question, doubt or reservation.

He played and replayed the day's events in his mind, going over every detail. What had worked and why. What hadn't worked and why. Great leaders did that. Analyzed, strategized, reorganized.

He'd watched the fight between the two alphas from afar, glorying in the frustration that had grown in Vivienne. The sexual tension in the air from the Loup Garous had been so strong it created its own bubble around the entire compound, causing Vivienne's spells to weaken.

But it hadn't negated them as she'd thought. That was one thing she didn't know and would never find out—if he had anything to do with it. Had she pushed a bit harder, she might have broken through.

The alphas had felt the spell hit them, surround them. They'd fought against it, putting more energy into tearing into each other. His money had been on Milan, but alas, because of her he wasn't able to watch either Milan or Warden succumb to death. By their own hands anyway.

The stupid wench hadn't realized that her binding spells and calming spells had been the reason Warden and Milan hadn't killed each other. She kept repeating them over and over, spewing out her ridiculous, rhythmic words. Her own frustration level had done her in.

And the fact that four Benders had arrived like knights on black horses didn't worry him one bit. Sure, they managed to take out a few of his people with their stupid baton toy from time to time, but that was only a battle or two. No way they'd stop the war.

As commander in chief, he'd had a small taste now of victory with the Originals, and refused to let anything or anyone get in his way when it came to taking them all. And that included the Triads.

He was so thrilled with how well all had gone today, he felt a giggle threaten to rise in his throat. He held it back. Leaders, especially powerful ones, didn't do ridiculous things like giggle. Truly, after waiting so many years, centuries, just being ordinary from time to time wasn't so bad.

All those years ago, he'd known he'd been born for greatness. He'd known from a very young age. His parents had never recognized his potential for supreme power. They'd cared for him as one would a family pet.

Now the time had come to prove his greatness to the world. To the universe.

They would know his army, his goal, his dream. They'd watch as he gathered every monstrosity from the underworld. The Nosferatu, the Loup Garou, the Chenilles and all their bastard subspecies—vampires, werewolves, zombies, leprechauns, fairies, the djinn. Every creature large and small, some immortal, all with unique and dangerous powers. He would take those powers unto himself, meld them with his own and make himself the most powerful creature the universe had ever known.

The netherworld was the key, for those creatures were stronger, offered so much more than humans. Although those from the netherworld feared at times and each bore its own Achilles' heel, they hungered for human flesh, blood and bone. What they feared was the mentality of humans and their resourcefulness in killing not only those of the netherworld, but each other.

For him, there would be no fear. Only greatness. He'd have no worries about whether it was night or day or what he might have to feed upon.

He looked over the small squadron of Cartesians that stood before him, all standing with pride, many still soaked in blood from their recent conquest. How they made him proud.

In the natural world, they were stronger, more terrifying than any netherworldly creature known to man. They stood well over eight feet tall, bodies covered with thick scales that were overlaid with heavy fur. Their fangs were five times the length of any Loups or werewolf, and their claws were razor-sharp killing instruments.

Nothing would stand in their way. Their size, power and talents were all of his making. His first victory dance had been the day he'd discovered his ability to weave in and out of dimensional folds. He taught each of his Cartesians to do the same. Such beauty and wonder to watch them duck and dodge time and space and wreak havoc of monstrous proportions. Then simply vanish as if they'd never existed at all.

He'd discovered over the last forty decades that bending time and space took effort, but with the right amount of determination and focus, it was easily done. He had experimented with each fold, pushing farther each time.

The farthest he'd managed was the sixth dimension and by the time he'd reached it, he'd been so exhausted, it had taken him nearly a decade to return to the third. He allowed and even encouraged his Cartesians to experiment as well, but none were allowed past the sixth dimension. He was unclear as to whether or not they'd be able to return if they went beyond that.

Even restricted to the sixth, what his Cartesians were able to accomplish was far greater than he'd ever hoped. He kept most on standby in the fourth dimension so, should he sense a breach into the third, all he had to do was issue the command. In the blink of an eye, his troops would pounce through the breach and collect their bounty.

For years, it had been one Cartesian here, another there. Two fairies, four or five subspecies of vampires or werewolves, but nothing on such a grand scale as today's slaughter.

The fact that their conquest had been the Loup Garou, one of the original breeds, untainted by another species, made it all the more delicious. No other creature, save for a Cartesian, would have dared cross that line. The protection over the Originals had always been too strong, too consistent. But time evidently changed things. One just had to be patient.

And he had been the victor in that arena over Vivienne. She'd lost patience, and her frustration had taken hold and controlled her. That was not the mark of a great leader. That was the demise of stupid wenches who had been named Triads. How bogus. How superfluous.

No rift in any dimension had produced so much fruit. Not of this magnitude. And for all intents and purposes, it was one to be repeated again very, very soon. He felt it down to his own scale-and-fur-covered bones.

The thought of it made him shiver with delight—with power—with ecstasy. Soon it would all be his for the taking.

With that thought front and center, he raised his monstrous arms and roared in triumph. He was Lord—he was Master—he was God.

Chapter 9

Viv didn't know how long she'd been out, but she must have been sleeping the sleep of the dead. The next thing she knew, Socrates was yelling in her ear, and it was dark.

"Get up!" Socrates yelled again.

Viv swatted at him. "Stop. Let me sleep."

"*He's* back in the house, Vivienne," Socrates hissed. "All four of them in fact."

"Huh?"

Socrates gave her an incredulous look. "The men from earlier, remember? Or did you leave your brain behind in REM sleep?"

Her brain finally kicking into gear, she stumbled off the chaise, gave her eyes a second to adjust to the darkness, then went to her bedroom door and opened it a crack.

She heard Gilly's and Evee's voices coming from downstairs along with Nikoli's. She'd recognize the man's silky baritone anywhere. Then Lucien spoke, and Gavril responded.

Furious that Nikoli had the audacity to come back to their home after she'd told him to leave, Viv slapped on the lightswitch and blinked against the harsh brightness. She was about to yank the door open, then realized she had on the same clothes she'd worn since showering that morning.

She headed to her closet, Socrates followed at her heels.

"What are you doing?" he asked. "Those men are back. Why aren't you going downstairs, Vivienne?"

"I am," she said, pulling out a clean pair of jeans and a maroon V-neck blouse.

Socrates sat on his haunches, watching as she stripped off the clothes she'd fallen asleep in and jumped into her clean ones. "My word, this is absurd," he said. "I knew it. I simply knew it."

Viv gave him a warning glance. "Knew what?"

"I tell you those strange men are back and instead of rushing downstairs to rid the house of them, you're changing your attire. The only explanation for such a ridiculous reaction is as I assumed. You're in heat, and for the man they call Nikoli."

"Oh, shut up," Viv said. "You don't know squat." After dressing, she hurried into the bathroom, checked her reflection in the vanity mirror and saw her hair sticking out of her braid like straw from a worn broom.

"Shit." She quickly untangled the braid, brushed out her hair, then wove it back into place.

Shoving her feet back into sneakers, Viv headed for the bedroom door. "Stay put, understand?"

Socrates yawned in response.

"I mean it."

With that, Viv left her bedroom and headed down the stairs. She glanced at the antique grandfather clock near the foyer as she followed the sound of the voices. She paused, staring at the time. 10:00 p.m. If the clock hadn't gone on the fritz, it meant she'd slept for almost six hours, something she never did during the day. It unnerved her.

As before, her sisters and the Hyland cousins were in the sitting room, almost in the exact positions they'd been in earlier that day. Except this time, Nikoli stood just inside the entrance to the room, his hands behind his back, head down as he listened to Gilly talk about her Chenilles.

Viv stormed inside, ready to give Nikoli a piece of her mind, when Socrates jumped out in front of her as if he meant to land on the occasional table that stood near the back wall. His acrobatics caused Viv to twist and duck so as not to get clawed in the head. Landing face first on the hardwood floors seemed imminent until an arm snatched her around the waist and stood her upright.

They were Nikoli's arms. And in that moment, her clairvoyant gifts chose to shift into high gear.

She no longer saw the sitting room, her sisters or

Nikoli's cousins. She had been mentally transported to a different place—a different time...

Where Nikoli's lips were on hers, full and soft. They kissed hungrily, greedily, his tongue darting into her mouth, devouring it. His lips moved across her chin, down her neck. The width of his broad chest pressed against her breasts, which were bare. She felt her nipples aching, hardening when he stepped back ever so slightly to allow his hands access to her body.

His touch sent fire coursing through her, and she moaned unabashedly for more. He lowered his mouth to her left breast, flicked her nipple with his tongue, his teeth grazing gently across it until she cried out.

At the sound of her voice, he lifted his head, pressed her tightly against him once more, sought her mouth with his own and moved his hand down to the small of her back.

His touch sent heat, passion and something Viv couldn't identify flowing through her like lava. It awakened every nerve ending in her body, opening her up, yet closing her off at the same time, so all that existed or mattered was Nikoli's touch.

As his kisses grew more fervent, his hand slid lower—lower still, until she felt his fingers slide over her buttocks, then between her legs. One of his fingers edging closer to the center of her heat. She felt an orgasm forming in her core, growing higher and higher, like a tsunami of such magnitude it had the power to shift the earth on its axis.

The next thing Viv knew, she heard a whisper in her ear.

"Are you all right?" Nikoli asked.

Viv blinked, embarrassed. She'd just experienced a clairvoyant episode while still in Nikoli's arms. Her legs felt like rubber, and she trembled as she stood upright. She wanted to say something but feared gibberish might pour out of her mouth.

"Sorry," she finally said, throwing him a quick glance. The look in his smoky gray eyes appeared heated, like he'd been in the moment with her and had basked in their passion.

Viv turned away, still shaken. She wiped her sweaty palms against her pant legs and tried not to wobble as she went to sit by her sisters.

"Are you okay?" Gilly asked Viv. "Your cheeks are flushed."

"Maybe she has a fever," Evee said, her brow furrowing with worry. She put a hand on her sister's forehead, and Viv quickly brushed it away.

"I'm not sick," Viv said, then glared at Nikoli. "What are you doing back here?" she asked him.

"Viv," Evee said, her voice filled with shock. "How rude. He told us what you had to do at the compound, and my heart breaks for you, sister, but the attack wasn't his fault."

Now Viv felt heat wash over her face. "They came here saying they wanted to help. Do you call seeing the aftermath of a slaughter of a hundred-plus Loups helping? If Benders are supposedly commissioned to help us… What the hell?"

Gilly reached over and touched Viv's knee. "I feel

for you, I truly do, but you've got to cut these guys some slack."

"I don't have to cut anyone anything," Viv said, growing furious. How dare her sisters side with the Hylands.

"You're right," Nikoli said, and all three sisters looked at him stunned. "If given the chance to do it over again, we'd have gone directly into hunt mode and found our way to the compound. I'm to blame for the error. I chose courtesy first. I realize no amount of apologies will ever right the situation, but please accept mine."

Viv didn't quite know what to say to that. Gilly and Evee elbowed her gently on either side of her ribs as if to say, "See?"

Feeling sandwiched between traitors, Viv stood and faced Nikoli. "As I said before, what are you doing here? The damage is done and can't be undone. It's over, so you can leave now."

"Unfortunately, it's far from over," Ronan said from where he sat.

Viv glared at him. "What do you mean?"

Nikoli stepped closer to her, and Viv felt her heart rate jump up a notch. "The attack at the compound was only the beginning," he explained. "Now that the Cartesians know the whereabouts and have had a taste of the Originals, they won't stop until they've killed them all."

Viv felt her mouth drop open, then she quickly regrouped. "All of my Loups?"

"All of the Originals," Nikoli said. "Your Loups, the Nosferatu and the Chenilles."

Turning to her sisters, she said, "Surely there's a spell we can cast to protect them."

"Spells might save some," Nikoli responded. "But far from all."

Gilly and Evee got to their feet and walked over to Viv. "They've offered to come with us during feeding time. They feel that having all the Originals in one place is exactly what the Cartesians are waiting for."

Viv looked back at Nikoli, her heart now thudding with fear. "All of them?"

He nodded solemnly. "They want all of them."

Swallowing hard, Viv felt she had little choice but to accept their offer, despite how she felt about the earlier attack.

"We leave for the docks at 2:50 a.m.," Gilly said.

"If you are all in agreement, we'll be at the dock then to make certain we don't miss you."

Evee nodded and nudged Viv, who gave a hesitant nod.

"Please be prompt," Evee said.

The three cousins, who were seated, rose and walked over to Nikoli.

"We most certainly will," Ronan said.

After Gilly led the men to the front door and escorted them out, Viv headed for the stairs to stave off any questions from her sisters.

"Wait," Evee called after her.

Viv stopped midstep and looked over at her.

"Grimoires before feeding tomorrow morning, re-member."

Viv nodded and hurried up the last few steps.

When she finally made it to her bedroom, she closed the door and rested her back against it for a few sec-onds, her heart beating like a marching band had taken residence there, her mind whirling in too many direc-tions. Cartesians, all of the Originals, the deaths of her Loups—the clairvoyant vision of Nikoli.

Of all the things that were going to feed or be fed in the next day or two, Viv knew without question that she would be one of them.

Chapter 10

Stepping out of the shower, Nikoli wrapped himself in one of the hotel robes, then headed for the sitting area of one of the adjoining suites they'd been able to score at the Hotel Monteleone.

He appreciated the spaciousness of the suites and the architecture of the old hotel, as much as he appreciated the city. From the moment they'd landed, he'd felt all the energies roiling through New Orleans in a huge wave. It was as if their destination hadn't been the city but a person. You either smothered or fell in love with her.

For Nikoli, it had been love. In more ways than one.

Lucien and Gavril sat on a paisley-upholstered couch in the sitting area, and Ronan in a straight-back chair. All three men wore jeans and were bare-chested.

When they had arrived at the hotel earlier, they had gorged on a huge dinner. Afterward, Lucien and Gavril claimed the showers, and while waiting his turn, Nikoli had fallen asleep across one of the queen beds. Ronan, who shared a suite with him, had snored softly in the bed next to his.

Thanks to food, sleep and now a shower, Nikoli felt like a new man. Unfortunately, after all they'd experienced since arriving here, he considered that it might take more than feeling like a new man to accomplish this mission.

As if reading his thoughts, Lucien said, "I think we're in over our heads, cuz."

"Yeah, man," Gavril said with a nod. "Like twelve feet over our heads."

Nikoli let out a sigh, went over to the minibar and grabbed a bottle of water. He drank deeply, thinking about what his cousins had just said. He capped the bottle and set it on the counter, then turned to Ronan.

"What do you think?"

Ronan looked at Lucien and Gavril and gave a slight shrug. "I think we just need to strategize. We have three witches responsible for some pretty large sects. Some in the city, some outside of it. Besides, with all that's happened so far, even if we did call for backup, other Benders wouldn't reach us until we'd lost half or all of the Originals. We can't just sit around and wait. We have to establish a plan."

"I agree," Nikoli said.

Lucien tapped the seat of the couch he sat on with a finger. "If we called for backup right now, even if we wind up in the heat of battle before they arrive, at least we'd know the cavalry was on the way."

Nikoli studied him for a moment. "If you keep your head focused in that direction, we've already lost the mission before we've started. Look how long it took us to get here from New Zealand. Other Benders are in parts of the world unknown to us."

"Maybe," Lucien said with a frown. "But our fathers would know where to locate them."

"If you want to call your daddy and have him bring your little nursemaid along to hold your hand, go right ahead and do that," Nikoli said. "We're grown men, trained Benders, and we need to handle the situation."

"That's harsh, bro," Lucien said.

Nikoli scrubbed a hand over his face. "Didn't mean for it to come out that sarcastic. Look, I'm just as concerned about this situation as the three of you. But if we keep a positive, straightforward mind-set, I think we have a good shot of accomplishing this mission. I know there had to have been generations of Benders before us who faced the same challenge. Maybe not with Originals, but a serious challenge nonetheless. I've never heard of any team of Benders calling in for backup, have you?"

His three cousins shook their heads simultaneously.

"We haven't even fought here yet," Nikoli continued. "I'm not ready to throw in the towel and run to Daddy saying, 'I can't do this, it's too hard.'"

"Yeah, he's right," Gavril said. "It's like Ronan said. We just need to have a strategy, a game plan as to how we're going to take this on."

"Good," Nikoli said. "Now let's look at this. Problem number one is that we have Originals spread throughout the city. At least the Loup Garous have been contained in one compound, which makes it easier."

"The Chenilles," Gavril said, "are spread out in three or four different cemeteries. There's no way we can keep hopping from one to the other. We can't watch them all at one time."

"The Nosferatu are in one place," Lucien said. "That's not really a big help because it gives us yet another place to monitor. You have one North compound, three or four cemeteries, and the catacombs at St. John's. I know my math isn't the best in the world, but the way I figure it, that's at least five locations, possibly six. And there are only four of us. If we split up, how will one of us handle a horde of Cartesians that can suddenly decide to drop from the sky?"

Gavril nodded. "Another problem is, since we have the Originals in separate areas, which will keep us hopping from one place to the other—or separate us so we each taking a territory or two—we won't any time or opportunity to scout for Cartesians *before* they make a hit. We'll just have to wait at our assigned territory for them to appear. We'll all be dealing with surprise attacks."

"Good point," Ronan said. "What do we do about our inability to spread out and search for them? And—side note here—I don't know if any of you noticed, but there are subspecies in the city. Vampires, werewolves—"

"Where did you spot them?" Lucien asked.

"I smelled them the minute we got off the plane," Ronan said.

Nikoli sighed again. Just what they needed. Ronan had the gift of enhanced smell, just like he had the ability to amplify his hearing. If Ronan claimed he smelled vampires and werewolves, you could bet your life they were around.

"I think we need to stay focused on the Originals," Nikoli said. "That's where the Cartesians are going to hit first. They've already tasted first blood, so the sub-species are not going to be a priority."

"So what do you suggest we do?" Lucien asked.

"Split up and take different territories," Nikoli said. "Each of us should pair up with a Triad. They'll help keep their sect in line."

Gavril snorted. "Let me guess, it just so happens that you plan to pair off with Viv, right?"

Lucien tried to hide a smile behind a hand and failed.

"What are you talking about?" Nikoli asked.

"Aw, cuz, come on," Lucien said. "We saw the way you looked at her. I thought you were going to trip over your tongue. You went all mushy-eyed the second you saw her. That woman has you crossed six ways from Sunday."

"Me?" Nikoli said. "What about the three of you? Gavril, you were so far up Gilly's behind, always asking where she was and if she was coming, that a flea couldn't have farted between the two of you. And Lucien and Ronan, the same goes for you two and Evee.

Lucien and Ronan looked at each other, and Nikoli spotted the slightest hint of competition flash between them.

"I've got no problem taking Evee," Lucien said.

"Fine," Nikoli said. "But that either leaves one man out alone, which I highly disapprove of, or Ronan makes one of us a threesome. It's your call, Ronan."

A hint of a grin played around Ronan's lips. "I'll pair with Lucien and Evee."

Nikoli saw Lucien's eyes darken.

"All right," Gavril said. "But I'm not sure about all this. Let's face it, they may be witches and Triads, but they're still women. You get what I'm saying? We have to fight Cartesians and watch out for our own behinds so they don't get chewed up by an Original or a wandering subspecies. Now we're throwing women into the mix. We'll want to protect them. It's going to be hard to stay focused."

Lucien huffed. "Get real, cuz. It's going to be hard for you to focus because they're so beautiful, not because you only want to protect them."

Gavril shrugged. "Well, so? What's the difference? It's still going to be distracting."

The room fell silent for a moment, and Nikoli was sure each man was thinking about the Triad he was attracted to. He wondered if his cousins' fathers had experienced the same challenge.

When Nikoli was twenty, his father had warned him against getting involved with a woman while on a mission. He had told his own story about the time he'd been in France, fighting Cartesians alongside Nikoli's uncles, and how he'd met a woman named Maria. The most beautiful woman in France, he claimed.

She was the daughter of a man in charge of a group of vampires who'd been attacked by the Cartesians. He'd daydreamed and fantasized about being her husband, had even wondered what their children might've looked like. Just thinking about Maria so incessantly had put that group of Benders in danger. To this day, his father still carried the scar left by a Cartesian's claw on his left shoulder.

His father had also warned him to never tell his mother the story or she'd hound him about it until his last breath.

Nikoli and his cousins were born within two blocks of each other, just outside of Chicago, but they hadn't stayed there long. In fact, they didn't stay anywhere for very long. When his father decided it was time to move due to an extended mission, his three brothers and their wives and children moved right along with them. The cousins were homeschooled and watched over closely by their mothers, who worried incessantly about their husbands.

When Nikoli decided at the age of ten that he wanted to be a Bender like his dad, his three cousins jumped on the same train, as well. Now, when Nikoli thought back on it, he wondered how they hadn't given their mothers a heart attack at an early age. The four cousins refused to remain underfoot. They were always sneaking out, exploring new territory, using sticks as if they were scabiors and pretending to kill every Cartesian that ever existed. They were invincible, courageous.

They were the Hylands. Just because his father was a Bender, it hadn't meant that Nikoli would automatically inherit the title. A man wasn't born a Bender. It was something he chose to do.

And just because Nikoli chose to be a Bender, it didn't necessarily mean that the dream was going to come to pass. He and his cousins had to go through extensive training, not only from their fathers, but from other Benders. If at any time a Bender thought a trainee was unsuited for mission work, he was ousted immediately, no questions asked, no explanations given.

Luckily, Nikoli and his three cousins had passed their training period with flying colors.

The job wasn't always as glamorous as others assumed. It was dangerous, exhausting and trying work. Although Nikoli had never confessed to his cousins, it had been more than once that he questioned his decision about becoming a Bender. When a man spent his life fighting one Cartesian after another, all the while watching others go about daily life with wives and children, love and companionship, it caused him to struggle with focus.

He had to keep the bigger picture in mind. A Bender's job wasn't just to remove Cartesians. His job was literally to save the world from the monstrosities. Without the Benders, the world, the very universe as they knew it, would be destroyed.

Ronan got to his feet and stretched, breaking Nikoli's reverie.

"You still with us, cousin?" Ronan asked Nikoli. "Caught you daydreaming for a while."

Nikoli grinned. "Busted. I was thinking about when we were kids."

Lucien slapped a hand to his forehead and laughed. "Well, that's sure a side-step from what we were talking about. Don't know what brought that up, but we had some good times back then."

"Yeah," Gavril said, grinning. "I don't know how we survived to reach our thirties. We were hellions."

Ronan laughed, something he rarely did. "Hellions is an understatement," he said. "How we didn't kill somebody or ourselves is beyond me."

Gavril gave a hearty laugh. "Remember the time we built that missile? That big plastic tube with the bottom panel loaded with fireworks?"

Lucien gave Gavril a light punch on the shoulder. "Hell, yeah, I remember. We put Miss Lunenburg's cat, Pansy, in the tube because we needed an astronaut. How we didn't kill that cat when the fireworks went off, I'll never know. My mom grounded me for a month over that little experiment."

Nikoli grinned. "Mine did, too."

Gavril and Ronan chimed in at the same time, "Me, too!"

They all laughed over the memory, and Nikoli let the laughter die away on its own before he signaled a time out. "But back to our previous discussion, where were we?"

"The Triads," Ronan said.

Nikoli snapped a finger. "Right. The witches will help keep their sects fed, subdued and corralled in their assigned territories. We simply do surveillance of each den and watch for the Cartesians."

Ronan cleared his throat. "Cousins, no one's mentioned this, so I'm going to. We've admitted that all of us are attracted to one Triad or another. They are intelligent, beautiful, powerful women. Who wouldn't be attracted to them? But they will be of danger to us, costing us focus. You know all the energy and concentration it takes to properly operate our scabiors, to make certain we're on target. We really need to be honest with one other. If we don't separate ourselves from the Triads emotionally and mentally, we're in serious trouble."

"So what happens if we blow off the Triads and wind up having a pack of Originals, suddenly looking at us like we're dinner?" Gavril asked.

"That's why we definitely have to partner with the Triads," Nikoli said. "They'll keep an eye on their own while we watch for the Cartesians. Ronan brought the issue out in the open. So let's be fair with ourselves. We have to break off emotionally, mentally from the witches and really concentrate. We have a lot to lose here. We're not talking about just any old mission. These are the Originals. How do you think it will look in the Benders' history books if we are the generation that allowed them to be destroyed? Now, Viv told me earlier that some of the Chenilles and Nosferatu—also some Loups—work and have chores in the city so they can learn to interact with humans. Some work during the day, others at night. We need to make certain that doesn't happen until we get the Cartesians under control. We have to make certain all of the Originals are kept in their dens. We can't have a bunch of Originals running haphazardly through the city while we're at the compounds and other locations, watching for Cartesians."

"I agree," Ronan said.

"I don't think we'll have a problem convincing the Triads of that," Nikoli said. "Not after what happened today."

Nikoli sat on the arm of the couch and looked from one cousin to the other. "All right, just to make sure we're in agreement. When we meet with the Triads, the game plan we present will be to pair off. Lucien and Ronan with Evee, Gavril with Gilly, and me with Viv. They are to keep their sects in their dens, not allow them to work or tend to other chores outside of their assigned area. Gavril, see if you can talk Gilly into collecting all of her Chenilles into one cemetery. I know Viv had a challenge corralling all of her Loups into one compound, but she managed it. Gilly might be able to accomplish the same, which would make it a hell of a lot easier on everybody. All of the Nosferatu are in one area already, so they're a nonissue. This way, we narrow the territory. All of the Loups in one compound, the Chenilles in one cemetery and the Nosferatu beneath the cathedral. I think this would make things easier to control."

Lucien nodded. "Makes sense."

"Yeah," Gavril said. "I'll convince Gilly to do it."

Nikoli gave him a thumbs-up. "Now remember,

cousins. Keep your mind on the job and your dick in your pants. Stay focused and strong."

They all nodded, leaned forward, and all four stacked their right hands on top of the other in agreement.

Nikoli leaned back. "Okay, let's finish dressing and head out there."

Silently the cousins dispersed and went on the hunt for their clothes.

While Ronan went to the bathroom, Nikoli dressed. The silence in their room gave him time to think.

He was already screwed. Somehow, and he didn't think it was by spell but simply by being, Vivienne François had stolen something from him. His heart. Every moment he'd been away from her since this morning, he'd hungered for her, like a man who hadn't been fed in years.

Truth be told, if anybody had a challenge during this mission, Nikoli did.

Chapter 11

Viv had just tucked her Grimoire away when she heard a soft tapping on her bedroom door.

"Yeah?" she called out.

The door creaked open, and Gilly and Evee's heads popped out from around the corner of it.

"You okay?" Evee asked.

Gilly pushed the door open wider, and she and Evee stepped inside, their familiars perched on their shoulders.

"Yeah," Viv said. She walked over to her bed and sat, causing Socrates to meow in protest and move farther up on the bed toward the pillows. "Y'all don't have to babysit me. I read the Grimoire. My mirror's still gray by the way."

"We didn't come to check on that," Gilly said. She

sat next to Viv. Evee quickly followed suit. "With everything that happened with your Loups today…" Gilly glanced over at the alarm clock sitting on the nightstand near Viv's bed. "Well…yesterday…I knew you would read it."

Viv plopped her hands in her lap, wove her fingers together and tapped her thumbs against each other. She looked down at her hands. "Sorry I acted like an ass earlier."

Evee put an arm around Viv's shoulder and gave her a quick squeeze. "No apology needed. We understand. I can't imagine what it must have been like, seeing your Loups that way. Having to burn—"

"Can we not talk about that?" Viv said, standing abruptly.

Startled, Elvis chirped and ran from Gilly's right shoulder to her left. Hoot let out a screech, and his head bobbled.

Viv started to pace. "I've been having a hard enough time getting that vision out of my head as it is. All I want to concentrate on now is how to save the rest of our broods."

"And ourselves," Gilly added.

"What do you mean?" Evee asked.

Viv gave Gilly a stern look. Out of the three of them, Viv considered Evee a magnolia among thorns. Gilly carried herself with far more grace than Viv did, but she had a temper like a startled cobra and a mouth to go with it. Evee, on the other hand, had a huge, tender heart and always saw the good in people and situations.

Viv and Gilly were usually peeking around corners to find the bad hiding in both.

"She has to know what we're facing," Gilly said, frowning at Viv. "Leaving her in the dark won't help her defend herself."

Evee slapped her hands against her thighs, and Hoot's head did a one-eighty. "Stop all the twisting and turning of words," she said to Gilly. "Just spit it out. What did you mean when you said 'ourselves'?"

Gilly looked up at Viv, who walked up to Evee.

"Honey, if those Cartesians want the Originals for their power, there might be a chance they'll want us for ours."

Evee's eyes grew wide. "But we're human. Ronan and Lucien said Cartesians hunt those from the netherworld. They said it straight out. So that doesn't include us, right?"

Viv took Evee's hands in hers and immediately caught a vision of her sister injured and bleeding profusely. She wanted to jerk her hands away but knew that would frighten Evee all the more. She tried to offer her sister a small smile, something that might give her a bit of hope, but failed. All she knew to do was make the truth as palatable as possible.

"We really have no idea what those monstrosities will do or what they're capable of when it comes to Triads," Viv said softly. She released Evee's hands and gave her a small kiss on the cheek. "Let's hope for the best and prepare for the worst, okay?"

Evee looked over at Gilly as if for confirmation.

"Right, right," Gilly said. "What she said. Prepare for the worse, just in case, that's all."

Viv rubbed her hands over her face, then asked Gilly, "Were you comfortable with Gavril hovering in your shadow all the time, being up your butt, checking to make sure the Chenilles were safe?"

"He's thorough, that's for sure," Gilly said. "Only had one problem with the guy."

Viv felt anger prickle her spine. "What problem?"

"I couldn't stop staring at him. That's one good-looking hunk of flesh right there. It's distracting."

Evee lowered her head and tried to hide a smile. "Same here. Only I had two of them to stare at."

Gilly and Evee looked up at Viv simultaneously, and Gilly asked, "You?"

"Yeah, Nikoli is easy on the eyes, but I had too much on my plate to worry about his looks."

"Damn, I'm sorry, Viv," Gilly said. "Forget what I said. I'm just an insensitive asshole."

"Yes, you are," Viv said and offered her a little smile. "Now, look, we've got to figure something out. Our broods cover a lot of territory. Even with the Hylands, I don't know how we're going to keep an eye on everybody."

"We could split up," Evee said nervously. "Cover more ground that way. My Nosferatu are already in one place at St. John's, and Viv, you've got all your Loups around the city in the North compound. That narrows the territory we have to watch over a little."

Gilly stood, and Elvis chittered. She blew out a loud breath. "My Chenilles are spread out across three cemeteries. I'm going to have hell to pay with the heads of my packs, but I'll bring them all to Louis 1. It's the closest cemetery to St. John's. But that only puts two of us near each other. Viv, that leaves you out at the North compound alone, and we just can't chance that."

"She wouldn't be alone if we pair up with the Hylands," Evee said.

Viv, who'd been staring out of her bedroom window, listening and mulling over what Gilly and Evee had said, whirled about. "We just met those guys, and you want me to trust them with your lives?"

"What other choice do we have?" Gilly said. "Viv, you've got to at least consider it. I think they're legit. You were right when you said Gavril was in my shadow. He was. But in a good way. Very protective and an absolute gentleman."

"Same for me," Evee said. "I'd feel safe with Lucien and Ronan. Do you have a problem with Nikoli, Viv?"

Viv began pacing again. Yes, she had a problem with Nikoli. Her clairvoyant visions of seeing him and her naked and the fact that she'd treated him like shit. "I really railed on him," she admitted to Evee and Gilly. "Like bad. Even if we decide that pairing up is the way to go, they may not want to. And even if they do, Nikoli might not want to be paired with me." Saying it out loud made Viv's stomach churn.

"As if," Evee said. "He's a man, Viv, not a little boy. I'm sure he understands. And look, there's nothing stopping Ronan from going with you and Nikoli with me and Lucien."

Viv signaled for a time-out. "We'll figure out the

Hylands later. One other thing we need to discuss is putting our broods on lock-down. No going to work or running errands. At least until this fiasco is over."

Evee sighed. "My Nosferatu will give me hell about that, but you're right. It's the only way to keep them safe."

"You do realize that if we take away their outside privileges, we're going to have a lot of infighting," Gilly said.

"I know," Viv said. "Boy, do I ever. Remember Milan and Warden?"

"Right," Evee said.

"I don't know why your binding spells didn't work on them," Gilly said. "But if you run into any issues again with jazzed-up alphas, maybe I can run out there and help."

"Thanks," Viv said, but shook her head. "I need to take care of my own. Y'all know we're going to have to talk to the Elders about all that's going on, right? Maybe they'll have some answers as to how we can better handle this situation."

"Guess we should have gone to them yesterday," Gilly said and pursed her lips thoughtfully.

"We'll make a point of seeing them later today," Viv said. "After the feeding."

Gilly and Evee nodded.

"And one other thing," Viv said. "If we do pair up with the Hylands, watch yourself. Remember the Triad curse."

"Yeah, yeah," Gilly said. "Can't marry a human or live intimately with a human. We know." An evil grin spread across her face. "But that curse doesn't say a damn thing about kissing them."

"Gilly..." Viv warned.

Gilly batted a hand at her. "You can't tell me that before you got into a tiff with Nikoli that you didn't want to kiss those luscious lips of his."

Viv waved a dismissive hand and turned back to stare at the window. No way was she going to let on to either of her sisters that she'd wanted to do more than kiss him.

A small shiver ran along her spine as she remembered her vision about Nikoli. The shiver came from a bite of pleasure and a huge gulp of fear. She had no idea what they were in for next. All she had to go on was the vision she'd caught when she'd held Evee's hands.

Sister trumped an X-rated vision, hands down.

Chapter 12

Nikoli's global wrist unit had allowed him to locate the docks without any problem. Fortunately, the streets from the hotel to the dock had been relatively empty, save for an occasional cab and a wandering drunk or two.

Nikoli let instinct guide him through the cool October night to the Françoises' ferry.

"Are you sure this is the right one?" Lucien asked, running a hand through his hair.

Before Nikoli could answer, he heard the lapping of water and saw a shadow move ahead to his right. A gray shadow meshed with the darkness, as no lights illuminated the wharf. He didn't need light to know it was Viv. His body recognized her immediately, which disturbed him.

Back at the house, when Viv had fallen against him

and he'd caught her to keep her from smacking onto the floor, he'd inadvertently been swept up in what must have been a clairvoyant scene.

He felt a little ashamed of himself. He should've stood her up more abruptly, disconnected from that vision, but he'd chosen to ride it out with her.

It had taken every ounce of willpower he possessed for him not to physically react to what played out in Viv's mind. In that close proximity to his cousins and the other two sisters, it would have been difficult to hide a boner.

What had been impossible for him, however, was to get the images out of his head. That concerned Nikoli the most. He had to stay focused on this mission. It was too big, too much was at stake for him to be distracted.

He parked the Camaro near the loading area. As he and his cousins walked closer to the pier, the sight of Viv grew clearer in the moonlight. She wore jeans, a white T-shirt and a light denim jacket. Understated attire for one who carried such magnificent beauty.

She walked over to them, hitching her thumbs into the front pockets of her jeans. "Thank you for being on time."

Nikoli nodded.

"Please wait here a moment," she said.

Nikoli watched as Viv walked aboard the ferry and headed for its bow. She stood at the railing, her back to them. He saw her arms drop to her sides, then extend slightly. She formed an O with each hand, her thumbs and forefingers pressing together. She lifted her arms a bit higher.

Nikoli tilted his head and held his breath, a trick he'd learned to increase his ability to hear things at a distance. He listened to Viv chant.

"In shadows formed by moonlit night,
let all but vision remain in sight.
In cover walk thee hand-in-hand,
to my voice—to my voice, my immediate command.
Rocknigh—foring—tramore—naught."

She stood there a few seconds longer, then dropped her arms and turned toward them.

"Where is Evee?" Lucien asked.

"And Gilly?" Gavril asked.

"They'll be here soon," Viv said. "As soon as I make it to the North compound, they'll be following right behind."

"Shouldn't we wait here for them?" Gavril asked.

"No," Viv replied. "You'll come with me." She turned her back to them again, leaned over the railing at the front of the ferry, then threw a hand out, like she was casting dice.

The ferry began to move, much quicker than Nikoli remembered from his last ride. Although he saw the shore on the opposite side of the river, a ferry traveling at its normal speed would've taken fifteen to twenty minutes to reach shore. They were mooring onto the opposite dock in less than five.

As soon as the ferry was secured, Viv hurried over to the pickup parked under the lean-to. The cousins followed her, Nikoli pulling up the rear.

"All of you should be able to fit in here if you squish together," she said. "If you want to stretch out, two of you can ride in the cab, and the other two can hop in the bed of the truck. It's a little cluttered back there, but you're welcome to it."

Nikoli tagged Lucien and motioned for him to follow him into the cab. Gavril and Ronan caught his signal and jumped into the bed of the truck.

Sliding onto the bench seat, Nikoli allowed himself to be sandwiched between Viv and Lucien. The positioning couldn't have been more wrong.

He felt it difficult to breathe, being so close to her. Viv's hair was still braided, and the braid lay over her right shoulder and came to rest in her lap. A black mane of exquisite beauty.

Viv looked around Nikoli to make certain Lucien had closed the passenger door, then peered over her shoulder to check on Gavril and Ronan in the bed of the truck. It was as if she purposely avoided eye contact with him.

Nikoli didn't take offense. After his unintentional walk through her erotic vision, he couldn't blame her. She probably suspected that he had watched.

After slapping the truck into gear, Viv gunned the accelerator and the truck roared off. It was then that Nikoli heard the motor from the ferry start up again. He looked back.

"Is someone else on the ferry?"

"No," Viv said.

"But I know you shut the engine off when we moored. Now it's on again."

"I know."

"Do you have an automatic guiding system on it?" Nikoli asked.

Viv cast a wry smile his way as they bumped along a dirt road. "Um…yep, what you said. It's headed back to pick up Evee's brood."

After five minutes of bouncing and jostling down partially graveled roads, Viv swerved onto another dirt road that led to a giant set of wrought-iron gates. Each iron panel had the initial F planted in its center.

She pulled out a remote from the console of the truck, pressed a button and the gates chugged open. She drove past them and turned into a heavily wooded area.

The path they followed was only wide enough for one vehicle. Tree branches scraped and slapped the sides of her pickup as they barreled forward. The farther they drove, the denser the foliage became and the darker the night. It wasn't until they were completely canopied that Viv turned the headlights on.

Moments later, they bounced into a clearing and she veered left. Her headlights suddenly speared two men standing a few yards away. They appeared to be twice Nikoli's size.

"You have company," Nikoli said.

She nodded. "The one on the left is Jaco, my East pack leader. You've already met him. The one on the right is Aaron, who takes care of the West."

Viv finally pulled the truck to a stop and got out, leaving the engine running. "The four of you stay put until I signal all's clear," she said. Not waiting for a response, Viv closed her door and walked toward the two Loups.

With the headlights still on and the driver's window down, Nikoli watched her tall, slender body move with grace and power. She reminded him of a cougar.

When she came face-to-face with the two men, she tossed her braid over her shoulder so it fell down her back. The tip of it landed between her buttocks, which caused him to shift uncomfortably in his seat. Without prompting, a vision of his hand wrapped in that braid pulling her toward him flashed into his mind. He squeezed his eyes shut a second to block it.

"Those are some big dudes," Lucien said. "Think we're going to have a problem with them?"

Nikoli motioned for him to be silent, then leaned closer to the driver's window to see if he could pick up any of the trio's conversation.

They spoke in low voices, but hearing from great distances was one of Nikoli's specialties, one that had saved his life many times.

"Those men will not harm anyone," Viv said to Jaco and Aaron. "I'll make certain of that."

"But you never bring strangers here," Aaron said.

"Bringing them here was not wise, especially after what happened yesterday," Jaco said. "Terrible idea."

Even from this distance, Nikoli saw something waver over the faces of the two men, their features appearing to undulate. Not drastically, but enough to be noticeable.

He realized he was witnessing two Loups struggling to keep from morphing into their true nature, and it was Viv's presence that kept them in human form. The night was lit with a brilliant three-quarter moon.

A time for Loups to howl, feed and mate. He was impressed at the power and confidence with which Viv addressed the Loup Garous. She stood at least five foot seven, but looked to be child-size in the presence of the two men. Yet she seemed to control them effortlessly.

"I see that you have repaired the gate and the fence," Viv said to Jaco and Aaron. "Is the back territory secure?"

"Yes," Jaco said. "You wouldn't have had us tend to the repairs if you didn't think we could manage by feeding time. Isn't that right?"

"Why are you giving me attitude?" Viv asked.

"I don't like those men here," Jaco said, his voice growing deeper, a soft growl rolling beneath it.

"Like it or not, they are here by my invitation," Viv said. "And you will respect that. Now let's prepare for the feeding. We're already running slightly behind schedule."

With that, the two men turned away and disappeared into a heavy thicket of trees. Once they were out of sight, Viv turned and signaled for Nikoli to turn off the engine of the truck and come meet her.

No sooner were Nikoli and his cousins by her side, than Viv walked over to a large oak tree. She put an arm around it as if she meant to hug the tree, then Nikoli heard the soft click of a latch opening. A six-inch section of tree bark opened like a door. He stepped back to get a better look.

Viv's fingers danced over a panel of buttons inside the door.

A loud whoosh suddenly sounded from a great distance away. It was followed by a rumbling that grew louder with each passing second until Nikoli felt the vibrations from it beneath his feet.

"What is that noise?" Gavril asked.

Viv pointed to a steel fence about seventy feet away. The fence stood over fifteen feet tall and in the moonlight, Nikoli saw that the barbs on top of the fence were tipped in silver.

"If you watch through that opening," Viv said, "just past that small clearing there, you'll see. This compound consists of five hundred acres. I have the West and East Loup packs cordoned off in the far back acreage. I made the decision to gather all of them in one place so they could be watched together until we sorted through this mess."

"Smart move," Nikoli said.

Viv tossed him a small, shy smile.

The rumbling grew louder, and soon Nikoli spotted the horns of a bull, then another and another. He squinted into the darkness and saw cattle rushing into the compound. That's when he noticed the fence within the fence. It created some sort of shoot that allowed the animals to head in only one direction. He heard the squeal of pigs, the neighing of goats. Hundreds of animals seemed to rush by.

"We feed in order," Viv said to the cousins. "To avoid conflict. Evee's Nosferatu go first since they only feed on the blood." She held up one hand and pointed a finger skyward and said loudly, "Come hither!"

At that command came the sudden braying of cows, squealing of pigs and screaming of goats. Nikoli saw treetops sway off in the distance. Though he couldn't put an eye on any Nosferatu or any of the animals once they'd cleared the shoot, he knew the feeding had begun.

"Is it possible for us to get closer so we can watch the feed?" Nikoli asked Viv.

She looked at him as if he'd grown a second head. "I'm not going to risk your life or endanger the Nosferatu by allowing you inside the compound. We allowed you to come here, so whatever you need to smell, go smell it, but do it from this side of the fence. You're welcome to investigate the perimeter, but inside the compound is off limits," Viv said with a scowl.

"If the Nosferatu are feeding right now, where is Evee?" Lucien asked.

"And how did they get into this area?" Ronan added. "It certainly wasn't from where we entered. I would've spotted them."

"Just as I have Jaco and Aaron," Viv said. "Evee has two leaders that help her at feeding time. My sister won't cross the river. She's afraid of water."

The information Nikoli had received prior to this mission indicated that Evee controlled the element of water, so he didn't understand her fear of it. He decided against questioning Viv about it.

"So how do you get all of the Nosferatu over here without them being seen?" Ronan asked.

A look of frustration crossed Viv's face. "You have your secrets, we have ours."

Time appeared to jump into fast-forward because

it seemed like only minutes later when Nikoli heard a shrill caw and the sound of many crows flying overhead.

Evidently seeing the puzzlement on Nikoli's face, Viv said, "That is Evee calling them back. Now if you'll excuse me, I have to tend to my Loups. They're next."

With no further explanation, Viv unlocked a wide steel gate and slipped through it. She relocked the gate, then disappeared into the forestry.

"I don't like all the secret-secret stuff," Lucien said.

"Me neither," Gavril said.

Nikoli held up a hand. "We're the strangers here. You wouldn't expect us to welcome strangers into our territory with wide-open arms and say, 'Sure, come on in, I'll show you everything we do,' would you?"

"But we're here to help them," Gavril said.

"Then let's help them," Nikoli said. "Once they're through with the feedings, we'll walk the boundaries of the compound from this side of the fence and see if we pick up anything."

"Why do we need to wait until after the feedings?" Ronan asked, then struggled to hold back a yawn. "They won't let us inside the compound anyway, and we don't need them to examine the outside of the territory."

"Be patient, cousin," Nikoli said. "Be patient. We may need them more than you know."

The night grew silent. The bawling, bellowing, screeching, screaming and neighing of the animals had vanished. Now the only sound that echoed to Nikoli's ear was that of gnashing teeth and the sound of mouths chomping on flesh.

It was a difficult sound to process. It sent Nikoli's protection instincts into overdrive. He knew all animals, whether they walked on two legs or four, had to eat to survive. Nature had its own process. But hearing all of it going on at one time made Nikoli feel sorry for the cattle that had to be used to feed so many that haunted the night.

This part of the feeding seemed to take longer than that of the Nosferatu for it was a while before Viv returned.

Once she was back at their side, she lifted a hand in the air, pointed a finger skyward and issued a command. "Come hither!"

The sound that followed was like hordes of hyenas had infiltrated the compound. Wailing, high-pitched laughter and squawking.

Gilly suddenly appeared out of the brush to their left.

Startled, Gavril swung about, his right hand grappling with a sheath that hung from his belt. Nikoli prayed his cousin's action didn't startle the sisters.

"Whoa there, boss," Gilly said to Gavril. "Is that a gun at your side? A knife?"

"Sorry, no, Abigail," Gavril said. "It's my scabior. We each have one."

Gilly frowned. "You have a what? And let's just cut to the chase. Call me Gilly, will you? Abigail sounds too stuffy."

Gavril smiled. "All right…Gilly."

Nikoli cleared his throat. "Our weapons are called scabiors. We use them to battle the Cartesians. I'll remove mine from its sheath so you can look at it, if you'd like."

When Viv nodded, he reached for the sheath hanging from his belt.

Viv took a step closer to him and Gilly walked over cautiously. Nikoli slowly pulled out the scabior, and laid it out across his left palm. The eight-inch steel rod glistened in the moonlight and the bloodstone at the scabior's tip winked when he turned it just so.

Gilly let out a snort. "That looks like a toy! That's what you use to kill those monstrous beasts you told us about? It looks like the most you'd be able to do with it is poke out your own eye."

Nikoli couldn't help but grin. He loved the openness of the Triads. Although they were more than courteous, they weren't afraid to say what they meant. "I know how it appears, but you'll have to just trust me. It does the job."

"Can I hold it?" Gilly asked.

"No," Nikoli said. "I'm sorry. If it's used in the wrong manner by an untrained hand, you could annihilate everything within this five-hundred-acre compound. It took years of training for us to learn how to use it effectively."

"All right, big whoop," Gilly said with a pout.

The sound of hyenas gave way to the crunching of bones.

"Are the Chenilles in there?" Ronan asked. "Are they making that noise?"

"Yes," Viv answered. "They ingest the marrow from the bones. That's why the different breeds are brought in a specific order. Once all of them have had their fill, we'll either settle them down in their sleeping habitat or send them off to tend to other chores before dawn. The Chenilles and the Loup Garous aren't sensitive to daylight like the Nosferatu. Many of them have jobs that we've assigned them to during the day, so they'd learn to coexist and interact with humans. The same goes for the Nosferatu, only they serve by night. This feeding time is to make certain they are satiated so the potential for an attack on a human is minimized considerably. We've decided, however, to put them all on lock-down until the Cartesians are dealt with."

"Another good call," Nikoli said, impressed with her foresight.

"So is that where Evee is now?" Lucien asked. "Putting her Nosferatu away before dawn? Tucking them in?"

Viv grinned. "Yes, they're being tucked in."

"Will we see Evee again later this morning?" Ronan asked.

Viv gave him a quizzical look, then said, "She'll be dockside, waiting for us when we're done."

"You really have one hell of an operation here," Nikoli said. "Fast and efficient. It's so well organized. I'm impressed."

"Thanks," Gilly said. "You should be. This is a lot of hard work." She looked at Viv. "I'm going to go gather them up now." She took off at a fast pace along the east side of the fence that cordoned off the compound.

Suddenly, Nikoli caught a nostril full of noxious gas and cloves, a sure sign that one or more Cartesians had broken through to their dimension. He took off, following where the scent seemed to lead. It happened to be in the same direction Gilly was headed.

Lucien, Gavril and Ronan immediately took off after him, evidently picking up the scent, as well.

"Wait!" Viv shouted.

Nikoli heard her clap her hands twice. He glanced over his shoulder and saw her hands held out as if signaling for them to stop. Before his brain could register that she was casting a spell, he heard her utter a short incantation. Immediately he and his cousins were brought to an abrupt halt, as if they'd slammed into an invisible barrier.

"No, no!" Nikoli shouted. "Release—release, the Chenilles will be killed if you don't."

Gilly whirled about, her expression one of fear and utter confusion. She looked from Viv to Nikoli, then back to Viv. "Release, Viv! Let them go!"

Viv heeded her sister's request and clapped her hands twice more. The abrupt dissolution of the barrier caused Nikoli and his cousins to fall to the ground.

Nikoli scrambled quickly back to his feet and took off running, Gilly ahead of him.

"Where do I go?" Gilly shouted. "Viv!"

"Right behind you!" Viv yelled.

"Stay back!" Nikoli warned. "Let us get there first."

"How will you get to them?" Gilly asked, her breath coming in short bursts. "You can't enter the compound this way. The gate's back there!"

Nikoli nearly gagged on the smell of sulfur and

cloves. The farther they ran, the thicker the scent became. He stopped suddenly and pointed due north.

In that moment, the sky appeared to split open and four creatures with heads the size of two buffaloes melded together burst through the opening. Their arms were the circumference of a gigantic oak tree. Razor-sharp claws grabbled for Chenilles.

Shrieking laughter filled the night, and Nikoli caught sight of Chenilles running in every direction. Long, lanky bodies, some hairless, some spotted with fur. All of them terrified.

"No!" Viv and Gilly cried in unison, then both yelled out a binding spell. Unfortunately, all it did was appear to piss off the Cartesians for they turned in the sisters' direction.

Fearing Viv and Gilly might be attacked, Nikoli immediately held his scabior out in his right hand as did his cousins, and they aimed the weapons at the Cartesians. Before they could get a bead on them, two more Cartesians appeared, instantly capturing a Chenille apiece. They bit their captives' heads off, then sucked at the necks as if they meant to extract all of the innards, heart and soul.

Gilly screamed, but her voice barely reached an audible volume before Viv was at her side. Both women stood motionless, mouths open, as Nikoli, Lucien, Ronan and Gavril aimed their weapons, gave two quick twists of their wrists, twirled the scabiors between their fingers and took aim again. Bolts of lightning shot from their bloodstones and hit their target.

Nikoli heard the first deafening pop as the lightning

bolts hit the Cartesians on their heads and pushed them back to the fourth dimension. Another pop—the fifth dimension. Then the hole in the sky closed up tightly, and they were unable to push them back any farther.

Gilly was on her knees now crying, her hands covering her face. Viv hovered over her, trying to comfort her as best she could.

With the smell of sulfur and cloves fading in the night air, Nikoli and his cousins shoved their scabiors back into their sheaths.

Nikoli walked over to Viv and Gilly. "You two okay?"

They looked at him, dumbfounded.

Nikoli sighed. "I don't think many more explanations are needed about who we are or what we do or what Cartesians are, are there?"

Viv looked up at him. And a tear slid down her cheek. Her world and mind were being torn apart by polar opposites. Her growing need to be near Nikoli, and the desire to run as far away from him and the creatures he fought.

Chapter 13

After the death of the two Chenilles, it had taken some time to calm Gilly down enough so she was able to get the remaining members of her brood across the river, then head home. Viv would've gladly taken on the chore herself, but she had no control over the Chenilles, nor did Evee. Only Gilly. Just as Gilly had no control over her Loups or Evee's Nosferatu.

The ferry had returned for her and the four cousins once Gilly had offloaded city-side. By the time Viv and the men made it across, Evee was standing at the edge of the wharf, looking shaken to the core and about to jump into the water she so feared. Gilly had filled her in on what had happened.

It was then they'd parted ways with the Benders. And Viv, as much as she didn't want to admit it, hated to see Nikoli go. Yes, he was easy on the eyes, that was a given. Only it wasn't his looks that caused her to want him to stay. It was…him. His strength. His touch, as brief as it might have been made her ache for more. And his eyes, the confidence and compassion she saw in them. The softness and hunger she felt for him every time he looked at her. She and Evee had thanked them profusely and agreed to meet up with the men again later that evening at the triplets' home. Benders and Triads were still human, and despite the severity of any situation, a human had to eat and sleep at some point.

When Viv and Evee had finally returned home around 7:45 a.m., they'd found Gilly crying in the kitchen, attempting to make some kind of tea to help calm her nerves. Viv had taken over the task and set a pot of tea brewing with valerian, an herb for over-active nervous systems, passion flower for worry and St. John's wort for depression.

While she poured the tea, Evee had called one of her managers at Bon Appétit to let them know she was under the weather and wouldn't be coming in today. Her staff was more than competent enough to handle the café on their own.

The sisters sat at the kitchen table and downed the tea in silence, all three too exhausted and overwrought to talk, much less ask questions or ponder the morning's tragedy. No one was hungry.

Once the herbs kicked in, they'd gone off to their separate bedrooms to sleep. And sleep they did. Viv didn't wake until two o'clock in the afternoon. Gilly and Evee woke shortly thereafter.

They managed to eat some leftover lasagna, then decided it was time to go talk to the Elders before meeting with the Benders that evening. They needed answers from someone they knew and trusted. Someone and someplace safe.

The Elders lived in a two-story Victorian located in the older section of the Garden District, a good distance from the triplets.

The walk there did the three of them good. The afternoon was cool and relatively quiet, save for the occasional ringing of a trolley bell. Mostly older tourists interested in architecture ventured out this way, so there was no bustle or hassle of crowds.

When they reached the house and rang the doorbell, Arabella answered the door, flanked by Vanessa and Taka. Hugs were exchanged, then Arabella led everyone to the dining room. Tea was already steeping and six cups were laid out, along with colorful petit fours shaped like bonnets.

Viv would have preferred a shot of bourbon.

For over an hour and a half, the sisters filled in the Elders on the initial Loup Garou fight, the massacre at the North compound, the arrival of the Benders and the Cartesian attack on Gilly's Chenilles this morning. Viv, Evee and Gilly took turns interrupting one another's conversation, adding details whenever one or the other forgot something.

Everyone, including the Elders, appeared out of breath when the triplets finished.

"So where do we start?" Vanessa asked with a sigh.

"From the beginning," Viv said. "Are you aware of these Benders and the Cartesians?"

Arabella nodded. "I'm familiar with both. Although, I've not had the pleasure to meet a Bender and am fortunate to have never met a Cartesian."

Gilly threw up her hands. "You knew and didn't tell us during our training?"

"I guess we figured your mother or her sisters had told you," Vanessa said. "I mean, you did train under her up until the blessed dear passed on."

"Mother never told us a thing about them," Viv said. "Neither did Aunt Rose or Aunt Madeleine. As soon as Mom passed away, her two sisters high-tailed it to some other country, dumping their responsibilities into our lap."

"Be nice," Taka said to Viv. "You shouldn't talk about your aunts that way."

"She didn't say anything mean," Evee said defensively. "She told the truth. Rose and Madeleine took off right after Mom died. Period. There's no other way to put it."

"Maybe they were just a bit hasty in their departure," Vanessa admitted.

Arabella let out another sigh. "All of that is irrelevant. What's important is what's going on right now." A sad look crossed her face. "I'm sorry we made such a gross assumption. We should have made certain you knew about both. For no other reason than having the knowledge. You see, what we know about the Benders and Cartesians comes from what was handed down to us. It's not firsthand information."

"What do you know about them?" Viv asked.

"As we've been told, the Cartesians have been around since the 1700s."

"Fifteen," Taka corrected. "They've been around since the 1500s."

"Oh, you're right," Arabella said to Taka, then turned to the triplets. "That's about the same time that the Nosferatu, Loup Garous and Chenilles became Triad responsibility."

"What?" Gilly said. "Some Elder back then just woke up one day and decided to make the Triads responsible for them?"

"Oh, dear," Vanessa said, giving Arabella a disconcerted look. "They don't know about that either."

"Know about what?" Viv asked, suddenly realizing that through all of her years as a Triad, she'd evidently missed, intentionally or unintentionally, some crucial parts to the Circle of Sisters story.

Taka sighed. "The Triads are responsible for the Originals because they created them."

"What?" Viv and her sisters said in unison.

Arabella nodded. "I'm afraid so, my dears. Your grandmother, thirty times removed, and her sisters, were responsible for the Originals. They created them out of anger and spite, and you know what our laws say regarding that. It's quite clear. "

Viv, Evee and Gilly stared at each other, dumbstruck. Viv knew that the Triad screw up had been generations ago, and the curse meted out to them fell on their shoulders, as well. But creating the Originals out of anger and spite... That was a major screw-up.

They were fortunate any Triad survived after the initial incident.

"But you're wrong about one thing," Taka said to the triplets. "I told you about the Cartesians when you were small."

"I remember that," Evee said. "But it sounded like a story, make believe. You know, like the bogeyman."

"Oh, they are bogeymen, that's for sure," Taka said. "Only very, very real. We've heard stories over the years about how many vampires, werewolves and the like they've killed. The last attack was somewhere in New Zealand, I believe, not that long ago. They've never been able to touch an Original, though. Until now."

"When did the Benders come into play?" Viv asked.

Vanessa lifted her arms and stretched. "From what I understand, not until a century or two later. Is that right, Arabella?"

"Pretty close. It did take quite some time before someone took action. No spell seems to affect Cartesians. Not then or now. It wasn't until a Cartesian massacred a group of humans that churches got involved. They founded the first group of Benders. Sort of like the Knights Templar, only for the netherworld. Of course, the church would have never commissioned such a group for vampires and the like, but once humans became involved, everything changed."

"The Benders who are here told us the Cartesians are only after factions of the netherworld," Viv said. "Because of their powers. They said they weren't interested in humans."

Arabella shrugged, then eyed Viv. "Every group has a wayward son or daughter. Fortunately, that Cartesian's mistake of attacking those humans wound up being to our benefit."

Viv picked at a crumb on the tablecloth, feeling ashamed of herself. Her North pack Loups and Gilly's Chenille were dead because of her big mouth.

"So we can trust these guys?" Evee asked the Elders. "The Benders who are here now, I mean?"

Taka huffed. "You think? After what you witnessed this morning, you're still wondering if you can trust them?"

Arabella nodded. "Absolutely. You can. I thank the elements and the heavens that they've been sent to you. I would contact other members of the Circle of Sisters for reinforcement if I thought it would do any good. But I'm afraid adding others into the mix would only put more of our own at risk. No one but you can handle the Originals, and no one but the Benders can handle the Cartesians."

"How can anyone expect just the seven of us to battle these creatures all the while protecting our groups?" Gilly asked. "Those sons of bitches just appeared out of thin air."

"The Benders will handle the Cartesians," Vanessa said and took a sip of tea.

"Yeah, we kind of noticed," Viv said. "But we and they can't be everywhere at the same time."

"I'm confident the seven of you will work the situation out," Arabella said.

"You say that like the only thing we have to battle is a hill of ants," Viv said. "I mean no disrespect, Arabella, but if you had witnessed what we did, you'd know how ridiculous that sounds. You'd be wishing for an army, not seven people."

"You know," Taka said, "I just thought of something. Do you think the sorcerers might be able to help in this situation? Maybe they have resources that we don't."

"Have you lost your mind?" Vanessa asked, her back stiffening in her chair. "Those subspecies humanoids are only interested in themselves. When have you ever known a sorcerer to help a witch? They don't. Because they're greedy, selfish ingrates. Don't you dare mention any of this to those three yahoos in the city, Taka. Do you understand?"

"You're not the boss of me," Taka said, lifting her chin.

"No, but I am," Arabella said. "Not one word of anything we've discussed this afternoon shall leave this house. Is *that* understood?"

"I won't say anything," Taka said, casting her eyes downward. "I was just wondering."

"Well, now you don't have to wonder," Vanessa said. She folded her arms across her chest and glared at Taka. "I can't believe you even thought of that."

"At least I'm trying to help find a solution to their problems instead of just sitting like a lump on a log," Taka said.

"The two of you, stop," Arabella said. "We have enough to worry about without both of you acting like five-year-olds." She turned to the triplets. "I'm sorry we don't have more direction to offer you, my dears."

"Can you at least tell me why my spells on Milan and Warden didn't work?" Viv asked. "That's where all of this started. What if it happens again? What if we're out there trying to protect our sects, just like we have been, and the plug gets pulled on our incantations?"

"Your powers didn't leave you at the time they were fighting," Arabella said. "The sexual tension between Stratus and those two alpha males might have weakened them, but it didn't steal them."

"But I told you nothing I did worked," Viv insisted, tapping a finger on the table for emphasis.

Arabella reached over and patted Viv's hand. "Had you kept a cool, clear head and called upon your elemental guide for assistance, things would be very different right now."

Viv blushed and pulled her hand into her lap. "Look, I know this is all my fault. I'm doing my best to fix it. I can't bring back my dead Loups or Gilly's dead Chenilles, but I—"

Arabella shook her head. "I'm not making accusations, just giving advice. The three of you must stay clearheaded and strong during this time of tribulation. Generations of Triads before you have kept these Cartesians away from the Originals. You have to stick together. Work with the Benders."

"Arabella?" Evee said. "Why are the mirrors in our Grimoires reflecting only gray?"

"That's not a good sign," Taka said with a tsk.

"She didn't ask you," Vanessa said.

Arabella held up a finger, signaling for the two Elders to be silent. "It's gray because the future has become uncertain. The images it reflected before were for the three of you to take heed. To show you what would happen if you shirked your duties. That mirror, like the universe, takes your words seriously. Now what's uncertain is who will survive this ordeal. It may not be a matter of any one of you leaving your duties behind. It may be given pause, wondering if the three of you will survive."

"Shit," Gilly said, then slapped a hand over her mouth. "Sorry, no disrespect meant."

Arabella gave her a half smile. "No worries, dear. I heard that very word and some far worse from your mother's mouth more than once."

"I want to know how their weapons worked when the Benders used them," Taka said. "We were never given that information before. It would be good to know, something to pass on."

"What?" Gilly said. "You mean in case we don't make it and die?"

"Well, there is that," Taka said.

"Don't be so crass," Vanessa warned, then turned to Gilly. "You're not going to die, dear. We're confident you and the Benders will be the victors in this battle."

"Yeah, yeah," Taka said. "But I still want to know how the scorpions work."

"They call them scabiors," Viv said. "The weapon isn't very big or impressive to look at. Had I seen it in any other setting, I would've thought it was an amateur witch or sorcerer's wand." Viv described the metal rods and how the cousins used them. "The Cartesians seemed to enter the world through a big rip in the sky."

"What did that rip look like?" Taka asked, her eyes bright with curiosity.

"Blacker than any black I've ever seen," Viv said. "But when that lightning bolt hit the Cartesians, it pushed them back into the hole, which seemed to create another hole, one even blacker than the first, behind it, and the Cartesians were pushed even farther back."

"It's called a dimensional rift," Arabella said to Taka. "The hole in the sky that Viv is talking about."

"A dimensional rit," Taka said, dreamy-eyed.

"Rift," Arabella corrected. "If this is something you plan to pass on, make certain you've got the information right. Look what happened with Evette. You told her about Cartesians, and the poor dear thought you were talking about bogeymen."

Taka waved a dismissive hand. "Just a little misunderstanding." She turned to Viv. "What happened after that?"

"I heard two loud pops, then the hole in the sky immediately closed up, taking the Cartesians with it."

"I didn't hear any pop," Gilly said, looking at Viv.

"How could you not? It was so loud."

Gilly shrugged, confusion on her face. "Maybe… I guess… Maybe I was in shock and just didn't hear it."

Vanessa nodded. "Funny thing about shock. It can do strange things to people, even Triads."

"And these Cartesians were as big as they say?" Taka asked.

"Massive," Viv said. "I've never seen a creature with a head or arms that big."

"What was their method of attack?" Taka asked.

"I told you," Viv said. "They came out of nowhere from the rift in the sky."

"No, I mean how did they kill the Chenilles?"

Gilly held up a hand, her brow deeply furrowed. "I don't want to talk about that. It was the most horrible thing I've ever seen."

"I know it must have been a very traumatic ordeal for you, sweet one," Vanessa said. "But for once, Taka is right. Where the Circle of Sisters is concerned, if there is valuable information that may help another sister at another time, we need to be informed."

Gilly put her elbows on the table and looked at Viv. "You can go ahead and tell them, but I don't have to listen." With that, she stuck a forefinger in each of her ears.

Viv looked at Evee. "I didn't give you all the gory details. You sure you want to hear this?"

"Not really, but I have to know what we're facing," Evee said grimly.

Viv nodded and turned to Taka. "The Cartesians bit their heads off. Then they sucked on their necks like they were trying to pull everything inside out. When they finished, all that was left was a rag of flesh."

Taka slapped a hand over her eyes. "I should've never asked. Now I'm going to have nightmares."

"Try living that nightmare," Viv said, then got to her feet. "We need to head back home now. The Benders will be returning this evening. Any further advice?"

Evee and Gilly rose from their chairs and waited for Arabella to speak.

The Elders stood up, and Arabella motioned everyone toward the front door. When they reached it, she touched Viv on the shoulder and looked deeply into her eyes to make sure she had her attention. Then she looked gravely at Gilly and Evee.

"The only other piece of advice I can offer," Arabella said, "is to remember the warnings of your Grimoires. The mirrors may be reflecting gray right now, but they weren't always that way. Remember." She tapped a finger over her heart. "Watch over your hearts and your heads, especially where the Benders are concerned."

Viv held back a groan. Deep inside her, she already knew that where Nikoli was concerned, she was about to screw up again. Big time.

Chapter 14

No sooner had they left the Elders than Viv felt a nervous twitch in her gut. Her mind suddenly filled to overflowing with chaotic images of Chenilles, Nosferatu and Loup Garous clashing into one another, running through the city among humans. Oddly enough, at the same time, she saw Chenilles carefully tucked away in the Louis 1 cemetery, the Nosferatu in the catacombs of St. John's and her Loups in the North compound. The conflicting images didn't make sense.

Viv allowed the twitch in her gut to decide which she should pay attention to.

"Evee, I think you need to check on your Nosferatu," Viv said as they continued walking toward home.

Evee came to a stop and stared at her. "Why? Did you pick up something?"

Viv and Gilly pulled up alongside her.

"Yes," Viv said and explained what she had seen. "It was a conflicting vision. So just to be on the safe side, you should check out your brood."

Gilly blew out a breath. "I'm going to Snaps and let my managers know I'll be out for the evening. Then I'll head to the cemeteries, check on everyone, then start moving those in the City and Lafayette cemeteries to Louis 1."

Viv nodded in agreement. "I'll go to the compound and talk to Aaron and Jaco to make sure things are copacetic."

Gilly gave Viv a wary look. "Are you sure you're telling us everything you saw? I mean, you're not holding back anything to protect us, keep us from freaking out?"

Viv shook her head. "I swear. I've told you everything, as senseless as it sounds. That senselessness is why I'm suggesting we check on our broods."

Without another word, the three sisters parted ways, each heading in a different direction.

When Viv made it to the ferry, she jumped aboard and pushed it to a speed that nearly tipped it starboard. As she flew across the water, Viv couldn't help but remember the last time she'd ridden the ferry.

Nikoli had been with her. The memory caused her to feel his presence beside her, and it sent heat flashing through her body. It frustrated her that no matter how dire the situation, his face always sent a flush to her cheeks. Part of her wanted to meld to him, side by side, never leaving his presence—his scent. Yet the re-

sponsible part of her, the side that had a habit of rain-
ing on her and her sisters' parade from time to time,
knew it best to stay away. Emotionally especially. They
couldn't, shouldn't be together.

The first thing Viv spotted when she made it to the
front gates of the North compound was Aaron and
Jaco arguing, circling each other as if ready to attack.

Viv pulled the old pickup as close as she dared to the
Loups, then killed the engine and hopped out.

"What's going on here?" she said to Jaco and Aaron.
She had to yell over their arguing. Both were so ab-
sorbed in slinging curses at each other that neither of
them noticed she'd arrived.

When the two Loups spotted her, they froze, their
expressions like two kids who'd been caught with cig-
arettes behind a woodshed. Both wore jeans and were
bare-chested. Their long hair gleamed with sweat, as
did their faces and chests.

"We have a situation," Jaco said.

"No, we don't," Aaron said. "They have to be somewhere around here. You didn't check the East section
of the North compound yet." Aaron looked back at Viv.
"The entire compound hasn't been checked." He jerked
his chin at Jaco. "He's too slow."

"If you're so smart and fast," Jaco said to Aaron,
"why can't you come up with a clean count on your
side of the compound?"

Aaron growled and Viv shouted, "Hold up! Hold
up!" She waved her hands and shook her head. "What
the hell are you two talking about?"

Jaco stepped toward Viv, his massive bulk towering over her. "We've been through a count twice," he said. "It looks like we have at least fifty Loups missing. Twenty from Aaron's pack and at least thirty of mine."

Viv felt her blood run cold and her eyes narrowed. "What do you mean by missing? Was there another attack?"

Jaco gave a small shrug. "We found no dead bodies, no blood. They're simply missing. We've been calling out to them, trying to connect with them for at least the last three hours, but no response."

Viv scrubbed her face with her hands. "How long did it take the two of you to get the fence repaired?"

"About an hour and a half," Aaron said, stepping up alongside Jaco. "We worked as fast as we could."

"Could they have escaped before the repairs were completed?" Viv asked.

"Not from my pack," Aaron said. "I didn't bring them over until the fence was secure."

Viv looked at Jaco. He lowered his head.

"If mine did escape while we worked, I'm positive I would have sensed that," Jaco said. "I don't see how... or when." He glanced at Aaron. "Maybe you lost your twenty while en route here. Did you consider that possibility?"

Aaron growled. "Shut your fucking mouth, dog bone. I watch over my pack. You might be able to use a broken fence as your excuse, but I watch over my own."

"Then how the hell do you lose twenty of them?" Jaco snapped.

Viv clapped her hands together hard to get their attention. "Both of you, quit acting like infants. If we have fifty Loup Garous missing and there are no dead bodies or blood, that can only mean one thing. They have to be somewhere in the city." She glared at Jaco. "Did you search every part of this compound?"

"The only section I've not covered yet is the far East side. I was about to head over there when smart-ass here decided to give me directions on how I should accomplish my search. I know this compound like the back of my hand."

"Then finish searching it," Viv demanded. She turned to Aaron. "I want you to go back into the compound and recount your pack, make certain the first count wasn't an error."

"I didn't miscount," Aaron insisted. "I have twenty missing."

Viv glared at him and said through clenched teeth, "I said go back and recount. We have to get a true picture of what we're dealing with here, and I don't want to work with erroneous information."

Both Loups gave her a quick nod, then made their way into the compound to do as they were ordered.

Feeling like she'd vomit at any moment, Viv got back in her truck and headed to the ranch house. Maybe Charlie, Kale or Bootstrap saw or heard something that would give her a clue as to her missing Loups' whereabouts.

When Viv reached the ranch, she found Charlie hammering on a fence post in the cattle grazing pen. When he spotted Viv, he waved and a smile creased his weathered face. He tipped his cowboy hat up a notch when she drove up beside him and stopped the truck.

"How you doing, Miss Viv?" Charlie asked.

"Fine, Charlie, thanks for asking," Viv lied. No way could she tell Charlie what was really going on. "Where are Bootstrap and Kale?"

"Oh, I sent them out to Abbeville to pick up a truck-load of hay bales. Got 'em for a good price from a farmer I know out that way. Even though the boys are gone, I can surely tend to whatever you need help with, Miss Viv."

Viv leaned through the driver's-side window and swiped a hand over her face. "I know I asked you this last time I came out here, Charlie, but I need to ask again. Have you seen or heard anything unusual coming from the back five today?"

"You're meanin' the place you told us we need to stay out of?"

"Yes," Viv said, feeling like a fool talking this way to someone nearly twice her age.

Charlie took off his hat, pulled a bandanna out of his back pocket, then wiped the sweat from his brow. His lips pursed. His brow furrowed. Then Charlie shook his head slowly as he stuck the bandanna back into his pocket and his hat back on his head.

"I ain't seen nothing, but you know, now that you mention it, I heard what kinda sounded like a bunch of coyotes yelping earlier today. I thought it was just a pack of 'em moving through the woods. Didn't see any though. Been keepin' a close eye on the horses and livestock just in case. Better they're out in the woods than here. Other than that, I haven't seen a thing but this ol' fence I've been workin' on."

Charlie tilted his head slightly and studied Viv's face. "No disrespect meant, Miss Viv, but you sure look like you're carrying a bucket full of worry. Are you sure there isn't something I can help you with?"

Viv worked hard at giving Charlie a smile. She wished she had someone else to talk to about the Cartesians, about her Loups, about everything that was going on. And if anyone could keep a secret it was Charlie Zerangue. But she didn't want to chance it. Knowing him, he would've stormed into the compound to help track her Loups, even if it meant risking his own life.

"Just a lot on my mind, Charlie. But thank you anyway." She pulled the gearshift into Drive and held the brakes for a moment. "You take care. I'll be talking to you again soon, I'm sure."

With that, Viv drove back to the compound where she found Aaron standing by the gate, toeing dirt with his boot. She pulled up next to him.

Aaron looked at her, frowning. "Twenty missing for sure," he said. "I don't know what to say. I don't know where they went or how they got out."

"And you brought your pack here after the fence was repaired, right?"

"Yes. No way I would've let my pack in here if it wasn't secure."

"There has to be a breach in the fence, somewhere," Viv said. "Loups don't simply vanish into thin air. They couldn't have jumped the fence, even if they'd morphed. It's too high. And, if by some freak act of nature one did make a jump that high, the silver tips on the barbs would've skewered the Loup. It would still be up there wailing for help."

Aaron nodded, looking lost for words.

In that moment, Jaco jumped out of the brush and hurried over to Viv. "Entire area searched. My count's the same. Thirty missing."

"Great," Viv said sardonically. "Not only do we have to watch over this compound, but we've got fifty MIA Loups. They could be running around the city for all we know. If we don't find them before feeding time, the gods only know what or whom they'll attack."

Aaron and Jaco simply stared down at her.

"Watch over this territory. Don't take your eyes off it. Stay inside the compound and walk its perimeter. Count and recount your packs to make sure we don't lose more."

They nodded in unison.

Viv slammed a foot on the accelerator and peeled out of the area, heading for the dock.

She had no clue as to how they were going to manage this mess. Although they'd narrowed the territory by putting the Chenilles in one cemetery, her Loups in one compound and the Nosferatu in the catacombs, the plan seemed futile. Now they had to worry about her Loups roaming the city, and the last thing they needed was a whirlwind of public attention. Up until now, she, her sisters and their broods had stayed under the human radar. She feared that luxury had just been shot to hell.

When Viv made it back home, she found Gilly and Evee pacing around the kitchen table. Gilly had obviously been running her hands through her hair because her pixie cut stuck out in little spikes, like antennae. Evee had dark circles under her eyes and they looked swollen, like she'd been crying. The sight of them twisted Viv's stomach into knots.

"What's wrong?" Viv asked.

"I have fifteen Chenilles missing," Gilly said, her eyes suddenly brimming with tears, something uncommon for her.

"And I've got ten Nosferatu gone," Evee said and leaned against the table as if needing the support.

Gilly and Evee looked at Viv.

"I have fifty Loups missing," she said quietly, perplexed by the missing Originals.

"Sweet Mother Earth, no!" Evee said. "Viv, what are we going to do? All of those Originals could be out in the city. They're going to miss feeding time. People will be in danger."

Viv put a finger over each of her eyelids to keep a headache at bay. She shook her head. "I have no damn idea. This is way out of hand. All we can do is take one challenge at a time and deal with it."

"Maybe we should go back and see the Elders. Let them know. Maybe they can help us find them," Evee said, her voice lilting with hope.

"They can't do shit," Gilly said firmly. "We're the only ones who can deal with the Originals. All the Elders would do is fret, talk over one another for an hour and serve us tea. I mean, really. Can you actually see Arabella, Taka and Vanessa running around the city looking for Originals? No. I don't know why we have Elders anyway. They're frigging useless."

"Stop," Viv said, her voice low with anger. "Those women took us under their wing when we had no one. They trained us, worried over us and still do. That's called family. And I don't want to hear you dissing family."

Gilly huffed and looked away.

"Look," Viv said, "the Benders will be here in about forty-five minutes. Maybe they'll have some ideas on what to do."

Evee tapped the table with a finger. "What if... What if we conjured up some kind of repellent spell? Something that would keep the Originals away from humans?"

Viv shrugged. "Might be worth a try. Let's get to our Grimoires before the Benders get here. Maybe we can find something in our books that will allow us to at least manage the missing Originals while we deal with the Cartesians."

Gilly and Evee agreed and the sisters took off for their respective bedrooms.

Viv trudged up the stairs, feeling angry, lonely and more afraid than she'd ever been in her life.

Chapter 15

By the time the Benders returned to the François home at 7:30 p.m., Viv felt wired with worry. The dark pressing up against the windows didn't help.

They sat around an antique dining table that held eight people. An expansive, eighteenth-century crystal chandelier hung overhead. The cousins were dressed all in black, though the shirts were different styles.

Viv wore jeans and a royal blue pullover sweater. Gilly had dressed in white linen pants and a pink, long-sleeved T-shirt, and Evee had chosen jeans with an olive-green button-down blouse. Simple but stunning against her olive complexion and copper-colored eyes.

They'd spent the last five minutes attempting small talk, and it had been halting at best. Even so, just looking across the table at Nikoli made Viv feel like she could breathe for the first time in hours. Something about him calmed her mind and riled her up physically at the same time.

The triplets' situation had worsened since the last time they'd been with the Benders and Viv was ready to push the small talk aside and get on to business. Oddly enough, as dire as things were, having Nikoli here gave her an uncanny sense of hope. No one else, except for her sisters, had ever made her feel that way.

"Things have changed since we parted this morning," Viv said, looking around the table at the cousins. "And not for the better."

"What changed?" Nikoli asked, his expression growing more solemn. "Did you have another attack?"

"It couldn't have been that," Gavril said. "We would've picked up on it."

"Not another attack," Gilly said. "I don't think so anyway."

"What happened?" Nikoli asked.

"I have fifteen Chenilles missing," Gilly said, and her lower lip quivered.

"What?" Gavril said. "Missing from where?"

"They're unaccounted for," Gilly said. "I went to open Snaps this afternoon, told my managers I'd be tied up for the evening, then went to take count at the cemeteries. I'm fifteen short."

"From one cemetery or all three?" Gavril asked.

"All three. Lafayette, St. Louis 1 and City."

Evee leaned into the table. "And I have ten Nosferatu that have gone MIA."

Viv saw the cousins eyeing each other and wondered what messages they were sending.

"I did a head count a few hours ago," Evee said. "That's when I found out they were gone. The two captains I have in charge at the cathedral had no idea they were missing, saw no one leave the catacombs."

"What about you?" Nikoli asked Viv.

"Jaco and Aaron told me we're at least fifty short. That's from all the compounds. If you remember, I told you I had brought everyone into the North compound. My sisters and I have our own way of calling our groups to us, and we've been calling out to them, trying to connect with them for hours. No response."

Nikoli sat back and folded his arms over his broad chest. "So now we have to add another challenge to the mix. Not only do we have to find a way to protect the Originals, we now have Nosferatu, Chenilles and Loup Garous on the loose. And they won't respond to their mistresses' calls. We have to assume they're roaming free in the city. Definitely not an ideal situation."

"You're not telling us anything we don't already know," Viv said.

"Did you let your Elders know?" Gavil asked. "Any possible solution from them?"

"We haven't told them anything," Gilly said tersely. She glanced at Viv before looking back at Gavril. "There's really nothing they could do. We're the only ones who can handle the Originals. No need to worry them just yet."

"And you can't even feel where your factions might be?" Ronan asked.

"No," Viv said, "which is odd. That's never happened before."

"If you can't feel them," Ronan said, "does that automatically mean they're dead?"

"Not necessarily," Viv said. "I've had a wayward Loup or two over the years that didn't respond to my call just to be hardheaded. I don't see fifty of them doing that, though."

"All right," Nikoli said. "We simply have to add this to our to-do list. My cousins and I came up with a game plan that we wanted to discuss with you. We think it's pretty solid, but now that we have some Originals missing and we have to assume they're milling around people, we may have to retool that plan."

"What were you considering?" Gilly asked.

"We thought about each one of us pairing off with one of you," Gavril said. "Now, because there are four of us and you're three of you, one of you—well, actually, we decided it would be Evee—would have two Benders with her. For example, Gilly, you and I would take care of the Chenilles. Evee, Lucien and Ronan stand watch over the Nosferatu. And that leaves Viv and Nikoli to tend to the Loup Garou. We also discussed something regarding the Chenilles. If it's possible, we'd like to see them all corralled in one cemetery, the way Viv has her Loups in one compound. That way we wouldn't be running from cemetery to cemetery."

Gilly tilted her head to one side, narrowed her eyes and pursed her lips. "We're five steps ahead of you. We took care of that before you arrived. And we even discussed pairing up with you."

Gavril shot her an admiring look. "That's great. How did you manage to put the Chenilles in one cemetery and not have them kill each other over territory?"

"I trisected the cemetery with a binding spell," Gilly said. Viv saw a blush rise in her cheeks.

"Very well thought out," Nikoli said. "This will be very helpful. We'll only have three places to monitor. One cemetery for you, Gilly. The cathedral for Evee, and the North compound for Viv."

Viv felt her heart flutter in her chest. "I like the divide and conquer thing, but what do we do about the Originals that are missing?"

"Since we've just found out about it, you'll have to give me a minute to think that through."

"What about having seven Benders instead of four?" Viv asked.

Nikoli's brow furrowed. "I don't understand."

"Well...do you have any more of those scabiors?"

"No," Lucien said. "Each Bender is given a scabior at the time of their training and it stays with them until their death."

"Can you get more?" Viv asked.

"No," Gavril said. "They're not like guns or knives. The way it works is one scabior to one Bender."

"What are you thinking?" Nikoli asked Viv.

"I thought if you had extras, that my sisters and I could use them, as well, to fight Cartesians. It wouldn't be just the four of you. I mean, I'm sure I could handle one. It didn't look that hard. I'd have to get used to that loud popping noise, though. Scared the hell out of me the first time I heard it."

Nikoli stared at her, seemingly frozen. "You heard that sound?"

"Yeah."

Nikoli turned to Gilly. "Did you?"

"No, I never heard a popping anything. But then again, Viv has great hearing. All of us have our own little specialties, you know? Like Viv hears really well and does this partial invisibility thing. I have a strong sense of smell and can astral project. Evee runs really fast, and she can channel and produce illusions. She can do things with water, too. I can do things with fire, and Viv with earth."

"I understand different abilities," Lucien said. "It's the same with us. Nikoli has exceptional hearing, Ronan can smell anything a mile away and Gavril runs faster than a gazelle. As for me, I can jump up five to six feet from a complete standstill."

"Wow," Evee said. "Very impressive." Her copper eyes twinkled with a smile.

Nikoli put a finger to his lips for a moment and the movement sent the scent of him wafting Viv's way. He smelled of soap and musk. So delicious.

He suddenly turned to Viv. "The Triads... I mean, the three of you are human, right?

"Of course we're human," Viv said, slightly taken aback. "We have different talents like the four of you do, but it's kind of like being a prodigy. We simply have the ability to do different things. Why do you question whether we're human?"

"Because until this moment, I've never heard of

another human being able to hear that popping sound. Only a Bender."

"Sorry to bust your bubble," Viv said with a shrug.

"What did you see before or at the moment you heard the sound?" Nikoli asked.

"I saw a big, black rip in the sky, like it had been unzipped. Blacker than anything I've ever seen. Then those monstrosities lunged out. When you did whatever you do with your scabior and that bolt of lightning shot out of the bloodstone, hitting the Cartesians right on their heads… Good shot by the way…"

"Thank you."

"I saw the Cartesians fold over in half, like they'd been punched in the stomach. Then I saw them get sucked backward into the hole in the sky. That's when I heard the first pop. There seemed to be an even darker place behind them that pulled them farther back. When they entered that darker space, that's when I heard the second pop. After that, the sky closed up. No more pops." Viv got to her feet. "Now, I hate to break up our little tête-à-tête but the clock's ticking. I need to go check on my Loups. See if anything else has changed."

Everyone at the table stood.

"I'll go with you," Nikoli said.

"I can handle it on my own," Viv insisted. "I've been doing it for years. Look, we have Originals on the loose and Cartesians dropping out of thin air. So what's the verdict? Pair up or spread out so we could cover more territory?"

"You and your sisters can't go out there alone," Nikoli said solemnly.

"Since when?" Viv asked, frowning. "Is there something you haven't told us?"

Nikoli glanced around the table at everyone before settling his eyes back on her. "I haven't even discussed this with my cousins yet because the thought just occurred to me. If the Cartesians, specifically the leader of the Cartesians, is so hell-bent on getting to the Originals, there's a good possibility he might take the three of you out so he can have easier access to your groups. It's like the old saying, if you want to destroy a beehive, you kill the queen. If he destroys the three of you, he has nothing to hold him back from the Originals. You wouldn't be around to protect them."

"Wait," Evee said. "You mean the three of us might be attacked by Cartesians?"

"We've discussed this already, Evee," Viv said, slightly annoyed with her sister and not sure why.

"The thought occurred to me," Nikoli said. "And I think it's a valid concern. We have to assume the worst. Think about it. What would you do if you were in the Cartesians' leader's shoes? You want to conquer every Original because you want their power. Because the ultimate goal is supreme power over the world. Over the universe. What would be the fastest way to accomplish that goal? It would be to get the three of you out of the way, leaving the Originals unprotected. He'd have complete control over all of them."

Evee held a hand to her mouth.

"Shit," Gilly said with a shaky voice. "That makes sense."

Gavril stood military straight and said, "I won't let

anything happen to you, Gilly." He looked at Evee and Viv. "To any of you. The three of you will be with one or two of us at all times. We'll get this figured out and taken care of. You have our word."

"But we can only do so much with what we have," Viv said. "That's reality. We have a responsibility to the city to protect the people in it. I can't just sit by the compound and wait for these Cartesians. I have to look for my missing Loups."

"The Nosferatu and Chenilles, too," Gilly added.

"Can you cast a binding spell around the Originals that are missing?" Nikoli asked Viv.

"Each of us did cast a repelling spell, hoping that will keep the missing Originals away from people. But since they're not even responding to our calls, we have no way of knowing if the spells will be effective or not."

Nikoli stroked his beard thoughtfully.

Viv let out a frustrated breath. "We need to figure out a way to secure the Originals we're controlling now. That way we can hunt for the ones that are missing."

"I have an idea," Ronan said, giving voice for the first time since they'd arrived. "I don't know if it will work, but it may be worth a try."

"Speak now, cousin," Lucien said, "or forever hold your peace."

"You remember the fencing around the North compound?"

"Of course," Nikoli said.

"And that big steel corner post not far from the entrance?" Ronan looked at Viv. "Do you have the same kind of poles on the other three corners of the property?"

"It takes more than four poles to hold up that much fencing," Viv said. "There must be at least forty."

"Perfect," Ronan said. "Now, do you have access to any bloodstones?"

"Oh, I have tons of bloodstones out in the work shed behind the house," Gilly said. "I work with a lot of crystals and gems."

"Wonderful," Ronan said.

"What are you thinking?" Nikoli asked him.

"Okay, hear me out before you blow me off, all right?" Ronan said.

"Go," Nikoli said. "Let's hear it."

"What if we set a bloodstone on top of each corner post at the North compound? The posts are steel like our scabiors, and with the bloodstone added, you'd basically have a gigantic scabior. If we had four of them aimed at each other and charged them with our real scabiors, they'd stay charged since no one's able to hold them. With the four posts aimed at the center of the compound, we'd basically be creating a huge electrical canopy over it. That way no Cartesian would be able to drop down into the center of it."

"Hmm," Nikoli said. "I've never heard of that being done before."

"Me neither," Gavril said. "But it sounds plausible."

"How are we going to move those huge, steel posts so they're aimed at each other?" Lucien asked.

"Does it matter if they're bent?" Viv asked. "Like

two or three feet from the ground, if they were bent from there and aimed where you want them?"

"I don't think it would make a difference if they're bent rather than hammered at an angle into the ground," Ronan said. "As long as they're aimed toward each other."

"Then the problem's solved," Viv said. "All I have to do is have Jaco and Aaron bend the posts. I don't know if you've ever seen a Loup in action, but the strongest of them can easily bend something like that."

"How do you keep them in the compound if they're that strong?" Lucien asked. "Aren't you afraid they'll escape?"

"One reason," Viv said, "is because the barbs on top of the fence and woven through it are dipped in silver, something none of the Originals can tolerate. And second, I would only have Jaco or Aaron bend those poles. I trust them. They know we're here to take care of them, feed them, protect them from people who would literally kill them for sport."

"So what do you say?" Ronan asked Nikoli. "Think it's worth a shot?"

"You may have something there, cousin. If we can make this happen at the North compound, we might be able to create a version of it around the cemetery where the Chenilles are and in the catacombs. If it works, that would protect the Chenilles, the Nosferatu and Loup Garous, who are already contained, from the Cartesians. That would give us some freedom to look for the ones that are missing and hunt for Cartesians before they figure out a way to get through the containment areas. It'll take longer to secure a cemetery since we're limited on manpower."

"Manpower won't be a problem," Gilly said. "My lead Chenilles can take care of that."

Everyone standing at the table exchanged glances.

"So what do you say?" Viv asked Nikoli. "Do we give this a try or what? Are you confident enough that you can charge those poles with your scabior?"

"No," he said. "As I said, to my knowledge, this has never been done before. I do know that if you aim a scabior at anything and activate it, something will definitely happen. Since we're talking steel and blood-stone, though, and no Bender handling it, it should stay charged. That's only taking into consideration the laws of physics and how the scabior works. My vote is we give it a try."

"I say yes, too," Gilly said.

"Same here," Gavril said.

"I'm in," Lucien added.

"Me, too," Evee chimed in.

Ronan shrugged. "It was my idea so of course I'm for it."

Viv nodded. "Gilly, why don't you and Gavril go take a look at Louis 1. Figure out where we'll set up this rig job. Evee, you can go with Lucien and Ronan to the cathedral to figure out how we'll set up scabiors in the catacombs. I'll collect the supplies we'll need and head to the compound so we can get Jaco and Aaron started on the posts. Let's plan to meet up at the ferry at our regular time, right before feeding. We'll com-pare notes then."

Everyone except Nikoli shuffled around the table and headed for the foyer. As Viv watched her sisters pair off with their respective Bender and leave the house, she offered a short prayer to the elements, asking for guidance and protection.

Nikoli called out to his cousins. "Stay sharp!" Then he looked at Viv as he continued to speak. "We have to protect what is ours at all costs."

Tonight could change everything. They'd either win or lose everything they'd ever known. He glanced over at Viv. Or treasured.

Chapter 16

Viv bit the inside of her cheek hard. The pain did little to stop her hand from trembling as she closed the front door of her home, sending her sisters and the other three Benders on their way.

Nikoli stood just behind her, which sent a flush throughout her body, and no amount of cheek biting changed that. She scolded herself silently. *You've gotta turn around, stupid. You can't just stand here, staring at the door. He's going to think you're dysfunctional.*

Viv turned to Nikoli, avoiding his eyes. "Okay, supplies. What are we going to need?"

Nikoli ticked a list of items off with his fingers. "Flashlights, bloodstones, rope or cable."

"What's the rope or cable for?"

"Just in case." He grinned. "We'll also need a ladder. My cousins and I are tall, but not tall enough to reach the top of the twenty-foot pole, even if it is at a forty-five degree angle. The bloodstones will need to go on top of each pole."

"We don't have to worry about ladders," Viv said, heading for the kitchen. Nikoli followed closely behind. "My Loups can shimmy up the poles and set the bloodstone wherever I tell them to. The same goes for Gilly's Chenilles and Evee's Nosferatu. Though I'm not sure how we're going to handle the catacombs. Twenty-foot poles and fencing will definitely not fit under the cathedral. There's not much height under there."

"We'll figure something out for the catacombs," Nikoli assured her.

When they reached the kitchen, Viv went to a supply cabinet and pulled out two flashlights. She handed one to him. "It's cloudy tonight. We'll definitely need these. No need to bother with rope or cable here. I've got some in the back of my pickup I keep parked under the lean-to across river."

Nikoli nodded, took the flashlight she handed to him and stuck the long handle of it into his back pocket.

Lucky flashlight.

She hurried out of the kitchen, Nikoli in tow.

When she reached the stairs that led to the second floor, she said to him, "I have a couple of items to get upstairs. If you don't mind, please wait down here. I'll be right back."

"Sure," he said. He placed a hand on the newel post and planted a foot on the bottom step. His eyes bore into hers. "I'll be waiting right here."

Those swirling, stormy gray eyes caused Viv to nearly trip on her way up the stairs. She had to get her head together.

She entered her bedroom, and Socrates, who'd been stretched out on her bed, confronted her with a loud hiss.

"Why, Vivienne," Socrates said, sarcasm in his tone, "what have you been up to?"

"Too much to go through right now. And besides, I know you, you little sneak. I'm sure you've been creeping and hiding around every corner and already know what's been said and planned. I don't think there's one bit of conversation we've had that you've missed. You know what's going on."

"Oh, I'm not talking about all the Cartesian hullabaloo and scabiors and what not. I'm talking about you and the Bender downstairs. The one who's anxiously awaiting your return. I can feel him, even from here. He's really struggling to keep himself together, you know. You seem to have an odd effect on him." Socrates lifted his head as if to sniff the air. "Hmm. His heart is beating faster, and he's fighting to keep his thoughts on the job. They keep bouncing back to you."

"Shut up already," Viv said and went to her closet.

"You know what you're planning is a stupid idea," Socrates continued. "Someone is going to get hurt or killed."

"I didn't ask for your opinion," Viv said. "I've got all the scoop on how dangerous it is, but I have no choice. My Loups are in danger. So are the Chenilles and Nosferatu. What would you have me do, stay home and play canasta with you?"

Socrates yawned. "You don't even know how to play canasta. I'm just warning you. It's my job." He shook his head rapidly, as if to clear his mind of sleep. "Humans can be so ridiculous at times. Take me for example. I know when to nap, when to eat, I know when to keep my nose out of certain situations so I don't get into trouble. Humans on the other hand eat fat-laden garbage from drive-through windows, carouse most of the night and manage three or four hours of sleep, thinking they'll be productive the following day. And they allow their asses to make decisions for them instead of their heads."

Viv came out of the closet with a satchel and headed for the nightstand on the right side of the bed. "You know I don't eat drive-through food."

"I'm talking about humans in general," Socrates said. "The thinking with your ass part, though, you have down pat."

Ignoring him, Viv opened the top drawer of the nightstand and pulled out a spool of red yarn. She threw it into the satchel.

"What?" Socrates said. "You plan to knit him a sweater?"

"No, Kitty Warhol. It's for emergencies. Holding spell."

"Ah, yes."

"Where are Hoot and Elvis?" Viv asked, suddenly thinking about Evee's and Gilly's familiars. "I haven't seen them around lately."

Socrates yawned again. "That ridiculous bird and rat have been in hiding since this Bender-Cartesian incident started. They have no backbone whatsoever. It's quite embarrassing if you ask me."

Viv waved a dismissive hand at her familiar. "I'm sure if Gilly or Evee needed Hoot or Elvis, they'd be there for them."

"Maybe," Socrates said and stretched.

"You on the other hand may not be in hiding, but you sure seem pretty chilled considering all that's going on."

"My job has always been to look after you, warn you of impending danger and offer advice, all of which you routinely brush off."

Viv headed for her bedroom door, then stopped and turned to him. "I take your advice into consideration… sometimes."

"My point exactly," Socrates said.

"I said sometimes because most of the time what comes out of your mouth is nonsensical ranting. You have an attitude, cat."

"A familiar mirrors his mistress," Socrates retorted.

Viv blew out a breath. "Whatever. I don't have time to argue with you. I want you to stay here. There's a lot going on, and I don't want you to get hurt. I know you've overheard about the Cartesians and that we're missing some of the Originals. I don't need to be worried about you, so stay put."

"Oh, I plan to," Socrates said. "But if I may…and even if I may not…I will leave you with this one piece of advice, Ms. François."

Viv rolled her eyes. "What?"

"The gentleman who awaits you downstairs…"

"Yes?"

"Be careful, Vivienne." Socrates looked at her solemnly. "Beware of him."

She frowned. "What are you talking about? Is he dangerous?"

"In more ways than you know. He won't harm you physically. In fact, he'll do quite the job of protecting you. It's your heart that concerns me."

"Well, don't let it."

"Vivienne," Socrates warned. "He may be your undoing."

"Yeah, yeah, I know. I remember. I can't marry or live intimately with a human. I don't need to be reminded of that *again*."

Viv left the bedroom, closed the door and hurried down the stairs. She slowed considerably midway down the staircase, when Nikoli swung around the newel post at the bottom step and faced her.

He was breathtakingly handsome. She wanted to jump from the middle of the staircase right into his muscular arms. And she knew without question he'd catch her effortlessly. So strong. So tempting. She'd give up half her Grimoire to taste his full lips.

"Are you all right?" Nikoli called up to her.

His voice startled Viv back into action. She clambered down the stairs. "Sorry. Just thinking about the supplies we need. Wanted to make sure I didn't forget anything upstairs. Now we have to go to the back of the house, to the workshop. That's where Gilly keeps her bloodstones."

Nikoli gave her a small smile, bent at the waist and swept his right hand out like a gallant knight. "After you, milady."

Viv squashed back a groan of desire, then held her breath as she scooted past him. If she had to inhale his scent one more time, all bets were off. She'd strip him naked here and now and have her way with him.

Keeping her eyes focused straight ahead, Viv meandered through the dining room, then into the kitchen and to the back door. She opened it, went down two steps and signaled for him to follow her outside.

The workshop was a thirty-by-forty-foot structure, painted beige with forest-green shutters. Evergreen foliage grew in planters that bordered the two front windows. It looked more like a cottage than a workshop.

They never locked the building, so Viv let herself in and flipped on the light.

She turned to motion to Nikoli and nearly ran into him as he was right at her back. Viv swallowed hard and pointed to the satchel hanging from her right shoulder.

"I'll get the bloodstones," she said hoarsely. "How many do you think we'll need?"

"Four for each holding area. So twelve should do it."

"All right," Viv said. "I'll bring sixteen just in case. You never know. One might break or we may wind up needing extras. Always better to have more than not enough, right?"

Nikoli gave her a sultry look. "I agree. It's always better to have more."

Viv cleared her throat and pushed her way past worktables covered with artist's palettes, paintbrushes, strips of canvas and jars of crystals and dragon's eye that they occasionally used for spells. Gilly was the expert when it came to understanding the properties of every gem and crystal known to man. To Viv, they all looked like pretty rocks.

Beyond the tables, near the back left corner of the cottage, Viv found a large woven basket sitting on the floor. It was filled with the bloodstones. Gilly had either hit a sale or had been hunting them on her own and hit the mother lode.

"Would you mind holding the satchel open while I go through these?" Viv asked Nikoli, who stood at her side.

"Of course." He took the satchel from her shoulder and opened it wide.

Viv squatted near the basket, and Nikoli followed suit. Trying her best not to bump into him, she started rummaging through the bloodstones, choosing the largest in the lot. She might not have been touching Nikoli, but there was no getting past his scent, a mixture of leather, musk and fresh, rain-kissed air. She felt her breath quicken.

What that man did to her should be against the law. No other male had ever affected her this way. A jumble of emotions flip-flopped within her heart and mind. And that wasn't even taking into consideration the physical reaction he caused in her. Her body seemed to disconnect from her brain and simply react to him. She was thankful for the sweater she'd chosen to wear, for she felt her nipples harden.

Viv narrowed her eyes and forced herself to concentrate on the bloodstones, rummaging through the entire basket.

"Are you certain we won't need a ladder?" Nikoli asked.

"Positive." Viv struggled to keep her eyes away from his mouth. So far she'd collected eight fist-size bloodstones. "The ones I put in the satchel are the biggest bloodstones we have. The rest are smaller."

"As long as they're larger than the one on my actual scabior, it should work. It just needs to protrude above the top of the post. By the way, those posts are solid, right?"

"Of course," Viv said. "Any Loup could swipe down a hollow post in a nanosecond."

"I figured as much," Nikoli said. He peered into the satchel, then stuck a hand inside and scrounged about. He glanced up at her. "What's with the yarn?"

"Backup," she said. "For emergencies."

Nikoli grinned. "You know I want to ask what emergency would call for red yarn, but you're a Triad, so I'll leave it at that. Red yarn it is."

Viv couldn't help but smile back at him. He knew when to press and knew when to pull back, the markings of an intelligent man.

She went back to rummaging for bloodstones, chose eight more of the largest remaining stones in the basket and placed them gently into the satchel.

With that done, Viv sat back on her haunches. "I think that's all we'll need. Oh...wait." She swiveled to her right, dropped to her knees and crawled to a small, white cupboard a foot or so away. She opened it and pulled out a pouch that had FIRST AID written across it in red.

She looked back and tossed the pouch over her shoulder to Nikoli. He caught it in midair, then dropped it into the satchel.

"I thought you did your own healing," he said.

"Oh, we do. But having a Band-Aid around never hurts." Viv crawled back over to him, all the while wondering why she just didn't get to her feet and walk out of the workshop.

When she reached him, she sat cross-legged on the floor. She dug through the satchel: bloodstones, flashlight, first aid kit, yarn. "I think we're good," Viv said, chancing a look at his face. Big mistake.

While she'd been taking inventory of the items in the satchel, Nikoli had evidently lowered himself beside her to check out the contents, as well. When she turned to him, they were but a breath apart.

Both of them froze, eyes locked, and in that moment the rest of Viv's world disappeared. All that existed was the scent of him, the brawn of him. His gorgeous face, his silky hair, his Van Dyke that she longed to touch. The only thing either of them had to do was move a fraction of an inch and their lips would meet.

Her body raged with desire. Her mouth went dry, her breathing labored.

Before Viv knew it, not knowing who made the first

infinitesimal move, she found her lips on Nikoli's. From the moment they touched, their kiss grew fervent, hungry, familiar. His mouth, his essence, felt like something Viv had never experienced before but had craved, starved for it for an entire lifetime.

She had no thought of the Cartesians or her Loup Garous. Of any mission or plan. All she had on her mind was the feel and taste of Nikoli Hyland. And the feeling that she'd die without more.

Nikoli leaned forward, gently pushing her onto her back. Viv's legs uncrossed naturally.

He sat beside her right hip, never moving his mouth from hers. His hands cupped the sides of her face, stroked her hair. His fingertips ran down the sides of her neck. His tongue probed the inside of her mouth, and she sucked on it greedily, wanting him to explore every inch of her. Wanted his tongue to run down the length of her body and back up again.

Viv had no conscious thought of time or place. They could have been in the middle of a public arena for all she cared. She wrapped a hand around his neck, pulling him down harder against her, and moved her other hand to his chest, feeling the tautness of him, searching for buttons. She found two and quickly unfastened them, her knee brushing against the hardness trapped behind his black jeans.

Finding a third button, Viv fumbled with it, then felt one of his large, strong hands grasp her wrist and gently pull it away. He held her hand against his chest, over his heart, and she felt the maddening beat of it. It matched her own.

Without breaking their kiss, Nikoli moved her hand from his chest to over her head, where he held it against the floor. The fingertips of his free hand roamed down the side of her cheek, traveled down her neck, then lower. Over her sweater, across her left breast. Lower still, until she felt his fingers find their way beneath her sweater.

The softness of his touch drove her mad. She wanted to rip off her clothes and press her naked body against him. She needed to be filled, to be fed.

Nikoli's fingers hesitated over the top of her half-cup bra that barely contained her rock hard nipples. That's when she finally broke their kiss and panted. "Yes—yes."

Viv closed her eyes and arched her back, encouraging him to take more. His fingers found her right nipple, and he rolled it gently between his thumb and forefinger. She groaned loudly, felt her body quiver. She had never been touched so completely. The sensation went beyond flesh on flesh. It reached down to her core. Viv heard herself begging, pleading, "More… more."

Nikoli didn't hesitate to oblige. He lowered his mouth to her nipple, ran his tongue over it, let his teeth softly scrape over it, and Viv felt her hips rise and fall. Rise…fall, as if she rode the hardness that gave claim to his own arousal.

As his lips and tongue worked their magic over her right breast and nipple, his hand moved to her left breast, where he found it swollen with passion, that nipple just as hard as the other. He gently rolled it between his finger and thumb, then tugged on it—released it, then ran his thumb over it.

Viv became blind with need. She groaned with desire.

When Nikoli's mouth and tongue moved slowly across her sternum to her left breast, Viv thought she'd lose her mind. She desperately needed him inside her.

"More," Viv cried out. "Oh, Nikoli..."

The sound of his name seemed to trigger something in him, for his fingers traveled quickly down her stomach to the top of her jeans. He unfastened them, and she felt his fingers work their way inside.

"Yesss," she panted and lifted her hips.

His hand moved lower, his fingers inching their way beneath her panties. Then finally...finally—his hand cupped her heat.

Viv groaned loudly and arched her back again. He lowered his mouth to hers once more, and his tongue pushed its way into it. It darted in and out of her mouth. Soon his middle finger dipped into the swollen wetness of her and took on the same rhythm as his tongue. In...out, his finger reaching to the farthest depths of her being. Viv felt a wave of pleasure build up inside her. Higher, stronger, and she held her breath, waiting for it to crest and wash over her.

She didn't have to wait long.

With his fingers stroking, probing, pressing deep within her, Nikoli's palm brushed against her swollen nodule of lust, and Viv cried out. His palm brushed against it again, his fingers plunging deeper, and in that moment the tsunami that had been building inside her reached its peak and crashed over her again and again. Her mouth flew open, but she remained wordless— mindless, as the powerful orgasm consumed her.

She finally let out a guttural moan of pleasure so loud it deafened her own ears. Nikoli held still as her body contracted around his finger. The waves of pleasure seemingly endless. Viv shuddered until the waves calmed.

She never felt him remove his hand or refasten her jeans. The next thing that drew her consciousness to here and now was the touch of his hand on her cheek. He kissed her lips, her nose, her eyelids.

When she opened her eyes, he was looking down at her, smiling softly. His eyes never left hers as he straightened her bra and lowered her sweater.

Warm butter seemed to flow through Viv's body, and she didn't want the sensation to ever end. She wanted to stretch like a cat and curl up next to him and sleep. She didn't want to let this moment go. She didn't want the peace she felt within her body and mind to leave.

His hand moved over her lips, and Viv smelled her own passion on his fingers, which sent a flare of heat through her body once more. Nikoli must have sensed it because he drew his hand away and placed it at his side.

He kissed her gently. "You're so beautiful, Vivienne. So much woman." He let out a deep sigh. "We must go now," he whispered and released her hand that he'd locked over her head.

She tugged at him. "But...you..."

"Shhh," he murmured and kissed her again.

"There'll be time for that later. Right now we have things to tend to. Come."

Viv wanted to say, "I just did," but kept the comment to herself. She felt as though she'd been left to wander in déjà vu-land. Her premonition the night she'd first met him had been spot on, almost to the exact moves.

She felt light-headed when Nikoli helped her to her feet. He took the satchel and hefted it over his right shoulder.

On wobbly legs, Viv followed him out of the workshop. He closed the door behind them, then took her hand and led her to his Camaro.

"Are you okay?" he asked, opening the car door for her.

"Yes," Viv said softly. The world still looked glossy through her eyes.

He smiled at her, and they loaded into the car and headed for the ferry.

Despite where they were headed and all that faced them, Viv had never felt more alive in her entire life.

Chapter 17

As they drove to the dock where the ferry was moored, Viv found herself wishing the car had a bench seat so she could sit closer to Nikoli. They rode in silence, but she kept her eyes on him as he watched the road. Every so often, he'd cast a look in her direction. At times his expression held the appearance of ultimate satisfaction. Other times, he appeared disconcerted. A confusing combination.

Viv didn't want to think about what had happened in the workshop. She just wanted to feel it. The residual power of it still echoed in her body. If she overthought it, like she did most things, she'd miss out on the simple sensation of pleasure.

It didn't take long, however, for her mind to take

the reins and say, *Bitch, what did you just do?* She grimaced at the voice yelling in her head.

What *had* she just done? When Viv thought back on it and tried seeing it through Nikoli's eyes, she imagined him thinking her to be a wanton harlot in heat. Condemnation and embarrassment attempted to override the pleasure she'd tried so desperately to hold on to.

Viv folded her hands in her lap and rolled her shoulders forward. The last thing she'd ever want was for Nikoli to think of her in such a negative way. But there was no way for her to undo what had already been done.

She peered over at Nikoli and caught him watching her with a smile. They'd stopped at a red light at the corner of Toulouse and Dauphine.

"Uh…" Viv said, unsure of how to say what she needed to tell him. "Back there… I mean at the, uh… the workshop. I—I don't know what came over me." She lowered her head and wished for once her hair wasn't pulled back in a braid. Her cheeks felt like they were on fire. "I just wanted to, uh…to say I—I'm sorry. I don't know what—"

Before Viv could finish, she felt Nikoli's hand gently take hold of her chin and turn her face toward him. Holding her there, he steered the car over to the side of the road with his free hand, came to a stop, then shoved the gear into Park.

He turned to her. "Vivienne, don't ever apologize for being who you are. You're one of the most beautiful women I've ever known. Not only physically, but your heart, your mind. I was drawn to you the moment we met. You never need to apologize for your passion. It's refreshing, exhilarating. You're open, not only in what and how you think, but in your sexuality, and you allow your body the freedom to express itself honestly. I lo—appreciate that about you."

"But isn't a woman's body reacting to sex normal?" she asked.

Nikoli arched a brow. "Far from it. Some women, for whatever reason, have trouble letting go. They need to be coaxed to give their body permission to experience sexual pleasure. Others see their sexuality like an old shoe, ready to slip onto anyone's foot."

"Oh," she muttered. "Guess I need to get out more."

He chuckled. "Whatever you do, don't change. And never compare yourself to another woman or think you need to blend in with some fashion group, who, for the most part, can often times come across as fake and vain. Stay just the way you are. You're perfect."

Nikoli glanced over at the windshield for a moment, then turned back to her. "I'm not sorry about what happened, and I don't want you to be. Ever. Okay?"

Seeing the sincerity in his powerful gray eyes, Viv nodded.

"Promise?" He stroked her chin with his thumb, then released it and trailed his fingers down her cheek. "I don't want you to ever regret it."

Viv gave him a small, still-embarrassed smile.

"Good," he said, then turned back to the steering wheel, shifted gears on the car and pulled back onto the street.

They drove in silence for a while. Traffic appeared unusually light and pedestrian traffic even more so. Viv stared out of the passenger window, thinking but not really seeing anything that went by.

"Have you alerted Jaco and Aaron about our arrival?" Nikoli asked.

"No. I never tell them when I'm headed out there. I just show up. That way they don't have time to prep anything or clean up a screw-up before I arrive. Keeps them on their toes."

"Smart lady."

He turned right onto St. Ann Street, then drove down four or five more blocks to Decatur and took another right.

They were still on Decatur headed for the street that led to the wharf when Viv caught sight of something out of the corner of her eye. She squinted to get a better look out the passenger window and spotted a tall, pale figure with a bald head darting into an alleyway between two shotgun houses.

"Stop the car!" she said.

"What's wrong?"

"I think I saw one of Evee's Nosferatu over there." She tapped a finger against the window.

Nikoli quickly pulled the car over to the side of the road, the passenger side wheels climbing the sidewalk.

As soon as he came to a stop, Viv opened her door and jumped out of the car. She heard a rumble of thunder. "Be right back," she said without looking back at Nikoli and took off for the alley.

No lights shown through the windows of the houses

on either side of the alley, indicating that either no one was home or the dilapidated buildings had been abandoned.

Having forgotten her flashlight in the truck, Viv squinted into the darkness and slowly made her way to the entrance of the alley. She pressed her back up against clapboard siding and inched her way forward.

Something rustled ahead, and Viv froze, straining to hear more clearly. The rustle of leaves, like someone walking through them in short, halting steps. The darkness proved unforgiving. Even squinting, all she saw was more darkness. She wanted to kick herself in the ass for having left the flashlight behind.

When the rustling sound stopped, she started to inch forward again, being careful not to rustle anything herself. As she moved, Viv considered a game plan.

She had none.

What the hell was she supposed to do with a Nosferatu? She had no power over them, just as Evee had no power over her Loups.

Viv contemplated one option. She might not be able to control the Nosferatu, but she could certainly put a boundary spell around herself, keeping the creature away from her. Of course, that plan would only work if it didn't pounce out of the darkness and kill her first.

Suddenly, the rustle of leaves started up again, only louder. Whatever made the noise had managed to get much closer to her, and it now sounded like it was running in her direction. She stood stock-still, holding her breath—holding her ground, still unable to see. What good was there in being a witch if she didn't have infrared vision or couldn't produce it?

Viv felt a presence drawing closer, faster. She pressed her back firmly against the wall and just when she felt the presence almost on top of her, a beam of light flooded the alley. It blinded her for a moment.

She whipped her head from right to left and saw Nikoli standing with a flashlight in the alley. He aimed the light toward the opposite end of the alley, and she saw, not five feet away from her, a Nosferatu, hunched over with its arm thrown over its eyes.

Man-made light did no harm to the Nosferatu, not like natural sunlight, but she was sure that looking directly into a flashlight beam burned the hell out of its eyes.

The creature's head was bald with one large, bulging vein running from the bridge of its nose to where a hairline should have been. The vein branched off like a tree, spreading across the top of its head. It had large, black eyes, skin like an albino and cauliflower ears. Its fangs weren't its incisors, but its two front teeth. Sharp, needle-like and deadly. Its fingers were twice the length of a normal man's, and its nails, yellow and gnarled, were at least four inches long.

Nikoli lowered the beam of light to the creature's feet, which were bare. Its toes abnormally long and contorted.

The Nosferatu hissed at Viv, threw its arm to its side, then crouched.

She knew it was ready to pounce.

"Get out!" Viv shouted to Nikoli. "Go back to the car!"

The creature hissed again and inched forward awkwardly, seeming uncertain about its next move.

Nikoli didn't budge, and Viv yelled at him again. "Go!"

Remaining where he stood, Nikoli turned the flashlight so the beam once again hit the Nosferatu directly in the eyes, causing it to shrink back and hide its face. "I'm not leaving you here. If I go to the car, you're coming with me."

"This is one of Evee's Nosferatu. I can't leave!"

Viv turned to the creature and shouted out a binding spell.

Heed my voice, ye creature of night.
I bind thee now from taking flight.
Inside or out, it makes no matter.
Boshnah, morva, benlu, sonah!"

Nikoli moved the light beam to one side, evidently checking on the spell's effect. The creature lurched forward, causing Viv to reflexively drop into a crouch. The beam of light returned once again, searing the Nosferatu's eyes. She might as well have been singing "Mary Had a Little Lamb" for all the good the binding spell did.

The next thing Viv saw was Nikoli running toward her at full speed. He sprang right for the Nosferatu, hitting the creature mid-chest, dropping it to the ground on its back. The flashlight flew back in Viv's direction.

Viv scrambled to her feet, grabbed the flashlight and cried out, "No, Nikoli! It's too strong!"

As she predicted, the Nosferatu freed itself like a snake, slithering out from beneath its captor's grip, and got to its feet before Nikoli had a chance to turn around.

The creature grabbed him by the throat and held him up with one hand until Nikoli's feet dangled in the air.

Viv saw Nikoli immediately cross his arms over his chest, draw in a deep breath, then do a half twist in midair, which released him from the Nosferatu's hold. Landing on his feet, Nikoli threw an uppercut, catching the creature under the jaw. Its head snapped back, but the punch did little more than piss it off.

The creature hissed loudly and lunged for him. Nikoli dropped onto his haunches, then met the Nosferatu lunge for lunge, throwing all of his weight into a punch that landed against the creature's left temple. This time it knocked the Nosferatu back a couple of feet.

Viv knew no spell would stop it and nothing she could say would stop Nikoli from trying to protect her from it. That left her with only one option.

While creature and man struggled for the upper hand, Viv raced to the car, grabbed the red yarn from the satchel, then ran back to the alley.

Holding the spool in one hand, she found the loose end of the yarn, pulled it free and continued to unspool it, estimating the length she'd need.

When she reached eight feet, she mumbled a short cutting incantation, and the eight feet of yarn immediately broke free from the spool. She glanced down the alley, the flashlight still on the ground, casting light and shadows over the fighting creature and Nikoli.

She hurriedly attached one end of the eight-foot piece of yarn to a crevice in the clapboard siding on her right, then pulled the remainder of it across the alley to the house on her left.

With the red yarn stretched across the north end of the alley, she shouted a holding spell.

"Yarn of red, spirits blue,
Hold what's captured firm like glue.
Yarn of red, binding real,
By my command, ye shall be steel.
Steel of gray forged near a river,
Ye shall now become a coil of silver."

Viv grabbed the spool of red yarn and ran at breakneck speed around the house on her left until she reached the south end of the alley. There, she repeated the process with the yarn and issued another holding command.

Now that both ends had been secured, Viv ducked under the clothesline of yarn and yelled at Nikoli, who had just drop kicked the Nosferatu onto its side. "Holding spell!" She pointed to the red yarn. "This way. Hurry!"

He looked puzzled but darted off in her direction. He was only ten feet away from her when the creature flew through the air and pounced on Nikoli's back, dropping him to the ground and knocking the breath out of him.

Without a second thought, Viv ran toward him.

Straddling Nikoli's back, the Nosferatu lifted its head, eyes blind but for the kill, and bared its fangs. It barely had time to lower its chin, much less drop its head to Nikoli's throat before Viv landed a side kick to the creature's face, pitching it off Nikoli's back. Having no time to ask permission, Viv scrambled for the sheath attached to Nikoli's belt and yanked out the scabior.

The creature sprang toward her, fangs bared, and she rammed the handle of the scabior into the Nosferatu's left eye. It fell to the ground, shrieking in pain. Viv pulled out the scabior, which made a sickening *schtuuck* sound and she hurried over to Nikoli, who'd gotten to his feet.

Before the creature regained its footing, Viv grabbed Nikoli's shirt and ran for the end of the alley. She yelled, "Duck!" just before they reached the yarn. She ducked, scabior still in hand, and Nikoli's shirt yanked free of her grasp as he did a duck and roll.

The creature, now flailing mere inches behind them, shrieked like a banshee the moment its body touched the yarn. It screeched in fury, backed away, then ran full speed ahead, back in their direction, one eye glaring at them like a rabid dog, the other leaking thick pus-colored fluid.

Nikoli pulled Viv off to one side, and they both watched as the Nosferatu hit the red yarn at chest level. Smoke rose from the black sarong that covered it, and the rest of its body appeared to flatten as if it had hit a thick pane of glass. The creature screeched in pain and fell onto its back, then rolled from side to side.

Viv signaled for Nikoli to follow her and she hurried off to the car. He matched her step for step.

"Red yarn?" he said after they'd both jumped into the car.

"Holding spell. It won't stop a Nosferatu from attacking, but it'll hold it in place until Evee can send one of her leaders over to collect it."

The car engine roared to life and they were soon speeding down the street, tires screeching.

"Do you have a cell phone?" Nikoli asked, not taking his eyes off the road.

Viv looked at him quizzically. His hair was tousled, his cheeks streaked with dirt and scratches. "No. Do you?"

He shook his head. "We never carry one."

"Why? Electromagnetic field interference?"

"Yep. Screws with the scabiors."

"Same here. Only it messes with our incantations. Throws them off."

"So how are we going to let Evee know about her Nosferatu?" he asked.

Viv tapped her right temple. "I already have." Earlier, when they'd run for the car, Viv had wordlessly issued a yearning spell for Evee, along with coordinates to her Nosferatu.

She leaned her head back against the seat for a moment to catch her breath, then remembered something.

Sitting upright, Viv held out her right hand. "I believe this belongs to you." She handed Nikoli the scabior.

He did a double take from windshield to scabior and reached for his sheath as if to verify it was missing. His expression was one of amazement and disbelief.

Obviously finding his sheath empty, Nikoli took the scabior from her and grimaced at the stickiness on the handle. "How...? When...?"

"Had to borrow it. Nosferatu needed eye surgery," she said. "Sorry about the eye goo on the handle. I didn't have time to clean it.

"I—I..." Nikoli's mouth dropped open, then snapped shut.

Viv smiled and dropped her head back onto the seat and closed her eyes. She was glad Nikoli hadn't been bitten. He would have either died or turned into a similar creature.

And no way would Viv ever have sex with a Nosferatu.

She turned her head and peeked through eyelashes at the gorgeous hunk of man sitting beside her. Besides, she'd already been bitten—by a Bender.

Chapter 18

He'd had fun watching all of the action over the past couple of days, but now he grew bored. It was time to clean house.

It's not that he'd been surprised by the Benders' arrival. He'd expected it. Those four pathetic losers always brought their toys when no one had invited them to play. No matter where he sent his Cartesians, the four fools or others like them—showed up, flipping and twirling their little batons. So they took out a Cartesian or two. No big deal. The size of the army he was building would dwarf any army from the Benders' world. Collectively, they'd certainly be able to handle those four little twerps.

So far, he'd gotten the biggest kick from the death of the Chenilles earlier. It had been as easy as shooting fish in a barrel. Right under their noses. Oh, and the crying Triad—extra icing on the cake.

Sure, now he had to wait until the Carties that the Benders had shot with their batons made their way back to him. When a Cartesian either pushed its way into or had been thrust into other dimensions, it took some time for them to return. Always waiting on a rift.

Always.

Fortunately, his Carties had only been pushed to the fifth dimension. Only one away from him. Their return might take a while, but not centuries. No. Those little baton-twirling majorettes had only shot them two dimensions away from their world. They'd find their way back to him. To their god.

He was a patient leader. They'd be back soon enough to watch the sinking of Atlantis—the Originals—the Triads. His glorious victory.

There were plenty of games to play to occupy his time until then. Not only was he patient, he was ingenious. Who else would have thought to shove some of the Originals out of their dens instead of killing them? Only he had the brains to come up with a plan like that. Which was as it should be. Great leaders thought in great ways.

Missing Nosferatu, Chenilles and Loup Garous kept the Triads running in all directions. Along with those dickless Benders. Distraction. Diversion. Dictator. That was the name of this game.

The one thing a Triad couldn't do was clone herself. How else were they going to hunt for the missing while protecting the cloistered—and themselves?

And what could the stupid Benders do with all of that mess flying in every direction? Why, even now they were scurrying about wondering, "Where, oh, where do I stick my baton now?"

He'd show them where to stick it.

This was survival of the fittest, and he was king of that game.

Too often it appeared that humans had no fittest, only mentally and physical challenged nitwits who called themselves leaders. By the time he was ready for them, for the humans, the pickings would be as easy as berries on the vine. He'd crush those berries and serve them up as wine to his Carties.

How did that saying go? As a man thinketh, so shall he be. Or some kind of crap like that. And therein lay the human demise. They blurted out words that had no meaning in them. Blah, blah, yada, yada. See how big my dick is.

He, on the other hand, did and meant what he said. To himself, anyway.

By tonight, or tomorrow at the latest, he'd be well on his way to acquiring the victory he'd been planning, preparing for and dreaming of for centuries. Someone with a lesser mental capacity would probably consider his actions a form of revenge. And if he was honest with himself, and on occasion he was, he'd have to admit that was partially true.

He'd been an innocent bystander, minding his own business, going about his own life, living by his own creed when someone decided, without his permission, to divert his personal journey and make it their own.

Little did they know that their meddling would change the very course of history. For the Originals, whose innocent lives had also been diverted, for the Triads, who, in secret, he'd always coveted, for the world, something they had no business toying with in the first place.

He'd been fortunate over the years, that the meddling few had created multitudes of species that had kept his Cartesians fed and growing in number for centuries. The vampires, whose powers tasted like honey right off the comb. The leprechauns, albeit with lesser strength, held the unique aftertaste of gumdrops stolen from a candy vendor. The werewolves, an acquired taste, like snails and caviar. The djinn, like a strong, heady wine.

Each unique, diverse. His for the choosing. It simply depended on what his palate craved on any particular day. No, those responsible for their existence had no idea just how tasty they were.

Had they not realized, all those centuries ago, that no secret stayed hidden forever? They'd sat, so haughty, filled with false righteousness and self-designated authority, pointing fingers at whom they considered the lowly, and changed the course of lives. All the while, thinking no one would ever know, ever find out. How wrong they had been. How gloriously wrong.

The truth would not only be revealed, it had become his weapon of choice.

He had to admit, however, that he carried a secret of his own. He'd coveted generations of Triads. Often daydreamed of how, once destroyed, their power would taste on his tongue. Sweet? Salty? Or strong and heady, like the finest fruit from a champion winery?

Soon.

He'd find out soon.

Now, though, he had the luxury to play for a while, which he planned to do. The Triads would know more misery, worry, heartache and temptation than they'd ever experienced in their miserable little lives. He'd show them, the wenches who played queen with the Originals like they owned the netherworld. He'd show them exactly who owned and controlled what. Once he'd had his fill of playing with them, he'd slowly savor their destruction.

If he had any regret, it was that he'd never see the Originals or the Triads bow at his feet. On a positive note, however, they would *become* his feet—his arms. His brain and heart. His weaponry for ultimate, universal control.

As for the meddling Benders, he would squash them like bugs. Or simply use them to clean his teeth after he'd snacked on Triads and gorged on Originals.

Chapter 19

Hoisting the satchel onto his right shoulder, Nikoli boarded the ferry and watched Viv at the helm. He held onto the railing, expecting her to rocket across the water as before. Suprisingly, she kept the ferry moving at a slow and easy pace across the muddy river. It gave him time to study her, not that he hadn't already. Every time he saw her, in fact. Nikoli couldn't help it. She fascinated him to the point of distraction.

The cool night air blew tendrils of hair from her head, and the tip of her braid slapped between her buttocks. How he longed to wrap a hand around that braid and pull her toward him—to kiss her, make love to her, make her his own.

Nikoli didn't know whether to be angry with himself for feeling this way and for what happened in the workshop earlier. Or to be excited to know Viv yearned for him as much as he did for her.

Logic snapped at him in his head. *How can you be angry over something that's so completely out of your control?*

Back at the shop, when Viv had turned to him, she'd been so close that he'd felt her breath on his face. In that moment, something more powerful than anything he'd ever experienced overtook him.

Nikoli was far from a teenage boy with raging hormones. As a Bender and in his midthirties, Nikoli rarely, if ever, lost control due to a woman. Granted, he was no saint, but he'd always kept romantic dealings, of which there'd been few, and Bender missions separate. He'd learned from Lucien's and Gavril's mistakes that mixing the two held the potential for disaster. About five years ago, both had been suspended by an Elder Bender for four months for chasing after skirts instead of taking care of business.

Thinking about his cousins, Nikoli wondered how things were going on their end. They didn't have telepathic abilities, nor could they conjure spells in order to communicate. They ran strictly by instinct. He didn't feel that Lucien, Gavril or Ronan were in danger, not from Cartesians or from any Original anyway.

What concerned him was their undeniable attraction to the Triads they had been paired with. Each time he'd seen Gavril stare at Gilly, the man's eyes took on that hound-dog yearning look. Then he had Lucien and Ronan. He sensed both were vying for Evee's attention and was curious as to which one would pull ahead in the race.

Seeing Ronan interested in Evee had Nikoli intrigued. He'd never seen that particular cousin, a very private man, show any outward attraction to any woman. Nikoli knew he dated when they weren't working, but Ronan always kept any and all information about the woman very hush-hush.

Lucien, on the other hand, they often called Butter Man, for rarely did he cross a woman who didn't instantly turn to butter when given his attention.

Not that Evee or Gilly were easy catches by any means. But the truth was none of them should have been trying to win or vie for any of the Triads' attention. They had a serious situation at hand. But who was he to judge? Nikoli had not only crossed the line he always harped on, he'd high-jumped it like a hurdle.

Viv glanced back at Nikoli and smiled at him. Her straight, white teeth, her full, to-die-for lips made his heart and body ache with need.

He returned her smile, knowing full well that, for all intents and purposes, he'd breeched that creed earlier. He'd managed to keep his pants zipped, but that was semantics. His cousins weren't stupid either. If Nikoli had noticed them ogling Gilly and Evee, they must certainly have seen his tongue hanging down to his kneecaps for Viv.

"I know we have a lot to do at the compound," Viv suddenly said to him from over her shoulder. "But I wanted to make this ferry trip slower so you'd have a chance to see the Mississippi. I don't sense any trouble from the compound, so we have a little time."

Nikoli nodded and smiled.

Grinning, Viv motioned with her chin. "Why are you standing so far away?" she asked. "Why don't you come up here, feel the breeze on your face and smell the water? It may be brown and muddy, but the scent is bayou—South Louisiana. The only place you'll catch the scent."

Nikoli watched her, not knowing what to say. If he stayed where he was she might take it as an offense, thinking he didn't want to be near her. Which was the farthest thing from the truth. He wanted, needed to be close. Wanted his arms wrapped around her.

He'd been doing his best to keep some distance between them so he'd have his mind on the mission. But distance hadn't helped that one bit. The mission was crucial, but he didn't want to hurt Viv's feelings. One was just as important to him as the other.

"Come on up," she said again.

This time Nikoli gave in and went to meet her at the bow of the ferry. He hooked his hands onto the railing, tilted his head back and closed his eyes, took a deep breath.

Viv had been right. The water here did have a unique scent. It didn't smell like the Atlantic or Pacific, both of which he'd traveled many times. Although he'd boated across the Gulf of Mexico a time or two, the trips had been far from the coast of Louisiana. Even there the water had looked and smelled different. It was almost as if this water was the core of New Orleans. It had built her, fed her, and had been essential in creating the beauty that was the city.

He glanced over at Viv. "It's beautiful."

She smiled. "Only place like it in the world. I know other bodies of water have white sand and blue-green waters, but those waters and sand seem to suit the cities or countries they surround." She shrugged. "I guess it's different for everyone, water I mean. This—" she waved a hand to indicate the waters below "—is part of home."

Viv's hands came to rest on the top railing, and, unable to stop himself, Nikoli reached over and put one of his hands on top of hers.

She looked down at their hands, then up at him.

"Waters often reflect the nature of the inhabitants who live near it," Nikoli said. "And this is no different." He gave her hand a gentle squeeze. "You are as unique as these waters, Viv. Very different than any woman I've ever met before."

Viv lowered her eyes shyly and said, "Oh, I'm sure you've met tons of women around the world. Beautiful women, sensual women, rich and smart women. Women who don't have baggage like the Triads carry."

Nikoli didn't think it was a good idea to admit to any woman that he had in fact known quite a few, even though Viv had stated it as common knowledge. He knew women well enough to know that responding to the statement in the affirmative carried its own set of problems. With Viv, however, in his heart of hearts, Nikoli wanted nothing but transparency.

"It's true, I've known quite a few women around

the world." He took her hand that he'd been holding on to and placed it over his heart, tapped it against his chest. "But trust me when I tell you, despite the number of women or the country they came from or the time I knew them, I've never met anyone as beautiful and unique as you. You're bright, intelligent, strong-willed, yet conscientious and caring."

Viv pursed her lips, cocked her head, gave him a wary look, then laughed. "You've either practiced that line in front of a mirror ten thousand times or you're the best bullshitter on the planet."

"Honestly, I would never tell you anything that wasn't true, Vivienne."

She smiled, then sighed and looked ahead, lifting her head to catch the breeze of the night. "You're pretty special yourself," she said, not looking at him.

Nikoli didn't respond, hoping she'd share more of her feelings.

She did.

"When I first met you and your cousins, I thought this was all bullshit," Viv said. "I mean, we'd never heard of Benders before. But I have to admit, I was immediately attracted to you. All of your cousins are very handsome but there was just something about you that really stuck with me. As hard as I tried, I couldn't help but think of you in a romantic way. There's just something about you that causes an urgent tug inside me. That's never happened to me before, and I don't even know why I'm blabbering on about it. It's a little embarrassing." She looked up at him. "No...it's a lot embarrassing."

"Please don't be embarrassed," Nikoli said. "I've never told any other woman the things I've told you just now. I hope you'll always feel free to tell me what's on your mind."

"Well, now that you mention it…" Viv paused mid-sentence as they pulled up to the docks across the river. She moored the ferry, made certain it was locked down, then turned to Nikoli. "You know, I've seen the way Gavril looks at Gilly and the way Ronan and Lucien look at Evee. That worries me. You seem stronger, emotionally and mentally, than your cousins, more focused, more able to retain control. I haven't seen your cousins in action, though. If the three of them have gone gaga over my sisters, do you feel confident they can stay focused enough to protect them? To protect the Originals they're responsible for?"

"They wouldn't be with them if I didn't," Nikoli said. Having heard the concern in her voice, he squeezed her hand reassuringly.

She nodded, offered a small smile.

The soft look in her eyes, the fullness of her lips, the hint of dimples when she smiled. She'd drop any man to his knees. Her ability to think quickly on her feet, her confidence when taking charge. Nikoli could've stood staring at her, listing a million reasons why she was special.

It was then Nikoli realized, with some trepidation, that he was falling in love with Ms. Vivienne François.

Chapter 20

By the time they finally reached the North compound, Nikoli drew in a deep breath through his nose. He smelled the faint odor of cloves, residue from the previous Cartesian attack.

All appeared quiet. A little too quiet for his liking. And dark. Clouds had thickened overhead, blanketing the moon and stars. He reached for the flashlight he had stashed in his back pocket, then glanced over his shoulder to Viv, who walked a step or two behind him. She carried the second flashlight and had it aimed at the ground, sweeping the beam from left to right, surveying everything around her closely.

"No new tracks," she said when she caught him looking back at her.

He nodded, then, for no other reason but reassurance, touched the sheath attached to his belt to make certain his scabior was securely inside.

Though he'd never admitted it to Viv, he'd been unnerved when she'd handed it to him in the car. Having someone take the scabior from its sheath without him realizing it felt like an assault. Like someone who'd fallen asleep with two arms, then woke only to discover they now had one. And no clue as to the when, who and how of it all.

Nikoli remembered Viv's attack on the Nosferatu, how she'd jabbed it in the eye. He hadn't known then what weapon she'd used. Only assumed, given that she was a witch, that she had conjured up whatever tool she'd needed. Recalling the fight with the Nosferatu, Nikoli suddenly wanted to slap his own forehead.

He aimed his flashlight at Viv's feet. "I'm sorry," he said. "I forgot to thank you."

"For what?"

"Back there, with the Nosferatu. You saved my life."

She batted a hand in his direction. "I didn't do much really. You handled yourself pretty well."

"Yeah, until he knocked me on my ass. I saw it coming. Its fangs were ready for the kill before I could even catch my breath."

"I'm confident you would've kicked right back, breath or no breath," she said.

"Do you always take compliments and appreciation that well?" He grinned.

Viv smiled back at him. "Okay, all right... You're welcome."

"I owe you one," he said.

She gave him a mischievous look. "Oh, I think we'll run into plenty of opportunities to even the score."

Nikoli couldn't quite define the look that suddenly crossed her face. A little confusion—an undertone of danger—excitement. Simply put, Vivienne François mystified him. Aside from her beauty, her mysterious nature was probably the reason he was so attracted to her in the first place.

He glanced away for a second. He felt he should mention how deeply her taking his scabior without his knowledge had affected him. And he would. But not now. She'd just saved his life for heaven's sake.

"Come this way," Viv said, motioning to him with her flashlight. "Let's check out the tracks Jaco showed us earlier. See if there are any fresh ones near them."

She led him closer to the compound gate, then veered off to the left, about fifty yards. As they walked, Nikoli aimed the beam of his flashlight into the compound. He came to a halt when he spotted two Loup Garous dodging between trees in the dense forest.

He'd never seen a morphed Loup up close before. They amazed him. Their bodies were larger than that of an average werewolf. They had pointed ears, a longer snout and, from what he saw, thicker fur. They ran through brush like lightning, dodging trees, jumping thickets, heading for the back acreage of the compound. Evidently the beam from his flashlight had frightened them, and they sought a safe place to hide. They were so agile and quick, if he would've blinked at the wrong time, he'd have missed them.

"Over here," Viv called, signaling with her light.

When he turned his flashlight toward her, Nikoli saw her kneel on the ground, her flashlight now poised over a spot in the dirt right in front of her. It was the tracks Jaco had shown her.

You could've seen the tracks from a helicopter. They were that huge, but no surprise to him. Nikoli had seen similar many times before.

"That must've had you scratching your head when you first saw them," he said.

"It scared the shit out of me. I couldn't imagine an animal big enough to create a print this big. I thought it might have been a bear, but Jaco said even the biggest grizzly couldn't have made prints this size. I understand now what he meant."

"Do you see any others?" Nikoli asked. "Anything new nearby? If there are, I might be able to detect their travel pattern from point of entry."

"Nothing near the first ones," Viv said, then aimed her flashlight farther ahead. "We should have a look around the brush up ahead."

Before Nikoli knew it, Viv was on her hands and knees crawling on dirt and grass and swiping her way through a heavy cover of bramble and thickets.

He followed her.

The farther they crawled, the thicker the bramble became and the thicker the grass beneath their hands and feet. Tree branches and foliage lay thick overhead like a canopy. It felt like Mother Nature had cocooned them in her arms. A safe, quiet hideaway.

"Find anything?" he called out to Viv. He had to keep his head turned slightly to the left because right in front of him was her perfectly proportioned, heart-shaped ass, which made crawling all the more uncomfortable for him.

"Not yet."

They crawled a bit farther before he asked, "Have you contacted Jaco and Aaron to let them know we're here? We should get started on those posts."

Viv stopped and peered over her left shoulder at him. "No, I haven't. But I will, soon enough." She turned back and resumed crawling.

When they were about a hundred feet inside the cocoon, Viv stopped again, then turned and sat on the ground. She brushed grass and dust from her jeans. Nikoli pulled up next to her and sat, as well.

"I haven't found any tracks up this way so far," she said. "The brush only gets thicker from here. Before we get tangled up in it, it'd probably be best to head back."

He agreed, but neither of them moved. He made certain to keep the beam from his flashlight away from her face and out of her eyes. Those beautiful, cobalt blue eyes with long, thick lashes. They mesmerized him. So full of expression, so fierce. So intense.

Her face was mere inches from his, and Nikoli heard her breathing become short and shallow. He felt her breath, hot against his face. Her entire body seemed to radiate the same kind of heat. She held an invitation in her eyes, a question, an undeniable hunger.

Nikoli didn't have to be asked twice. He reached for her, behind her, wrapping his hand in the braid of her hair and pulled her close. It was his fantasy unfolding into reality.

The moment their lips touched, his desire for her became an all-consuming inferno. Her lips, her mouth tasted of honeysuckle.

Viv reached for him, weaving her fingers through his hair and pulling him closer. She lowered one of her hands and dug fingernails into his back.

Nikoli marveled at her. An all-or-nothing woman. She gave all to her Loups, all in her kisses, in her passion. Gave her all to anything she wanted or demanded. And she slipped effortlessly from one compulsion to the next as if no distance varied the desire.

Remembering that he'd seen her Loups only moments ago, Nikoli reluctantly removed his lips from hers. "We can't. Not here, not now. Not this way."

Viv groaned and the sound quickly took on the tone of a low growl. She crossed her arms in front of her, grabbed the bottom of her sweater and quickly pulled it up and over her head. Then she reached behind her back and unhooked her bra, letting it drop from her breasts and arms and fall into her lap.

Her breasts were perfect. Full, firm. Her nipples dark and hard.

"Yes," she said, her voice low and husky. "Here. Now. And this way."

Before Nikoli had the chance to respond, she swung her legs about and sat astride his lap. She pressed her body against him, grabbed a handful of his hair and lowered his head down to her breasts.

Where they were and why they were there became lost to Nikoli. He inhaled the delicacy of her skin, her undeniably erotic scent—lilac with an earthy undertone. A scent that would drive any man crazy, making him beg for more.

He cupped her breasts, rolled her nipples between his forefingers and thumbs, tugged on them gently until she threw her head back and moaned with desire. Nikoli turned his head to her left breast and flicked his tongue over the nipple, nipping at it gently with his teeth. He took his time before turning his attention to her other breast. The heat from her, from between her legs, penetrated his body. A scorching fire that refused to be denied.

Nikoli struggled with not taking her right then and there. Her hands were still tangled in his hair, and she pulled hard, forcing him to look up at her.

"I need you," she murmured. "I need you inside of me." She held on to his hair with one hand and reached down between his legs with the other, searching for the fly on his jeans.

Nikoli gritted his teeth, reached down, grabbed her wrist and held tight. He looked deeply into her eyes. "Not—this—way," he said, his voice low and gravelly.

The smallest of whimpers escaped Viv. "Yes—this—way."

Unable to resist her, Nikoli leaned forward, pushing Viv gently onto her back. She unfurled her legs so her body lay flat on the brush beneath them. Her eyes were bright with hunger and need.

Nikoli swung both of his legs to one side of her and knelt near her waist. He leaned over, put his lips to her right ear, kissed behind it, beneath it and let his tongue slide down her neck. He bit into her flesh ever so gently.

The groan that escaped her sounded animalistic, feral. It injected his own desire with adrenaline that made Nikoli want to rip off the rest of her clothes and shove the hardness throbbing behind his jeans deep within her without any preamble. But this wasn't about him and his needs. Everything was about Vivienne. He longed to satiate the hunger within her more than he desired the air he breathed.

Lowering his mouth to her breasts again, Nikoli forced himself to slow his pace, take his time as he licked and caressed her breasts. Her moans echoed throughout their cocoon.

He slid his tongue down her sternum to her belly while his fingers worked the button loose on her jeans and lowered the zipper.

As he licked down the length of her belly and back up again, he worked her jeans and panties off one hip, then the other and tugged them off her buttocks. Viv had already kicked off her sneakers and she began working the jeans down lower with her feet until she'd freed herself from pants and panties.

Nikoli didn't have to touch her to know she was wet, swollen and ready. He smelled the sweet musk of her and moaned as he lowered his head to the core of her heat. He pressed the tip of his tongue between the slit that held the fire that raged within her. The heat emanating from her amazed him, devoured him.

As he pushed his tongue in deeper, tasting her

sweetness, Viv arched her back and lifted her hips. He knew what she wanted, but he knew what she needed.

He let his nose graze over her clit, and she bucked up against him.

"Yes!" she cried.

Keeping his tongue at her center, he pushed it inside of her slowly. In and out. Lapping up all she had to offer. He purposely stayed away from the swollen nodule that would cause her to explode beneath him.

Not yet.

Viv arched her back again and lifted her hips, a sure sign that she wanted, needed more. He worked his tongue inside her. In and out. In and out. In. Out.

When Nikoli felt she could bear no more, he quickly replaced his tongue with his right middle finger and covered her swollen pearl of pleasure with his mouth, his tongue flicking over it again and again. His other hand cupped her buttocks, lifting her hips higher and he drove his finger in deeper. Her heat became fluid, flowing out of her body and over his hands. She cried out loudly and shuddered with the violence of her orgasm. He lowered his mouth, dipping his tongue into the hot lava that flowed from her.

When her gasps became short pants, Nikoli sat back on his knees, lowered the zipper of his jeans and released the hardness that had been causing him physical pain for some time. He leaned over her, allowing the tip of it to press against the hot, wet opening of her. He kissed her and she greedily sucked on his lips, nipped them with her teeth, shoved her tongue into his mouth.

Nikoli entered her gently, a fraction of an inch, then pulled back until the tip rested against her heat once more.

Viv released her mouth from his, arched her back, thrust her hips upward, trying to drive the remaining length of him inside her. But he held back.

"More!" she cried, arching her back, her neck.

Slowly, purposely, he lowered himself into her. Each time she thrust her hips up to him, he'd pull back. Only when her buttocks rested in his hand did he push deeper inside her.

He heard his heart pounding in his ears, his body demanding more, feeling ready to implode if he didn't act quickly.

When he could take no more, Nikoli thrust the remaining length of his hardness into her. "Yes!" Viv screamed, then wrapped her legs around his waist, her hips meeting him thrust for thrust.

It took mere seconds before her body shuddered and she cried out with release. She bathed him over and over with sweet, hot lava, her body contracting around him, pulling on him as if she needed the whole of him inside her.

Only then did Nikoli allow his own release. He groaned with the intensity of it, was blinded by it, and he called out her name.

"Vivienne..."

When his own body stopped convulsing, he lay atop her, putting a hand to the ground on either side of her body to minimize his weight. He whispered in her ear. "Vivienne—my Vivienne."

Moments later, she lay in his arms, her head resting

against his chest. Nikoli held her tightly, stroked her hair and before he realized what was happening, he found himself silently mouthing the words, *I love you.* Although he hadn't said it out loud, those were words he'd never even considered saying to another woman.

Slightly unnerved by his emotions, he kissed the top of her head. Ever so slowly, his mind and body began to take on the weight of the responsibilities that awaited him. He kissed the top of her head again and was about to tell her it was time to get dressed when he caught the sudden scent of cloves. His arms tightened around her and he sniffed the air to make certain.

Cloves.

He hadn't been mistaken. It held only a hint of sulfur, which meant the Cartesians were working their way into the third dimension through some rift nearby.

Viv pushed away from him abruptly and sat bolt upright. "Cloves," she said.

"You smell it, too?"

"Yes." Viv scrambled for her clothes. Not bothering with her bra, she yanked her sweater over her head and wiggled into her jeans. She grabbed her sneakers and shoved her feet into them.

Nikoli pulled up his zipper and righted the clothes on his own body. When she finished dressing, he got to his hands and knees and crawled quickly toward the opening of their cocoon. Viv followed closely behind.

The closer they got to the opening, the stronger the sulfur scent grew. The smell of cloves became overwhelming, mixing with the sulfur, both growing thicker, heavier by the second.

When Nikoli broke free of the opening, he turned back to Viv. "Stay in there!"

"Screw that," she said and popped out from the opening.

Nikoli didn't have time to argue with her. The smell of the Cartesians was so strong that he knew the rift had already been opened. Lightning streaked across the sky and a clap of thunder shook the ground.

He reached for his scabior and realized it wasn't in its sheath. Shocked, he glanced down to make certain. No scabior.

Puzzled, he looked over at Viv, who stood beside him on the right. No scabior in her hands.

"What the hell," he said. "Viv—"

"I smell it, I smell it!" she cried. "Where are they? What direction?"

Thinking the scabior might have fallen from its sheath when they'd crawled through the cocoon or during the heat of their lovemaking, he shouted at Viv over another clap of thunder. "Stay put! My scabior!"

He quickly ducked back into the cocoon, crawling as fast as he could. The flashlights were still burning brightly inside. Three quarters of the way into the cocoon he found his scabior. Grabbing it, Nikoli put it between his teeth, then hurried back to the opening as fast as his hands and knees would allow.

When he reached the opening, he found Viv standing nearby. He jumped to his feet and spotted a wide, black opening in the sky to his left. He took the scabior from his mouth and held it out in front of him. He heard howling, yipping and roars of fury coming

from the Loup Garous inside the compound. Another
streak of lightning and Nikoli looked up at the sky. A
second rift had formed off to the right, and it yawned
open right before his eyes.

"Get behind me," he shouted at Viv over the howling and thunder.

She did as she was told, and he aimed the scabior at
the wider of the two rifts above them. He walked slowly
to his left, holding the scabior up and out. It only made
sense that the slit he was aiming for had been worked
over longer by the Cartesians. He was sure this would
be where they'd make their first appearance.

He zeroed in on the rift, allowed his breathing to
grow shallow. Concentrated.

It was then he heard Viv's loud scream.

Nikoli whirled about just in time to see a Cartesian
hanging out of the smaller rift. It swung its gigantic
claws toward them. Viv appeared frozen in place.

With a roar, Nikoli ran, then dove, tackling Viv and
dropping her to the ground. But he'd been a second
too late for her to go unscathed. The Cartesian's claws
swiped across Viv's left arm, shredding her sweater
and leaving long gashes in her flesh.

Shaking with fury, Nikoli quickly got to his feet,
aimed the scabior, twisted his wrist twice, twirled the
scabior between his fingers at the speed of light, then
took aim again. A bolt of lightning shot from the bloodstone and hit the Cartesian in the head. It folded over
with a high-pitched screech, and its body jerked back
into the rift.

Nikoli stood his ground, concentrated, putting all

his effort into sending the son of a bitch as far away as he could. If possible, he would've jumped into that hole and beat the bastard into a bloody pulp. He heard a pop, then a second. More high-pitched screeching.

A third pop, then a fourth—fifth. The screeching grew muffled.

Nikoli let his anger rage, wanting to push the electrical charge from the bloodstone farther. He heard a sixth pop, then a seventh. Only then did the second rift in the sky zip close. The first immediately followed suit.

Drawing in a shaky breath and half-dazed, Nikoli looked about for Viv. She wasn't where he had left her.

Panicked, he called out for her, "Vivienne!"

When she didn't respond, he took a step to start hunting the compound for her and tripped over something.

Flailing, Nikoli caught his balance and looked down to see what had been in his way.

It was Viv.

Lying lifelessly on the ground near his feet.

Chapter 21

Startled from a nightmare, Arabella Matthews sat up in bed and glanced at the clock that sat on a nightstand near her bed. It was a little after 11:00 p.m.

The nightmare had been so vivid it was as if she'd been living it right here and now. Arabella rubbed the heel of her hands over her eyes to scrub away sleep. The dream had involved the Triads, she remembered that. Something…something about one of the Triads hurt? No…dying. One of them had been seriously injured and died.

The Benders had been in her dream, as well. Four of them. And they'd been fighting so many Cartesians she couldn't count them all. Huge, terrible beasts with one mission. To kill and conquer.

Arabella remembered that in the nightmare, she'd

stood in the midst of the chaos, along with Taka and Vanessa. Spells. They'd tried so many spells. Binding. Protection. Submission. Nothing worked. Taka screamed. Vanessa cried. She had done both. The dream had felt too real to be a coincidence, which forced Arabella out of bed. She had to let the other two Elders know about it. Something had to be done, although she was clueless as to what.

She walked into Vanessa's room and shook her awake.

"Mmm, stop…" Vanessa said groggily. She opened one eye and peered up at Arabella. "What?" Evidently seeing something in the Elder's expression, Vanessa sat up quickly. "What's wrong? Has there been another attack?"

"I don't think it's happened yet. I had a dream. A nightmare. It felt too real to ignore. We need to gather and discuss it. It's important. You wake Taka. I'll go into the kitchen and get water boiling for tea."

As Vanessa scrambled out of bed, Arabella hurried off to the kitchen, filled the kettle with water and placed it on the stove. As she woke more fully, the dream didn't dissipate. The details remained vivid. Too vivid. It made her anxious and sweaty.

By the time Arabella had set china saucers and cups steeping with chamomile tea on the table, Vanessa came into the kitchen, wearing a white robe over her white, floor-length flannel nightgown. Her silver satin slippers whispered quietly across the hardwood floors.

Taka followed close behind, her white hair sticking up in wild, tangled tufts. She wore gray sweatpants, an orange, flannel hoodie and green socks with yellow smiley faces on her feet.

The two Elders sat at the kitchen table. Small and circular, it seated four and was where they usually ate breakfast. Arabella needed small, comfortable and familiar. The kitchen table was their usual meeting spot when the three of them needed to discuss Circle of Sisters issues or occurrences in the city that might affect them. Sharing her dream in a larger room would have made her voice echo. Just the thought of that put Arabella's last nerve on edge.

"What's going on?" Taka asked, then yawned. She took a quick sip of tea. "Vanessa said you had a bad dream. Is that why we're meeting?"

"I already told you what happened and why we're here," Vanessa said with a huff. "Don't you ever pay attention?"

Taka rolled her eyes and sipped tea again. "I pay plenty of attention." She turned to Arabella. "You sure your dream wasn't from indigestion? You know, from the pot roast we ate earlier tonight?"

"I'm sure," Arabella said. Before she could get another word in edgewise, Vanessa rapped the table with her knuckles.

"Look here, missy," Vanessa said to Taka. "I cooked that pot roast, and it was quite delicious if I do say so myself."

"A little too much salt if you ask me," Taka said, and rubbed sleep from her right eye.

Arabella held up a hand to silence both of them. "Stop bickering. Yes, I did have a bad dream, Taka.

A nightmare. Only I don't think it was just a dream. I feel it was a warning."

"What kind of warning?" Vanessa asked. "What did you see?"

"I saw the Triads in dire straits. One of them was killed."

Taka gasped loudly and her teacup clattered onto its saucer. Tea sloshed over the cup.

"Dead?" she asked. "Not just injured, but dead?"

"My word, how horrible!" Vanessa said and picked up her cup of tea. Her hands trembled so badly, she set the cup back on the saucer, then folded her hands on the table.

"I know," Arabella agreed. "I also saw Originals running through the city. All of them out of control because the Triads were fighting for their own lives. The three of us were in the nightmare, too."

"Including me?" Taka asked, wide-eyed.

Arabella nodded. "It was as if the entire city of New Orleans was in a panic and no matter what we tried, we couldn't affect any change. None of our spells worked, not one incantation. In the dream, it felt like we were… unplugged."

"The dream sort of makes sense when you think about what the Triads told us when they came here," Vanessa said.

"Yeah," Taka agreed. "Things weren't exactly okay. So what do we do? Do you have any ideas at all?" she asked, turning to Arabella.

Arabella sighed. "The only thing I can think of is

putting all we've got into one big protection spell. Wrap it around the Triads."

"Hell, we need to wrap it around the city," Taka said.

"What about the Benders?" Vanessa asked. "Should the protection spell include them?"

Arabella pursed her lips thoughtfully. "I'm at a complete loss when it comes to the Benders," she said. "I don't know if putting a protection spell around them will somehow negate their powers and effectiveness in fighting the Cartesians. And frankly, and sad to say, I don't think I want to take the chance."

"Good point," Taka said.

"They're here to fight the Cartesians," Arabella said. "So we need to trust that they are well equipped to do just that. If they're with the Triads, who will be protected by our spell…hopefully…then there shouldn't be any worry about an Original attacking the Benders."

"Sounds good on paper," Taka said.

"What are you talking about?" Vanessa said to Taka. "Do you see any paper on this table?"

"She's just making a point," Arabella said. "It sounds good as we're talking about it, but having it work is another story."

"Yeah," Taka said. "Another story."

Vanessa rolled her eyes, then said to Arabella. "Let's get started then. What ingredients do you want us to use for this particular spell?"

Arabella aimed her chin at Taka. "You take care of gathering the herbs. We'll need rosemary, sage, thyme, lavender and bay laurel."

"Got it." Taka nodded.

"Vanessa, would you please collect the stones we'll need?"

"Sure," Vanessa said. "Which ones?"

"Amber, to increase the power of the spell, jet, to absorb negative energy, amethyst, to cleanse, blue lace agate for healing, azurite for psychic ability, and clear quartz, which, as you know, is needed for all manifestation spells."

"But we're not manifesting anything," Vanessa said, looking confused.

"I want this protection spell to be so strong it will seem like a living, breathing organism," Arabella said.

Vanessa nodded. "Got it."

"Now, we'll also need a blend of bergamot, cypress and myrrh oil, along with three candles," Arabella said. "One green candle as it relates to physicality, a yellow one to clear the path for our spell, then purple for spirituality. I'll take care of the oils and candles."

"Okay," Taka said. She pushed away from the table and stood. "Let's get started."

Vanessa took a quick sip of tea, then stood as well and sighed. "I wish we'd put one of those gliding chairs on the staircase so we wouldn't have to walk those steps. The stairs are hell on my knees."

"Mine, too," Taka said. "And my bunions. But the pain'll be worth it. It's for a good cause."

Arabella wished for the gliding chair, as well. She knew what the two Elders meant. They rarely went upstairs anymore due to arthritis, bunions, hip aches and ankle pain.

She hated getting old. That was one slight when it

came to the Circle of Sisters' order. From the beginning of the order, they were able to conjure spells to heal but not when it came to aging. They believed in allowing nature to take its course, which meant graying hair, creaky joints and sagging body parts that used to be round and perky.

"Once we've gathered our ingredients, we'll come back here and use the kitchen table for the altar," Arabella said. "That way we won't have to keep running... well, keep going upstairs to check on the burning candles."

As the three Elders moaned and groaned their way upstairs, Arabella thought about the right words they'd need for the protection spell. This wouldn't be a standard "don't touch me" spell. It had to be bigger, stronger. Their words had as big a part to play in the conjuring of the spell as the ingredients they were about to collect.

When they reached the second-floor landing, the Elders split off in different directions, each headed for the rooms where specific items were stored.

Thirty minutes later, they stood gathered around the kitchen table again. Taka cleared away the cups and saucers, then wiped the table down with a dishcloth. Arabella laid out a circular black silk cloth in the center of the table. Then she placed the green, yellow and purple candles in a triangle along the edges of the cloth.

Arabella nodded to Vanessa. "Place the stones in a circle within the triangle of candles. Start at the point, next to the green one."

"Any specific order?" Vanessa asked.

"Yes, start with the clear quartz, then follow with the azurite, going clockwise. After the azurite, place the amber, then jet, followed by blue lace agate and close the circle with the amethyst."

Vanessa quickly did as she was told, and when her task was completed, Arabella went over to one of the kitchen cabinets and removed a stone bowl. She pulled open a utility drawer and took out a box of matches. She brought bowl and matches back to the table and placed them in the center of the crystals.

Arabella nodded at Taka. "Put the herbs in the bowl, please."

Taka made quite the show as she dramatically sprinkled sage, rosemary, thyme, lavender and bay laurel into the bowl. She dusted her hands off over the bowl to brush off any herb residue.

Arabella took a bottle from her robe pocket. She opened it and placed three drops of her special blend of bergamot, cypress and myrrh oil on top of the herbs.

The other Elders stood silently as Arabella took the matches, lit the candles, then placed the match onto the herb and oil mixture. Once it began to smolder, she brought the match to her lips, blew it out and flicked the used match into the kitchen sink.

"Let's join hands," Arabella said.

When they were connected, Arabella stared deeply into the smoldering concoction in the stone bowl and said, "Repeat after me... We call upon the elements of life—water, air, fire, earth—to aide us in our quest."

Vanessa and Taka obediently repeated her words.

"Anything or anyone intentionally set on harming

the Triads shall be thwarted. And the harm intended for the Triads shall be sent back to thee. We do not accept harm to them. Protection is their shield from all negativity and hatred, from injury and illness. They do not harm others, so others cannot harm them. So we speak this, so shall it be."

The two Elders holding onto Arabella repeated her words verbatim.

Arabella continued, "And we speak a second protection over the Triads. Protection against dark entities and demons. This shield shall keep out evil. This shield shall keep out harm. This shield does not allow demons or negative entities to pass through it. This shield shall be the Triads' domain, and they alone determine what is allowed to pass through it. So we speak this into being, so shall it be."

When Vanessa and Taka completed their repetition, all three of the Elders sighed.

"It is done," Arabella said.

"What about the people in the city?" Vanessa asked. "Aren't we going to put a protection spell over them?"

"We can try," Arabella said. "But without knowing each person, seeing their faces in our mind's eye, it'll be sort of like tossing confetti in the air. If we specifically blanket the city, that doesn't allow nature to take its course."

"What do you mean?" Taka asked.

"Tonight, somewhere in this city, people will die. Either by natural causes or unnatural causes having nothing to do with the Originals. We can't alter everyone's future. A person's time to die is their time to die."

"Well, that doesn't seem fair," Taka said. "Doesn't the same apply to a Triad? If it's their time to die, I mean?"

"No," Arabella said, a bit uncomfortably. In truth, Taka was right. But Arabella steeled herself and lifted her chin. "They belong to the Circle of Sisters. And we're responsible for them."

"We'll need more supplies if we're going to attempt a protection spell over the people in the city," Vanessa said. "I'll get more crystals."

Taka frowned. "Wait a minute. Since when, as Elders, have we ever gone off half-cocked when it came to conjuring spells?"

Both Arabella and Vanessa stared at her, blinking. It was one of the most intelligent questions Taka had asked in some time.

"We're not going off half-cocked," Arabella finally said. "We're only doing the best we know how. We weren't trained to stave off Cartesians and flight-risk Originals. As head Elder, I've simply formulated what makes sense."

Taka pursed her lips, then said, "I know neither one of you want to hear this, but since we're looking at such a serious situation, don't you think we should get some help? Like from someone who knows the city?"

"And who might that be?" Vanessa said warily.

"The sorcerers," Taka said.

Vanessa threw up her hands. "And here I thought her brain had just regained some logical use."

"We can't let the sorcerers know about this," Arabella said. "The last thing we need is Cottle holding everything that's going on over our heads, claiming we're powerless, useless. He already thinks he's a know-it-all."

"What about Shandor or Gunner?" Taka asked.

"Shandor is Cottle's lapdog," Vanessa said. "He'll run to him with the news in a heartbeat."

"Gunner?" Taka asked, her brow furrowing.

"We're not knocking your ideas, dear," Arabella told Taka. "I don't think it's safe to leak word of this, even to Gunner. I might trust him more if he wasn't always around Cottle and Shandor. I don't know what their connection is, but it's disconcerting and doesn't elicit trust, in my opinion. We can, however, contact others within the Circle of Sisters and have them conjure protections spells that will overlap ours."

"Good idea," Vanessa said. "That'll certainly give us some leverage."

Seeing the distraught look on Taka's face, Arabella said, "We've always taken care of our own. We simply can't take the chance that word will get out in the city."

Taka tsked. "Don't you think you're being a bit dramatic?"

"Our sisters weren't being dramatic when they were hung by anti-witch zealots back in the early centuries," Arabella reminded her.

"We'll call more sisters," Vanessa said. "It'll work. You'll see."

Taka scowled at Vanessa. "Are you, like…trying to comfort me?"

Vanessa snorted. "Absolutely not. Simply making a statement."

"I certainly hope our spell, along with those of our other sisters, are effective and in time to save the Triads," Arabella said. "And the people in this city from the Originals. If not, we might all be destroyed."

Taka stared at Arabella, her eyebrows knitting together. "All of us?"

Arabella nodded. "Every last one of us, just like the lynchings our ancestors suffered centuries ago. This could very well start off another witch hunt, another hunt to destroy all of the Originals and their subspecies. And we'd be stuck right in the middle of it all."

Chapter 22

Viv heard someone call her name. She wanted to tell them to hush. Her arm burned like hell, and she didn't feel well. She wanted to sleep.

Suddenly, it felt like a switch flipped on in her brain, and she remembered where she was and about the Cartesian. Her eyes flew open, and she found herself lying flat on her back on the ground. She'd obviously passed out, something she'd never done before.

Gazing up at the sky, Viv saw that the rifts were closed. She sat up, struggled to get to her feet and felt something grab her uninjured arm. She let out a blood-curdling scream.

"It's me."

She recognized Nikoli's voice.

"It's just me," he said again. "The Cartesian's gone."

Viv was finally able to focus on his face. She reached for him, clung to him and shivered.

He held her close. "It's okay, baby. It's gone."

She pulled away from him, her eyes wide and questioning. "I saw two… There were two holes in the sky. I…I don't understand. You—you were right about the Cartesians coming after us!"

"I think they used the two rifts as a trap," Nikoli said. "To distract us. Have me wonder which one they'd drop down from first." He shook his head. "I don't know for certain. Hell, they could have just as easily dropped down from both. What makes me think it was a trap was they waited for my attention to be focused on the larger rift before the Cartesian dropped out of the other one and attacked you. By the time I saw it, I ran as fast as I could…" He cupped her face with his hands. "God, Viv, you could've been killed."

Even though her arm hurt like hell, she took his face in her hands and kissed him hard. "Thank you. I think we're about even now, so no more close calls, okay?" Her eyes welled up with tears, and she scolded herself. *Don't cry! Don't cry!*

"No more," he said, then helped Viv to her feet. "We need to get you home so I can tend to the wounds on your arm."

She looked down at her arm and saw the sleeve of her sweater. It looked like it had gone through a shredder, and blood oozed from the gashes in her arm.

"On second thought, you may need stitches," Nikoli said. "We should go straight to an emergency room and have a doctor take a look at that."

Viv eyed him. "I'm a Triad, remember? We don't do hospitals and doctors. We heal ourselves with herbs, crystals—shit like that."

The frown on his face deepened. "So can you do a spell? Have the wounds close up and go away? Make the bleeding stop at least?"

"I'm a Triad, not a stupid vampire." She plucked at a piece of the shredded sweater sleeve. "Can you rip this off? We can use it to wrap the wounds, staunch the bleeding and keep the dirt out until I can tend to it better."

Pursing his lips, Nikoli took hold of the fabric of the sleeve closest to her shoulder and pulled. It ripped at the seam, and he continued to tease it loose all the way around her arm. When the last stitch tore free, Viv carefully tugged the sleeve down her arm and over her hand. She saw three long gashes on her arm. *Don't cry. Don't cry*, she repeated.

She held the material out to him, "Do you mind?"

"Of course not." Nikoli took the material from her and wrapped it around her wounds. "They're bleeding pretty good. In order to stop it, I'm going to have to put a little pressure on the wrap. Tell me if it gets too tight."

Viv nodded and gritted her teeth as he flipped, tugged, then tied the torn sleeve around her injured arm. She couldn't tell how deep the gashes were from all the blood.

When he was done, Nikoli said, "I really think we should go to—"

"Don't think," she said. "You've covered up the

wounds nice and tight, so it's all good. I'm not bailing over some little cut."

"They're not so little."

"It's my arm, so I get to call it. They're little." Before he hit her with a retort, Viv spun about on the balls of her feet, cupped her hands around her mouth and let out a loud, long howl, then two sharp barks and another howl. Her voice echoed far into the night, over the din in the compound, the thunder rumbling from every direction.

Viv looked back at Nikoli. He probably thought she'd lost her mind. "I'm calling for Jaco and Aaron. They usually respond right away. I hope they're okay." She waited a couple minutes and was about to send out another come-hither call when the branches of the trees in the thicker part of the forest to her left started to quiver.

Jaco suddenly appeared out of the brush. Standing in human form, he looked haggard and beyond exhausted.

"Where's Aaron?" Viv asked.

Jaco shook his head and shrugged. "He went missing about four hours ago. I don't know where he is."

"You've been dealing with all of the Loups in this compound by yourself?" she asked, stunned.

"Yeah." Jaco looked at the material wrapped around her arm but didn't say anything about it. He looked at her with weary, bloodshot eyes.

Viv felt sorry for her lead Loup and wanted to hug him for his loyalty and commitment to her. But she knew better. No personal contact. Not with the leaders. It would undermine her authority. She drew in a deep breath to clear her head. "There's only one more thing I need to ask you to do, then I'll assign two other Loups to patrol the compound so you can get some rest. We want to try something that might help protect the entire compound from the Cartesians."

Jaco suddenly lifted his head and sniffed. Viv's body went on alert. Though she still smelled residual clove, she didn't catch anything new.

"What's the matter?" she asked.

Instead of answering, Jaco let his nose lead him to the underbrush, where she and Nikoli had had sex. He leaned over and sniffed deeply, then turned to look at Viv, a steely expression on his face.

"I smell you and…" Jaco sniffed again. "Him." He aimed his chin at Nikoli, who stood a few feet away. "Does that mean that while I've been busting my ass inside that compound, trying to control all the in-fighting, worrying about when the next Cartesians were going to drop out of the sky, the two of you were in there, screwing like rabbits?"

Evidently overhearing Jaco, Nikoli took a step toward him, fury on his face. Viv held up a hand to stop him.

She turned her attention back to Jaco, feeling like she'd just been slapped. She firmed up her stance and kept her eyes hard. "Remember who you're talking to. The Triad who feeds you, who gives you a safe place to roam without fear. The one who protects you from human hunters. What I do is my business, not yours. Tell me, when you find a female in heat, have you ever known me to run up to your den and condemn you for fucking some little bitch in heat while I'm having so many problems elsewhere?"

Jaco's eyes went soft, and he dropped his chin to his chest. "I…I apologize."

"See that it never happens again." Viv forced her voice to remain strong and firm when what she felt was small and ashamed. Jaco was right. "Now, as I was saying, we have a plan, and I need you to do something for me. For this compound and all the Loups. Once you complete the task, I'll assign two other Loups to keep watch until I get back. You need some rest."

"What do you need?" Jaco asked.

"We're going to set something up that we believe will keep the Cartesians from dropping down into the compound. If it works, that'll give me time to search for our missing Loups."

"And if it doesn't?" Jaco asked.

"Back to square one," Viv said. "I wouldn't ask you to do this if I didn't think the plan had potential and knew you were the right Loup to help make it happen."

Jaco squared his shoulders. "What do you want me to do?"

"See that corner fence post?" Viv pointed to the thick steel post that braced one corner of the fencing. "I need you to bend that pole to a forty-five-degree angle so it's pointed at the center of the compound. Start about waist high."

"Why would you have me do that?

Viv gave him a stern look.

"O-okay, no problem. That it?"

"It's a start. Once it's bent, we can take care of the

rest. If it works, I'll need you to find the other three poles that square off this property and bend them the same way. All of them need to be pointed to the center of the compound. We're getting ahead of ourselves, though. Let's start with the first. See what happens."

Jaco nodded and scurried off for the first fence post.

Nikoli stood beside her as they watched Jaco stand at the base of the post, hitch up his denim pants, then wrap his arms around the post. He let out a loud "Huh!" and leaned over from the waist. The pole began to bend, creaking in protest. Once it leaned at a forty-five-degree angle, Jaco turned to look at Viv, and she held up a hand, signaling all was good.

She turned to Nikoli. "Do you have the bloodstones?"

"There're in the satchel over there." He pointed to the brown bag sitting on the ground next to the entrance of their hidey hole. "I'll get it."

Once Nikoli had retrieved the satchel, he pulled out one of the larger bloodstones. He held it up, examined it, then scowled.

"What's wrong?" she asked.

"I can't believe I didn't think about how we were going to attach these to the poles. Look at that angle. The stone's going to fall right off."

"No, it won't," Viv said and held out her hands. "May I have it, please?"

Nikoli handed her the bloodstone, and Viv quickly ran her hands all the way around it over and over, all the while muttering a holding spell.

"Stone of blood, spirit anew,

Bind thyself firm like glue.
Stone of blood, binding real,
By my command ye shall meld with steel.
Donda—Lorra."

When she was done, Viv called Jaco over to her and handed him the stone. "I want you to shimmy up the pole you just bent and place this on top of the pole."

"But it'll fall off," Jaco said, giving her a puzzled look. "That pole's at a forty-five,"

"Trust me," Viv said. "It'll stay in place."

Jaco jostled the stone in his hand as if studying it, testing its weight, then shrugged and headed back to the pole.

"You sure this is going to work?" Viv asked Nikoli.

He sidled up to her. "You've already asked me that. Sorry I can't give you a different answer. I really don't know if it's going to work until we try it. Like I said, it's never been done before."

She felt as if someone had just dropped a three-hundred-pound weight on her shoulders. This had to work. She couldn't accept anything but it working because the alternative was unthinkable.

Viv watched as her Loup shimmied up and across the pole one-handed. When he got within arm's reach of the top, he took the bloodstone, then reached under the pole and up and placed the stone directly onto the pole's center. He held on to it, glancing down and over at Viv.

She nodded, and Jaco released the stone.

The bloodstone remained in place as if it belonged there and had always been a part of the pole. A huge smile lit up her Loup's face as he slid down the pole and hurried over to her.

Nikoli, who'd retrieved their flashlights from the brush, aimed a light beam at the top of the pole. "Well, I'll be damned. That's some mojo you've got, lady."

"I know," Viv said. "And by the way, why would you do that to yourself?"

Nikoli looked down at her quizzically. "What?"

"Damn yourself."

He grinned.

Viv returned the smile, then dug through the satchel for three more bloodstones. She'd decided to have Jaco finish the job with the other three poles while they tested the first one. She didn't want him to be around and wind up being disappointed if something went awry.

After finding the largest of the remaining stones, she placed the satchel on the ground. One by one, she rubbed her hands over the stones she'd chosen, chanting over each one in turn.

"Stone of blood, spirit anew,
Bind thyself firm like glue.
Stone of blood, binding real,
By my command ye shall meld with steel.
Donda—Lorra."

"What now?" Jaco said when he returned to her side. "You going to test it?"

"Soon," Viv said. "Take these three stones and find the other three poles. Do the exact same thing you did to that one, okay?"

"Got it."

Viv handed him the stones, wincing from the pain in her arm. "Return to me as soon as you're done."

Jaco nodded and took off, soon disappearing into the forest's brush.

Once he was out of sight, she turned to Nikoli. "Show time."

"Fingers crossed," he said and reached for his sca-bior. Holding it in his right hand, he turned back to Viv. "Don't look so worried. I have confidence this'll work. Just because something's never been done be-fore, doesn't mean it can't or won't work."

"I know. You're right." Viv offered him a small smile. "Rock on, Magic Man. It's your show now."

She saw his eyes soften. He glanced at the makeshift bandage on her arm, and sorrow flitted across his face.

"Hey, it's all good," Viv said. "Don't beat yourself up. It's just a couple of scratches that'll heal in no time. You're forgetting the big picture. You saved my life, remember? How can you feel bad about that?"

"I don't," Nikoli said. "Your safety means every-thing to me. It simply hurts me to see you hurting."

Viv was taken aback by the emotion in his voice, the concern in his words and the depth with which his storm cloud–gray eyes studied her.

The wind suddenly picked up and stirred the cool night air. It wafted over her, and she breathed in deeply, appreciating the coolness against her fevered arm. She smelled the air charged with electricity, smelled the rain in its belly. They were in for a gully washer.

"You may want to get started before we get doused. Rain's coming."

"I smell it," Nikoli said and handed her the flashlight, then held out the scabior.

Viv watched in anticipation, but before Nikoli could twitch his wrists one way or the other, Jaco came bursting out of the brush over to her.

He was panting, out of breath. When he reached her side, he leaned over and put his hands on his knees and sucked in a breath. "They're—all—done," he said, each word coming out on the heels of a pant.

"You mean the poles?" Viv asked. "You've already finished them?"

Jaco nodded, sweat streaming down the sides of his face.

"Wow," Nikoli said. "That was fast."

Jaco scowled at him but smiled proudly at Viv. "You told me to return to you when I was done. Is there something else you want me to do?"

"Good job, Jaco," she said. "We're good for now. Go back to your den and get some rest. I'll assign two other Loups to watch the compound before I leave."

"When will you know if this plan you had will work?" he asked. "Having this compound under protection twenty-four-seven would be great."

"We'll know soon," she promised. "I'll give you an update when we find out." Lightning crisscrossed the sky, and Viv cringed reflexively. A loud clap of thunder quickly followed. "Go now before you get stuck in this storm."

Jaco gave her a formal bow from the waist, then hurried away.

Viv glanced over at Nikoli. He already had the scabior aimed at the pole.

A disconcerting thought suddenly struck Viv. "Wait. How are you going to get to the other three poles to charge them? At least two of them are only accessible through the compound."

"We don't have to physically be at those poles to charge them," he said. "This one, like the other three, is aimed at the center of the compound. If I'm able to charge this one, the electromagnetic field will immediately strike the bloodstone directly opposite of it, causing the second one to charge. The two charged poles will form a horizontal crossbeam that will ignite the other two poles."

Viv looked at him in amazement and for the first time since his arrival, she was grateful he was a Bender.

"Ready?" he asked.

"Past ready."

Nikoli spread his feet apart, firming his stance. He aimed the scabior, gave two quick twists of his wrist, then whirled the scabior through his fingers and re-aimed, his brow furrowing.

A bolt of lightning shot from the bloodstone attached to the scabior and hit the bloodstone attached to the pole. The large bloodstone shimmered, and sparks flew from it. Soon the pole began to glow an odd orange color, and she saw it sway slightly.

"You're melting it," she said to Nikoli and bit her bottom lip.

He held up his free hand, signaling her to be silent.

Viv knew he had to concentrate. Although she

feared the pole would melt into a huge puddle of molten steel, she had to trust he knew what he was doing.

In that moment, the bloodstone that sat on top of the pole shot out brilliant white light toward the center of the compound. And in a matter of seconds, like dominoes, three additional brilliant lights fell into place, all four linking as they should. Strobing, sparking, lighting up the compound like a football stadium during a game.

"It worked!" Viv shouted and had to work hard not to clap her hands and jump up and down like a five-year-old. "It worked! It worked!" Then, unable to stop herself, she clapped her hands and jumped once. Pain flashed across her arm from the gashes, quickly curbing her enthusiasm.

Nikoli stared up at the lights, his expression one of wonder and amazement. He shook his head slowly as if in disbelief. "Damn, it actually worked." He shoved the scabior back into its sheath.

Viv couldn't help but run to him and reached up to give his neck a hug. Her injured arm slapped her into submission. She threw her good arm around him and gave him a big wet kiss. "You did it! You made it work."

A sharp pain jabbed her injured arm again, and Viv grimaced and drew her good arm back to her side.

They stood side by side, watching as groups of Loups darted among the trees, dodging the light.

Out of nowhere, Jaco suddenly appeared at her side again.

"Where did you come from?" she asked. "I thought you were heading back for your den."

"I have news," Jaco said, glancing up at the lights in the sky, seemingly unimpressed. He looked back at Viv. "When those…things lit up, I was at the north end of the compound, near the back. I found Aaron."

Relieved, Viv looked about and asked, "Where is he? Why isn't he with you?"

The look on Jaco's face caused Viv's stomach to turn sour.

"He's dead," Jaco said.

Viv felt her mouth drop open, and she snapped it shut. "How? Where?"

"I have no idea how," Jaco said. "All I know is there's not much left of him. Found him near the fence out back. I don't know what all these lights are about, but I sure hope that whatever you're doing with them works."

Viv felt her brain struggle to grasp the fact that she'd lost another one of her Loups. This one a pack leader. The three-hundred-pound weight returned to her shoulders. She wanted to sit down. No, lie down. Close her eyes and sleep this nightmare away, then wake up to find things back to normal.

Unable to find any words to comfort Jaco, she watched him walk away. Her shock was too great to call him back.

Nikoli stepped up to her. "I heard," he said. "I'm so sorry."

She turned to him. This time she couldn't tell herself not to cry.

He took hold of her uninjured arm and pulled her in close. He held her head against his chest. She heard the rapid beating of his heart.

Viv remained too dumbstruck to say a word.

"I can't bring him back," Nikoli said. "None of them. But I'll do everything in my power to make certain nothing more happens to you or to the Originals. I'll bring order back to your world. You'll see."

Viv nodded slowly against his chest, wondering which would come first. His order to her world or her own death.

Chapter 23

Assigning two different alphas, Petros and Carlton, to watch over the compound had been tough on Viv. Aaron, her West pack leader, had been with her since she was a child. She still couldn't believe he was gone, that she'd never see him again—his soft brown eyes, his silky black fur and his signature birthmark—a pink ring of flesh around his left nostril.

Her only comfort when issuing the new assignment was knowing she was helping Jaco. He needed time to rest, to heal emotionally and physically. Something she didn't know if she'd ever be able to do.

So much had happened over the last two or three days. Viv couldn't even remember how or when all of this started. How long had it been since things were normal? She wondered if she would ever know times like that again.

Exhaustion beat on her, as did the pain in her arm. She and Nikoli had already crossed by ferry to city-side and were standing beside her truck. Only then did she allow herself time to feel.

"I'm going to miss that big guy," Viv said to Nikoli, fighting off tears.

He rested a hand on her shoulder. "I know you will. You've done a spectacular job caring for the Loup Garou. I don't know of anyone who cares about their charges the way you do. Who loves them the way you do. I'm sure you get frustrated at times. I know I do with my job. But you keep after it. You don't quit."

When she heard the word "quit," a tear slid down Viv's cheek. She quickly brushed it away.

"It's okay to cry," he said.

Viv looked away from him. "No, it's not. There's too much to do. We should let Gilly and Evee and your cousins know that the makeshift scabior worked at the North compound so we can start setting up their territories."

Nikoli tucked a finger under her chin, turning her head so she faced him. "It's a little after midnight already. We told them we'd meet them at the ferry for feeding time. That's only three hours away. Since they're going to meet us here anyway, why don't we use that time to look for your missing Loups?"

Viv drew in a deep breath. She wanted to be every-where at one time. At the compound, looking for her

Loups, helping Evee and Gilly look for their lost broods and protecting her sisters.

Her injured arm gave witness to the fact that the Cartesians were out to get them. What Nikoli had said about the leader of the Cartesians probably wanting them out of the way so he could get to the Originals freely had been spot on. They were all under attack. She didn't know where to put herself or know which direction to turn.

Evidently sensing her muddled thoughts, Nikoli tapped her gently on the nose with a finger. "Tell me what it feels like whenever one of your Loups is nearby but you can't see him. How do you sense them? By scent? By sound? By sensation?"

"Sensation," Viv said, not understanding where he was going with the question.

"Okay," he said. "Let's start with that. What does that sensation feel like?"

She thought for a moment, trying to find the words to describe it. "It starts out as a tingle at the base of my spine that works its way up to my neck, then my ears begin to ring."

"Do you feel anything like that now?"

She shook her head. "No. You think if I did that I'd be standing here right now?"

"I know, I know."

"Where are you going with this?" she asked.

"Bear with me. When your Loups are in the compound and not ordered to work—you know, they're simply hanging out, being Loups, going about their own business—what kind of sounds do they make?"

"I don't understand," she glanced over at Nikoli, and he looked deeply into her eyes. "What do you mean by sounds?"

"Think about it," he said. "When you and your sisters are just hanging out, not into any conversation, doing your own things, does Gilly hum to herself? Does Evee whistle a tune?"

"They don't do any of that," she said.

"Okay, but do you get the point I'm trying to make? When your Loups are just hanging out together, what kind of sounds do they make?"

"It depends. Sometimes they growl territorially, sometimes they howl, some bark or yip. A few make a clicking sound with their tongue that I've never quite been able to figure out. Other than that, they're usually quiet."

"Okay, that's a good start." Nikoli released her chin and leaned against the truck, crossing his feet in front of him. He pointed to his left ear. "Whenever I want to hear something more clearly that might be a great distance away, I have this trick I use to amplify the sound of whatever I have a bead on. Maybe if I show you that trick and you try it, it might amplify your ability to feel that sensation you get when you have a Loup that's nearby but out of sight. The reason I asked you about the sounds they make when they're not feeding or given a chore is so I can help you listen for them while you feel. That way the two of us will be like radars, seeking a missile."

Exhausted and hurting and trying to contain the ache in her heart over Aaron's death and frustrated over all she was unable to do, Viv didn't think she could feel one more thing. Still, Nikoli had piqued her curiosity. If there was a way to amplify the sensation, maybe that would help her find the missing Loups.

She turned to him. "Show me how you do it with your hearing."

Nikoli stood upright and patted his chest. "Back up against me. Put your back to my chest."

Viv eyed him suspiciously.

"No funny business. Here." He patted his chest again.

"Okay." Viv turned and backed into him. The moment her body touched his, she felt something spark inside of her, and she quickly squelched it. Something had to be seriously wrong with her for her to react the way she did every time she was near this man. The entire world could be coming to an end—much like hers was now—and she would still want to have sex with him. She couldn't help but wonder if all the hell breaking loose now had something to do with her sleeping with him earlier.

"Hold your arms out a little so I can get my arms around you without hurting your injured arm."

She did as she was told, and felt his hands wrap around her waist and settle over her diaphragm.

"Now, breath in deeply. Take in all the air your lungs can hold."

Viv drew in a deep breath through her nose. She smelled muddy water, gasoline fumes from the city and the rot of street garbage. She held that breath, waiting for Nikoli's instruction.

"While you're holding your breath, think about what the sensation feels like when an out-of-sight Loup is near. Think about it—concentrate on that tingling sensation that starts at your spine and works its way up your neck. Feel the ringing in your ears."

Viv felt herself grow calm under the sound of his voice, her body tuned to her Loups. She focused on the tingling that made its way up her spine, like a hundred spider legs jittering their way up her back.

"Now slowly let out that breath through your mouth. Release all of it, still thinking about that tingling sensation."

Viv released her breath slowly. As she came to the end of that breath, Nikoli pressed in and up on her diaphragm and another puff of air escaped her lips.

"See?" he said. "There's always a little left over. You need to make sure that entire breath is released. So just when you think you're at the end of it. Push a little harder. There's always a little more." He eased the pressure off her diaphragm and slowly removed his arms from around her waist. He turned her to face him. "That's the trick," he said. "It's all in the breathing, letting the oxygen go all the way to your core, and concentration. Once you tune into that sensation, you can turn slowly left or right, and the sensation will grow stronger, just like sounds grow louder for me, when you're facing in the right direction of the target you're looking for. When I do that, it feels like all of my senses suddenly wake up, especially my hearing. Now, let's try it again, only this time I won't touch you so nothing will distract you."

Viv was a little disappointed she'd be doing this on her own. She liked having his arms around her and having his body pressed against hers made her feel safe.

"Does it make a difference if they're in a location they're supposed to be in, like the compound," Viv asked, "versus them just taking off, nobody knowing where they went or how they got there?"

"It doesn't. They are your Loups. The who, what, when, where and how don't figure into the equation. Remember, it's all about feeling, breathing, concentrating. Don't let all of the other stuff muddle your thoughts. Don't think about why they're not heeding your call. Just feel them."

"What if I can't?"

"At least try it. They are your Loups. It's not like you're trying to zero in on vampires or werewolves whose lives were never a part of yours. Those Loups have been a part of your life since the day you were born. They're part of you. So go ahead, give it a try. See if you pick up anything. Lean against the truck and close your eyes if it'll help you."

Viv felt a little foolish, standing at the end of a dock, near her truck with her eyes closed. You never closed your eyes at night while on the streets of New Orleans. Still, she heeded his advice, leaned against her truck and closed her eyes.

She drew in a deep breath through her nose and held it, the way Nikoli had shown her. She thought about the tingling, prickly sensation she wanted to feel, the spider legs that always started at her spine. She thought about how the spider legs traveled up her spine to the base of her skull. Then the ringing in her ears, almost like an alarm, letting her know a Loup was nearby.

She allowed herself to get lost in that thought and released her breath slowly, still thinking about the spider legs, forcing more breath out of her lungs. Thinking about the tingling up her spine—the ringing in her ears—spider legs.

Viv suddenly froze, holding back what little breath she had left in her lungs. She felt it, tingling at the base of her spine. Only this wasn't in her head. It was for real.

She remembered what Nikoli had said about slowly turning from left to right to see if the sensation grew stronger when she faced one direction versus the other. Keeping her eyes closed, Viv turned slowly to her right. The tingling at the base of her spine remained at a constant, but oddly enough, she felt a different, disconnected tingling in the middle of her back when she faced east.

Feeling her heart rate triple, Viv turned slowly to the left, and the tingling at the base of her spine grew stronger. The one in the center of her back now the constant.

"I feel something, she whispered, afraid to open her eyes. Afraid she might lose the sensation if she did.

"Think about your Loups," Nikoli whispered softly in her ear. "The ones missing. See them in your mind's eye. Let the sensation build. Grab on to it and hold tight, like it's a physical object."

Viv drew in another deep breath and the tingling she felt in the base of her spine grew stronger, more pronounced. So did the one in the center of her back.

Two separate places. The tingling didn't inch its way up her spine the way it normally did.

She released her breath and said, "It's still there, only stronger. I feel the tingling in two separate places. It's not crawling up my spine like usual. And they must be stationary because the tingling in both spots doesn't move in any direction. My ears aren't ringing, but I know it has to be them."

Nikoli whispered, "Now let your instincts take those feelings and guide you in the direction of your Loups."

"One's east, the other west," Viv said, already knowing the direction. "I think the ones in the east are a bit farther away because the sensation doesn't get as strong as the one to the west." Viv opened her eyes, pushed away from the truck and faced him. "Now what do I do with that? If we head west, how far do we go?"

"There's only one way to find out," he said. "Hop in the truck. We're heading west."

She didn't argue when Nikoli opened the passenger door for her, helped her inside, then ran around the truck and jumped into the driver's seat. He turned the engine over, lowered the window at his side and set the truck into motion.

"You concentrate on that sensation while I drive," he said. "Tell me when to turn left or right."

"How am I supposed to know which way to turn?"

"Your instincts will tell you and the sensation will confirm it. I'll keep an ear peeled for any of the sounds you said the Loups make when they're together. And considering you heard the pop from the scabior, I'd say your hearing is like radar. So ear alert."

Viv looked out through the windshield but didn't see anything in front of her. She kept her mind's eye focused on her Loups and the sensations in her back.

Ten minutes into the drive, she directed him to head north on St. Peter Street, which brought them through the French Quarter. As they closed in on North Rampart, the tingling at the base of her spine grew stronger, and she knew they were getting closer to some of her Loups.

"Take a right," she said. "Here on Rampart."

Nikoli turned right as she instructed. He drove slowly. There weren't many people out at this hour, not in this part of town. Even the tourists knew to stay clear of this area late at night.

By the time they reached Ursulines, the tingling at the base of her spine was so strong, Viv felt as if a live electrical wire had been placed beneath her skin.

"Take a left, take a left," she demanded, sitting at the edge of her seat.

He did as she asked.

Three blocks later, Viv could barely sit still. They were now at the corner of Treme and St. Philip, one of the most dangerous parts of town. "They're around here. Park, park!"

As soon as Nikoli pulled the truck over to the side of the road and killed the engine, Viv jumped out of the truck, paying little heed to the pain shooting through her injured arm.

She began to walk down Treme, concentrating with all her might, stepping slowly, carefully so as not to lose the radar now so alive in her body.

Viv heard the beep of the automatic lock on the truck, and Nikoli called after her.

"Wait up!"

She didn't want to wait. If she had this tight of a bead on her Loups, she didn't want to take a chance in losing it. Viv kept walking and heard the thud of footsteps running toward her.

When Nikoli reached her side, she saw he had a large coil of guideline cable resting on his shoulder. It was the same type of cable they used to repair the cattle pens back at the ranch. She'd had some left over in the back of her pickup, along with miscellaneous tools from the last repair job Charlie and Bootstrap had done. She meant to bring it to Jaco so he could cordon off a breeding area—something he'd asked for.

"Has anyone ever told you that you can be a little hardheaded at times?" he asked.

"What are you doing with that?" she said.

"Just-in-case supplies." He hefted the coil of cable higher on his shoulder. "Let's go."

She shook her head in bewilderment. "Something feels odd around here," she said, training her eyes straight ahead. "Gangs hang out around here. Drug dealers. They all come out at night but look, the streets are empty. That's unusual." What was even more unusual for Viv was that her clairvoyant abilities seemed to have gone by way of the dodo bird. She may have gained a new radar, but her tried-and-true abilities had somehow fallen asleep.

Nikoli put a hand on her shoulder and held tight to keep her from walking any farther. "Hold up a second.

Wait. I hear someone screaming for help. It's really muffled but I hear it."

Viv had been so focused on keeping her radar alive she hadn't heard anything but her own breathing and voice. She tilted her head slightly, strained an ear and finally heard it. The muffled cry of a woman. There was a short scream, then a loud gasp.

Breaking free of Nikoli's grasp, Viv hurried toward the sound. "There," she said, coming to a stop in front of two run-down, shotgun houses. Trash was strewn about their yards, and it looked like the mailboxes had been demolished with a baseball bat.

The woman's voice led them through an alley between the houses into the backyard. There sat an old beat-up sedan, its tires missing. Someone had propped the chassis up with cinder blocks. And three of Viv's missing Loups were beating on the windows of that car, trying to get to the woman trapped inside. The Loups were scraggly and scrawny, like they hadn't eaten in days.

Nikoli squeezed Viv's shoulder and whispered, "If we don't get them away from that woman—"

"The Loups will break the glass, and she'll be toast," Viv finished. "I know."

"Try a holding spell."

She raised an eyebrow at him and whispered, "You're telling me how to do my job?"

He gave her shoulder another little squeeze. "No way. Your ball game."

Viv inched closer to the vehicle, her arms stretched out in front of her, hands up, palms out.

"Heed my voice ye creatures three,
I bind thee now to follow me.
Inside out it makes no matter.
Boshnah, morva, benlu, sonah!"

The three Loups stopped beating on the windows, turned toward Viv and snarled.

"Oh, shit," she said. "It didn't work."

"Yes, it did," Nikoli said. "You got their attention away from the woman in the car."

"Yeah, but now they're going to come after us."

"Perfect." Nikoli removed the cable from his shoulder and held the coil in his right hand. He stuck his bottom lip between his teeth and let out a loud whistle. "This way, you ugly sons of bitches! You want dinner? Come get it."

He quickly turned to Viv. "For once, please, hear me and stay put. I'm going to call them out toward that big metal utility pole over there. Once I get them there, I'm going to use this cable like a lariat and lasso them to that pole."

"When did you suddenly become Roy Rogers?" She stared at him, wondering if there was any limit to the number of talents he possessed.

"Who's Roy Rogers?"

"Never mind. You're talking about taking on three Loups. That's like you trying to take on twenty men. You can't do that alone."

"I don't exactly have a cavalry to call. Look, when I see them running in my direction, I'm going to let them close in just enough to get the cable around them. The idea is to trap them between the cable and that pole.

When I toss the cable, you start a holding spell. By the time the cable loops back to me, you'll be done and the cable will be locked to the pole."

"I tried a binding spell, and it didn't work."

"We're talking holding spell with two inanimate objects. It'll work. Don't cause the cable to meld with the pole like you did with the bloodstones back at the compound. Just make it tight enough to hold the Loups until you can get one of your alphas out here to scoop them up."

"Got it," Viv said, amazed once more by his brilliance.

The three Loups howled, then growled. They moved a little closer to Viv and Nikoli, bumping into one another, like they weren't sure whether to leave a sure thing trapped in the car that they'd already been fighting so hard to get to or head for the two humans on foot.

Nikoli stepped away from Viv and walked a few yards away toward the utility pole, whistling for the Loups as he went. For once, she did as he asked and stayed put.

One of the Loups kept eyeing her, but each time Nikoli whistled, it whipped its head back in his direction.

"Here," Nikoli shouted. "Over here! You want dinner? Come get it."

The Loups rolled their heads from shoulder to shoulder and sniffed the air. They huddled together and as a group moved toward Viv, then lagged left and headed for Nikoli. They moved cautiously, evidently suspecting a trap.

Viv could tell by their actions there wasn't an alpha among them. All three were followers with no leader, so they were unsure of the direction to turn.

Nikoli, who'd finally reached the utility pole whistled louder and let the guideline cable unfurl. It looked to be about eight feet long. Keeping hold of one end, Nikoli whipped the cable with one hand and it whistled through the air like a bullwhip.

Viv watched as the Loups drew closer to Nikoli. She was out of their line of sight. Now they were dealing male to male, and Loups never gave up territory without a fight.

Nikoli suddenly growled at them, mimicking an angry Loup, one ready to fight. The three Loups growled back, and their united voice was deafening. They spread out in an attack formation, ready to encircle their prey. Had there been a fourth Loup, Nikoli would've been screwed. Viv didn't know how on earth he'd handle those three.

The Loups lowered their heads and hunched their shoulders, preparing to spring forward. Viv kept her eyes on them, hoping the woman in the car had had enough sense to get out and run while the Loups were preoccupied with Nikoli.

She'd barely finished that thought when the Loups charged. Nikoli moved behind the pole, letting them draw closer. He seemed to be counting. When the Loups were about fifteen to twenty feet away, he tossed the length of cable out wide, snapping his wrist so the flying end of it would return to him, like a boomerang.

The second Viv saw him release the cable, she yelled quickly:

"Cord of steel, home anew,
Bind thyself, firm like glue.
Cord of steel, binding real,
By my command, ye shall cling to steel!"

The Loups never knew what hit them when the guideline cable looped back to Nikoli. He released his end of the cable, and the thick guidewire caught the Loups from behind and slammed them against the utility pole. The cable held fast and the Loups yelped and howled, struggling to get free.

As much as she hated to, Viv cupped her hands around her mouth and howled for Jaco. She hated to disturb him, but he was the only one she trusted to come and get the three Loups.

From a great distance away, she heard Jaco's response. He'd heard her and understood.

A streak of lightning suddenly lit up the sky, and thunder rolled up behind it. A thunderstorm was about to let loose over their heads. And one thing that kept Viv from connecting with her Loups was a strong electromagnetic field. Lightning the greatest one of all. If they didn't hurry, she'd lose the connection she had with the Loups she'd felt in the East.

She saw Nikoli walking toward her. His hair was tousled, his face weary. Her heart still lunged at the sight of him. The connection she had with him had gotten too far out of hand. Viv wondered if her intimacy with Nikoli had been the reason for Aaron's death, for the missing Loups, for her own attack.

Although he didn't know it, Viv had heard when Nikoli had mouthed, "I love you," as they held each other within the confines of the forest. She wanted so much to say the same but had held her tongue. The curse of the Triad loomed over her like a concrete wall ready to collapse on her head. They could never be together. History had sealed that deal, and she didn't even know the entire story as to why.

It was all her fault. It was she who'd allowed Nikoli too close. Close enough to capture her body and soul. He was human, and she knew better.

It felt like karma had come back to slap her in the face. Viv shook her head, felt her heart drop to her feet. Instinct and conscience told her what had to be done to fix the problem, and the thought made her want to be swallowed up by Mother Earth, never to return.

She had no choice but to face a concrete resolution...

Viv had to let Nikoli Hyland go.

Chapter 24

After the Loups were bound to the metal pole and Jaco was summoned to come and get them, the sky opened up and rain pummeled them from every direction. Lightning flashed across the sky, and thunder rolled along with each flash. Viv felt the vibration of it in her body. The problem with a lightning storm was that the resulting electromagnetic field seemed to short-circuit her ability to sense her Loups and their whereabouts. All she was able to do now was recall the sensation, the spidery-like tingling in the middle of her back that she'd picked up earlier.

The fact that the sensation had been in the middle of her back, told her the remaining missing Loups were somewhere west of where they were.

Viv and Nikoli were already soaked by the time they

made it back to the truck. She noticed as he grabbed the steering wheel that his hands and forearms were scratched and bruised from handling the cable. She wanted to take each one of his hands and place healing herbs on them, kiss them, soothe them, comfort him. Then she remembered her steely resolve. She had to distance herself from Nikoli.

"Which way?" he asked. "Where do you want me to go next?"

Viv shook her head. "I'm not sure. With this lightning storm, I've lost all tracking sensation. The last time I felt it, I knew one group was west and another east. If you've got that hearing mojo you told me about earlier, we may have to count on that to find the others. Remember, when they're together and not on the hunt, they make yipping sounds or growl and bark. If they're all asleep—or worse, dead—you won't pick up any sound at all."

"Got it," he said.

"Won't it be hard for you to hear anything with all this thunder?" she asked.

Nikoli glanced over at her, and a look of puzzlement flashed across his face. She read it to mean, *Why are you sitting so far away from me?*

Evidently choosing not to address that question, he said, "I can separate the sounds, zero in on the ones that belong to my target."

Thankfully he didn't insist she move closer to him. She didn't know what she would have said if he had. As difficult as it was, she had to keep distance between them. The farther, the better.

"Since we've already hit our target west, it makes sense for us to head east, no? Since that's the direction you felt the other group?"

"That's about all we can do," she said. "Drive east and hope your Superman hearing picks up something."

Nikoli grinned. "Superman, huh?"

She gave him a half smile. "Yeah, well…"

Driving up Esplanade, they continued east until they were out of New Orleans proper. Fifteen minutes later, they came upon a commercial area with warehouses stacked one against the other. The road ended just past the warehouses and right at the Mississippi waterline. Very few security lights illuminated the area.

"I'm not hearing anything," Nikoli said. "But it's pretty dark back here. Good place for them to hide out."

"I have no idea," Viv said. "With all this rain and thunder, I'm not picking up a damn thing."

"All right, unless you want to head across the river, I'm going to get out of the truck and see if I can make a little Superman action happen."

With that, Nikoli parked, killed the engine and got out of the pickup. He squinted against the rain.

Not looking forward to another soaking, Viv reluctantly grabbed the satchel, hooked it over her right shoulder and got out of the truck, as well. She went over to him and concentrated on the rain beating a rhythm on her wounded arm instead of her close proximity to Nikoli.

She watched as he cocked his head to one side and closed his eyes. Viv felt his energy reaching out for a specific sound. They stood there for three or four minutes, soaked to the bone before he said, "I hear something, but it's not howling or yipping. It's like the gnashing of teeth and something being ripped apart. No, wait…"

Viv knew before he said any more that he had honed in on her Loups. The sound he described was the sound of them tearing into a fresh kill.

"I just heard a growl," Nikoli said and pointed ahead, into the dark, water-drenched night. "It's coming from out there, about three to four hundred yards away. I can't make anything out in all this rain. What's out that way?"

"An old, deserted factory," she said. "It's three stories high and has like ninety thousand square feet of space inside. It's been there for as long as I can remember. I think they used to manufacture some kind of oilfield equipment in there." She swiped a hand over her face to rid it of some water. "The company went belly up about twenty years ago. No one's been out there since. No rebuild. Nothing. The owner's just left."

"How can a factory be that far out there when we're standing so close to a shore? The factory would have to be sitting on the water."

"There's a peninsula down that way. It juts out into the water about five hundred yards or so."

"Can we get there by truck?"

"Not unless you want to spend the wee hours of the morning stuck in mud," Viv said. "There's no road or driveway leading to the factory anymore. Just a grass-covered peninsula."

"So we'll hike it," Nikoli said, then got back in the

truck to fetch a flashlight before heading off in the direction of the factory.

Viv followed, occasionally swiping water from her face. Her clothes stuck to her body like a second skin, and the braid hanging down her back felt like it weighed twenty pounds.

Now that she was soaked, Viv didn't mind the rain. In fact, she wished it would soak right through to her soul and wash away all she'd done over the past few days, sending it straight to a sewer. Maybe then the world would stop spinning cockeyed, and she'd save the rest of her Loups and be able to protect her sisters from the Cartesians. Maybe if enough water soaked through, it would cleanse her enough so there wouldn't be any more Cartesians. Who knew?

The wind shifted, sending a blast of cool air over Viv's body. She shivered. Okay, so maybe she did mind the rain.

When they finally arrived at the dilapidated factory, Viv saw a heavy chain strung between the handles of two iron front doors. A giant padlock had been attached to the chain, denying entry to anyone without a key. Old buckets and other plastic debris littered what was once a front lawn, and from what she could see in the dark and rain, it looked like every window in the old factory had been shattered with either a rock or pellet gun.

She was relatively certain some of the city's homeless had made this place their permanent residence. She might have been a witch, but the place still creeped her out.

Viv walked around to the side of the massive building with Nikoli at her heels and spotted a side entry door standing slightly ajar. She held a finger to her lips, signaling to Nikoli that they should proceed quietly.

He shifted to one side and peered through the crack in the side door. "Can't see anything inside," he whispered. "Too dark. I hear the chomping noise, but I can't even make out what's making the sound. Don't know if they're your Loups or not."

"Let me see," Viv said quietly and ducked under his arm. She pressed an eye to the crack in the door. It was so dark inside it felt like she'd pressed her eye up against a black wall. The building held a noxious odor of fresh blood, urine, oil, wet fur and mildew.

The sounds she heard, however, left her little doubt that some or the rest of her missing Loups were inside. She knew the sound of feeding when she heard it. She stood listening for a while, then decided they'd never get anything accomplished just standing out in the rain.

Nikoli must have been thinking the same because he pushed gently against the door. "We're not getting anywhere like this. I'm going in."

The door creaked so loudly when he pushed on it that Viv heard it over the pounding rain and thunder. When it was wide enough, he slipped in sideways. Viv followed right behind.

They stood inside for a moment, letting their eyes adjust to the dark. Viv tapped Nikoli on the back. "Let me have the flashlight." Somewhere between here, the docks and Treme, she'd managed to lose hers.

He handed it to her. "You turn that light on, and they're either going to attack or scatter."

She flicked a finger against his back. "They're my Loups, remember?"

"Yes, ma'am," he said quietly, and she heard the smile in his voice.

Holding her breath, Viv flipped the switch on the flashlight.

In the middle of a vast, oil-stained concrete floor were at least twenty of her Loups, all fighting over what remained of a human body. All that was recognizable was a foot still trapped inside a worn-out sneaker with no laces. The sound of chomping, chewing, snarling echoed loudly through the building. It made her sick to her stomach.

Startled, the Loups huddled, ducking their heads, protecting their eyes from the light. Some of them yelped. A few growled and turned in their direction, faking a pounce. But Viv knew better. None were going to leave dinner behind.

No amount of cable was going to capture this group. Viv blew out a frustrated breath. "How on earth are we going to get all of them back to the compound?" she asked Nikoli.

He swiped a hand through his hair, then his beard. "Any spell come to mind?"

Viv tsked. "For some reason I can't even hang onto one Loup with a binding spell. What's it going to do with twenty?" Her Grimoire suddenly came to mind, and Viv mentally went through the worn pages she'd read morning after morning for the past fifteen years.

One spell stuck out in her mind, and she considered it. She hadn't attempted this spell before but remembered the word verbatim. She had no idea if it would work or fall flat like her binding spell. But there was only one way for her to find out.

"I'm going to try a teleportation spell," she said. "See if I can get them back to the compound in one fell swoop. I don't know if it's going to work or piss them off. Just saying."

"What can I do to help?" Nikoli asked.

"Watch my back." She handed him the flashlight, and the jittery Loups looked over in their direction, then back at dinner. She knew when they looked over this way, all they saw was a beam of light. But there was no discounting their sense of smell. As soon as they finished the meal they'd already started, the greedy Loups would be looking for more. Since there was little left of their fresh kill, Viv knew she needed to get with the program or get out.

The spell called for Viv to sit on the floor with her legs crossed and her arms on her thighs, hands palm up, and her eyes closed. Not exactly thrilled with the close-your-eyes part, Viv slowly lowered her body so as not to startle the Loups, then finally sat.

With a slow, fluid motion, she sat cross-legged and placed her arms on her thighs, keeping her hands palm up. She glanced one last time at Nikoli, then over at the Loups before closing her eyes. She blocked out the feeding sounds and rain beating against the old structure, the wretched smell of the building. All she allowed in her mind was a vision of her Grimoire. Then she began the spell.

"Par mon commandement,
laissez-vous le corps et l'ame,
a la place mon esprit maintenant.
rapidement se deplace.
Adhon—Fiontan—Uri—Ila!"

After reciting the spell, Viv didn't want to open her eyes and face another disappointment. While she was still in a zen state, Viv repeated the spell, hoping a double whammy would do the trick.

"Par mon commandement,
laissezvous le corps et l'ame,
a la place mon esprit maintenant.
rapidement se deplace.
Adhon—Fiontan—Uri—Ila!"

"They're gone!"

Hearing Nikoli's excited cry, Viv opened her eyes. Every Loup that had been feeding on the human, still smeared across the floor, had vanished into thin air.

"You did it!" Nikoli said and helped Viv to her feet.

Not wanting to get too excited yet, Viv hurried out the side door, into the night, where the pounding rain had turned into a lazy drizzle. She cupped her hands around her mouth and howled for Jaco to confirm the Loups' arrival. She had to howl twice more before she heard his response.

She *had* done it. The Loups were back in the compound! Viv whirled about on the balls of her feet, no longer caring about the pain in her arm. She wanted to fly into Nikoli's arms and celebrate.

No, no more, she reminded herself.

With great effort, Viv kept her demeanor business-like. "I need to get back to the compound before feeding so I can help Jaco. I'm sure he can use an extra pair of hands." She turned to head back to the truck and heard Nikoli call out.

"No. Not yet."

She turned to face him. "What?"

He motioned to the remains of the person the Loups had been feeding on. "I can't just leave the body here like that. I'm not sure if we should call the police or not."

"We can't call the authorities. That'll start an investigation. The Circle of Sisters will wind up being involved. My own sisters, too. I can't take that chance."

"But what about him—her? They might have family looking for them. Loved ones who are worried sick over their disappearance."

"I have to think about my family, Nikoli. No authorities."

He frowned, looked over at the body, or what remained of it. Then took the flashlight and walked across the length of the building, shining a beam of light into one corner or another.

"What are you doing?" Viv asked.

Instead of responding, Nikoli bent down and picked up an old shovel. The spade was still intact, but the handle was broken and only two feet long.

"I'm going to bury the remains. I know we're running out of time so I'll be quick. We just can't leave that body there to rot."

With that, Nikoli hurried past her and out of the building with his broken shovel. He didn't walk far before he started digging.

Viv watched as he managed to haul up three spades of dirt.

"There's an easier way to get that done," she said.

He looked up at her quizzically, and she motioned for him to step back a few feet. When he was out of the way, Viv held her hands out in front of her in a praying position, silently issued an incantation, then parted her hands like a book. The earth where Nikoli had been digging opened up.

Since there were so few remains left from the body, she'd called for a three-foot-by-three-foot hole, and that was exactly what she got.

Nikoli nodded as if this was a daily routine for them and went back into the factory. He came out moments later with his hands filled with blood and left-over innards. He walked over to the hole and gently placed them inside. When he did it, it was as if someone turned off a faucet in the sky because the rain abruptly stopped.

Nikoli made at least five trips carrying mangled flesh and bone. His last load was the foot still encased in the sneaker. Once that was safely in the hole, he grabbed the broken shovel and started tossing loose dirt into it, burying the remains.

Neither of them spoke as he shoveled dirt over the few remaining pieces of flesh and bits of hair and bone.

When he was about done, Viv took the flashlight and went to the entrance of the factory, where she'd spotted a few old buckets strewn about in the grass. She found one that sat upright and had about six inches of rainwater in it.

She carried the bucket back to Nikoli. He looked inside it, then dipped his hands into the water and washed off the blood and dirt. Viv watched him, her heart full, her mind quiet for the first time in her life.

When he was done washing, Nikoli stood, wiped his hands dry on the back of his pants, then quietly stared into Viv's eyes. She saw hunger in them, not just for her body but for *her*, all of her. It was as great a hunger as she had for him.

Nikoli held out a hand.

Viv took it with trepidation, and they walked away from the factory, hand-in-hand.

She didn't know if accepting his hand—accepting him, had just sealed her fate, but she'd had no choice. It felt like two universal truths had been set into motion from the moment they'd met.

Their hunger for each other existed for a reason.

And, from this day forward, their love, so full—so complete—so satisfying, would never again be denied.

Viv stopped for a moment and turned to Nikoli. Their eyes held, soft, deep, longing. Still holding one of his hands, Viv felt his pulse beat faster and was certain he felt the same from her. She had no idea when or how any of the reprecussions from the Triad curse might come to be. But one thing she knew for sure. The biggest curse of all would be living without him.

Then an intensity she had not seen before brightened Nikoli's eyes, yet his face remained sober. Her heart felt like it wanted to leap from her chest to touch his heart, and he obviously felt the same for his grip tightened on her hand.

And in that moment, as if the universe knitted them together, Viv and Nikoli whispered simunlateously, "I love you."

* * * * *